THE LAWYER'S HEART

CADENCE ELLIOTT LEGAL THRILLER
BOOK 3

J.J. MILLER

INNKEEPER PUBLISHING

© 2023 Innkeeper Publishing

All rights reserved. No part of this book may be reproduced or transmitted in any form or by any means, electronic or mechanical, including photocopying, recording, or by any information storage and retrieval system, without permission in writing from the copyright owner.

This is a work of fiction. Names, characters, places and incidents either are the product of the author's imagination or are used fictitiously, and any resemblance to any actual persons, living or dead, events, or locales is entirely coincidental.

Books by J.J. Miller

THE BRAD MADISON SERIES

Force of Justice

Divine Justice

Game of Justice

Blood and Justice

Veil of Justice

THE CADENCE ELLIOTT SERIES

I Swear To Tell

The Lawyer's Truth

Stay in touch with J.J.

Email: jj@jjmillerbooks.com

Facebook: @jjmillerbooks

Website: jjmillerbooks.com

J.J. MILLER

CONTENTS

PART I	1
Chapter 1	2
Chapter 2	10
Chapter 3	19
Chapter 4	27
Chapter 5	33
Chapter 6	40
Chapter 7	44
Chapter 8	49
Chapter 9	56
Chapter 10	68
Chapter 11	74
Chapter 12	81
Chapter 13	86
Chapter 14	93
Chapter 15	101
Chapter 16	108
Chapter 17	115

Chapter 18	121
Chapter 19	124
Chapter 20	132
Chapter 21	138
Chapter 22	146
Chapter 23	151
PART II	159
Chapter 24	160
Chapter 25	167
Chapter 26	175
Chapter 27	186
Chapter 28	193
Chapter 29	200
Chapter 30	207
Chapter 31	211
Chapter 32	221
Chapter 33	230
Chapter 34	234
Chapter 35	247
Chapter 36	252
Chapter 37	263
Chapter 38	274
Chapter 39	285
Afterword	300

PART I

Chapter 1

Sitting too low in her chair, Tessa Reeves reached down and tried to raise the seat higher.

"Don't bother," said the man sitting across the desk, her editor Wade Hampton. His eyes were focused on his computer screen when she had walked into his office and they had not strayed since. "The cylinder's shot."

"Why don't you get a new one?"

"A cylinder?" Hampton scoffed before tapping a few keys.

"No. A new chair."

Reeves knew she was wasting her breath. All the chairs at *DC Watch* were threadbare and most were hobbled in one way or another.

"It works fine enough."

In Hampton's eyes, the options for where his staff could park their butts were more than adequate. Their wages and benefits were competitive, the computers and smartphones he supplied were current enough, the Wi-Fi speed was passable and the network security almost top-notch. What more did a humming political website that punched above its weight need? It was a point of pride for Hampton that his workplace bore a certain Spartan aesthetic.

Still screen-focused, Hampton shook a couple of mints into the palm of his left hand and popped them into his mouth.

Tessa's nostrils flinched at the scent of peppermint mixed with cigarette odor. The list of things she did not like about Hampton was growing, but high on it had always been the smell of his office.

Her mind flicked back to the time when she viewed Wade Hampton as a mentor. It was exactly one year, two-hundred-and-fifty-one days ago—her first day at *DC Watch*. Raring to go, she had pitched him a great idea for her first story. Hampton said he liked it but proceeded to refine its focus. She was flattered and impressed. It was the mature guidance even she knew she needed. She was a young multimedia journalist with a knack for producing viral clips showing various subjects getting cornered by her sharp and bold questioning. Her "field" was social justice, and she found there was no shortage of targets in the capital of the world's most powerful country.

Her notoriety had drawn some interest from mainstream media outlets but they did not warm to her firebrand manner and her edgy looks. Hampton, though, believed Tessa could spice things up around *DC Watch* and pull in a younger audience via social media, a beast he openly admitted he did not understand. Like any website editor, he knew he needed clickable content and Reeves seemed a good way to get it. But since that first day Tessa had watched Hampton become ever less inclined to stick his neck out and back her ideas. Where she once saw professional courage in that lean-featured face of his, with its wrinkles and age spots and untamed nasal hair, she now saw timidity disguised as prudence. And this meeting was about to be another case in point, she just knew it. She was ready to kick serious butt with another great story, and he was about to jam a stick in her spokes. Again.

"I take it you read my draft," she said.

Hampton sighed and finally turned to face Tessa. "Look," Hampton said. "I'll just cut to the chase."

"Please do," said Tessa with a frown and folding her arms. The now familiar my-hands-are-tied resignation in Hampton's voice said it all. She knew exactly what was coming. She just wanted to hear him say it so she could point out all the ways he was wrong.

"Look, it's good but there's no way we can pull the trigger on this yet."

"I don't understand, Wade. I can get the first story done by Friday. The other two will be coming soon. It's a series. We can run them two weeks apart. That's plenty of time to get everything I need."

Hampton held up his hands to silence his young reporter. He, too, knew full well what to expect. "Did I say I was killing it? No. I'm saying it's on hold."

Tessa shook her head. "I disagree. Let's get this first part out there. Wade, this is what you've hired me for. I don't have everything now, but I don't need everything. Trust me, I'll pull it together."

"Tessa, once we run the first part we're committed to running the rest. And I'm sorry but you don't have all your ducks lined up. You think you do but you don't."

"This is big, Wade. You know it. I mean, it's got everything. Devious public relations companies, crooked politicians and rapacious big pharma. What more can you want?"

"It's a big chunk to swallow for a twenty-something reporter."

"I've got the stomach for it. I used to think you did too."

Hampton glared at Tessa. "Spoken like a true brat. You want all the glory and none of the responsibility. This company can't afford to defend itself against one defamation suit let alone the swathe that your story, as it is, would bring down upon us."

"It's not defamation when you can prove it."

"You don't have all the proof that you need. That *we* need. That's my point."

"What are you so scared of, Wade?"

The days when she hung on Hampton's every word were well in the past. Now she found just about everything about him annoying. She once took his lack of personal grooming as the mark of a dogged newshound. Now the disheveled mop of white hair just made him look uninspired. He shaved every day but he always managed to miss something and today Tessa found herself staring with disgust at the small patch of white stubble he had missed under his nose.

"Listen, Tessa. Quit giving me attitude about having the balls to run something or not. This is a Washington, DC outfit, not the *Chattanooga Gazette*. I do want a story on the rising power of PR companies. It's on point. It's—"

"It's more than that," said Tessa, trying hard to keep her indignation in check. "This is about PR firms subverting democracy. On behalf of their corporate clients like big pharma, they're running slick campaigns to brainwash people. It's about federal politicians being paid to sabotage state bills. This is about American citizens getting hoodwinked and screwed."

"I know all that, Tessa. It's in your draft. And it's good stuff. But you don't have all your ducks in a row."

"What I have is public relations companies trying to get Zellus Pharmaceuticals a monopoly of the drug addiction treatment market. And it's happening with the help of several elected officials. Men like your friend Senator Ron Nagle. So many people have already died as a result of their actions. People who were unable to get the help they needed because they could not afford what Zellus charged. Mothers. Fathers. Brothers. Sisters. Dead. And those bastards are getting away with it while we sit on our hands."

There was fire in Tessa's eyes and Hampton did his best to return in kind.

"Are you implying something? Are you saying I'm protecting Nagle?"

"He was in here yesterday. Sitting right where I'm sitting now. You guys were arguing. What was that about?"

"It was not about your story."

"Really?"

"Listen, Tessa. You need to cool your freaking jets. I didn't hire you to take pot shots at people whose business you don't like. I hired you because I thought you could develop into a great investigative reporter. You need to get irrefutable evidence for the whole series. Until you do, it's on hold. Got it?"

"Fine," Tessa said.

"You do know that it's not just you that's affected, don't you? I just told Luke that I'm holding his story until we run yours. You can imagine how happy he is."

"What's it got to do with Luke?" Luke Everson was the closest thing *DC Watch* had to a gossip columnist. He was well-connected enough to ensure his stories were the subject of much chatter around DC's most powerful water coolers. To

Tessa, Luke Everson was a politics lite kind of reporter. The kind of reporter she vowed never to be.

"You know as well as I do that this website does so well because it has both light and shade. You can't escape the fact that gossip sells."

"You mean clickbait sells."

"Sneer all you want but without those clicks we'd be nothing but a self-absorbed blog that no one reads."

"But it's not journalism."

"Really? Gossip is about the oldest journalism there is. Anyway, I've got a meeting. The long and the short of it is that, like yours, Luke's piece is on hold."

"What's his story, anyway?"

"Never you mind," said Hampton. "I never discuss your stories with him, and the same goes for you."

"Is there a crossover? There must be. You can at least tell me that."

"We're done here, Tessa. Just go focus on your story. Trust me, it's for your own good."

"What?" The way Hampton said it touched a raw nerve. "What are you saying?"

"Calm down, Tessa. I'm glad you're getting your teeth into a fresh story but I don't want to see you suffer like you did last year."

Tessa felt a pang of shame. The death of a friend of hers had prompted her to write a story about youth suicide. In hindsight, putting it together while she grieved the loss of her friend was not the best idea, and she found herself on a therapist's couch working through all the dark places her mind was taking her to.

"I'm fine, Wade," she said as convincingly as she could. "I'm fine with all that."

"This stuff is serious, Tessa. And you know I'm not just talking about your mental health. It's about your physical safety. Your security. There are a lot of people who wouldn't like you putting them in the spotlight. We need to be careful."

"Wade, please. I'm—"

"Look, Tessa. I've really got to wrap this up. We're done here. Please just do as I ask."

Tessa nodded.

"You need help, get Danielle. Okay?"

Danielle Farrell was *DC Watch*'s junior reporter who idolized Tessa.

"She's already helping," said Tessa. "She's been great."

Hampton nodded. "She's working on a follow-up to her technology and surveillance piece but I'm sure she'd love that."

"She's the one person in here that I trust."

The words were out before Tessa realized.

Wade's eyebrows went skyward. "Is that so?"

"I mean, besides you."

"I'd hope so. Now you've got a week, okay? Get back to me with the goods, or we park it and you go back to your normal duties. I don't have the staff to cover you."

With that Tessa got to her feet and left Hampton's office. When she got back to her desk, she noticed there was a text message on her phone.

She picked up her phone to read it and looked over her shoulder before she began typing her reply. Seconds after she hit send, another text appeared. Over the next few minutes, a meeting was arranged.

Later that night, Tessa Reeves left her home believing she would soon be marching back into Hampton's office with an offer he could no longer refuse.

She had a lead. One that just might be the key to getting her story out. It was a hell of a story. She knew it. And she could not wait to tell it to the world. Bigger prospects beckoned. The mainstream outlets would be falling over themselves to get her, happily finding a way to accommodate a strong-willed firebrand.

Soon Wade Hampton and Luke Everson would be nothing more than footnotes on her resume.

Chapter 2

Cadence Elliott read and chewed as she walked from the Hardwick and Henshaw break room back to her office. In one hand she had her phone, to which her eyes were glued. With the other, she balanced a cup of coffee on a plate of avocado toast.

> *The sudden death of our young, fearless reporter Tessa Reeves has us reeling in disbelief. In our state of profound shock, we can only begin to imagine the grief her parents, family, and loved ones must be feeling right now. We are united not just in grief but bewilderment. How could this happen? How could a young woman with the world ahead of her become the latest subway fatality? As I write, a police investigation is in progress but they are yet to rule out suicide. Such a state prompts us to wonder if we missed something here at DC Watch. Were there issues that Tessa was dealing with that we—and me in particular, as her editor—didn't pick up? From where I sit, though, Tessa had everything to live for. Like any great reporter, her passion in life was to expose truths and to right the wrongs of this world.*

> *She had the instinct to find a great story and the steel to go out and get it. She was following the great tradition of American reporting, the kind that led to Watergate. For now, we must wait for the investigation to unfold. But if there was some evil hand in her death, I will not rest until whoever was involved has been brought to justice. We want—no, we demand—the very thing to which Tessa Reeves devoted her life: the truth. — Wade Hampton, Editor*

Cadence was not a regular reader of *DC Watch* but news of Tessa Reeves' death was everywhere. Intrigued by the tragedy, Cadence followed a chain of stories before arriving at the website where the young reporter worked. Just about every online story linked to samples of Reeves' earlier video reporting. Anyone who watched them could tell she was a dedicated journalist, if a little overzealous. Sometimes her questioning got fierce and accusatory but the substance she put into the narrative indicated that she was very perceptive. It was not hard to see that Reeves needed to learn to keep her emotions in check. Still, she would not have been the first naive hothead to grow into a consummate investigative journalist. Sitting at her desk now, Cadence felt a pang of sadness for the passing of such a promising talent.

"Where's *my* toast?"

A voice at the door broke Cadence's train of thought. She looked up to see the welcome face of Bob Rhodes—investigator extraordinaire, all-round great guy, and just about Cadence's best friend in DC.

"What am I? Your slave?" returned Cadence with mock indignation. "I've got bread and avocado in the fridge. Help yourself. It's the container labeled 'touch this and you're dead.'"

Bob shook his head and entered. "I was kidding. I don't do breakfast."

Cadence raised a suspicious eye. "Since when?"

The idea surprised Cadence. Bob Rhodes kept himself fit by way of an active lifestyle rather than by anything resembling a training regime.

"Intermittent fasting," he said. "It's something I'm trying. No food between dinner and lunch."

Cadence thought for a second about her own rituals. Going without food after her daily morning workout would never do. This morning she had completed a boxing workout. Tomorrow would be a spin class, the next day the treadmill, the day after yoga. Up until a few months earlier she was getting her workout mostly by way of krav maga classes. She got into self-defense after being physically assaulted, and the practicality of the Israeli discipline appealed to her. She did it long enough to feel confident that she could incapacitate a male attacker. What put her off, though, was the unwanted attention of a fellow classmate. He seemed to take the class just to spend time standing too close to her. Soon enough, she did not want to go because all she would do when she woke up was wonder if the creep was going to be there. So she quit. She loved her all-girl boxing class and felt it was a great way to hammer out her frustrations on the pads and bags. And considering how much energy she spent every morning before she logged on for work, there was no way could wait until twelve o'clock to eat.

"In my world, that's an eternity," she said. "Come and take a seat. I'm going to keep demolishing my breakfast, if that's okay with you."

"Of course. I'm not proselytizing but fasting is fantastic. I feel lighter, more energetic."

Cadence took another bite. "Good for you."

She took a napkin and wiped crumbs from her mouth before tapping her phone. "Did you read about this girl Tessa…?"

"Tessa Reeves," said Bob, nodding. "Yes, I did. I know her boss Wade Hampton. He was around when I was in the White House press corps. Did you read his piece today?"

Bob was an award-winning newspaper reporter who saw print give way to online. When he waved the industry goodbye, he took his finely tuned snooping skills and launched a new career. In a short time he was in hot demand as a private investigator, but he had become almost like staff at Hardwick and Henshaw.

Cadence took a sip of coffee. "I just finished it. I don't know. There is something odd about it. It's like he's accepting that she killed herself but trying to come across as her valiant champion. Am I wrong?"

"Not at all," Bob laughed. "Those were my thoughts exactly. And that's the Wade Hampton I remember. He was always talking a big game, saw himself as a mover and shaker but never really delivered in that sense. He produced the kind of story that left you feeling like he hadn't quite delivered the killer blow. There was some kind of shortcoming, either lack of effort or talent, that meant he never really stuck the landing, if you know what I mean."

"Yes. Was he too polite for his own good?"

"No, I'd say it was more a lack of ambition. Nothing like Tessa Reeves, from what I gather."

Cadence smiled and folded her arms. "You know something. What are you sitting on, Mr. Rhodes?"

"Well, since you asked, it's my understanding that Tessa Reeves was working on the kind of story that makes powerful people sweat."

Bob said these words with a conspiratorial air. The fun of their banter was gone.

"Tell me more," said Cadence. As she said this, she checked her watch. "Geez, I've got to go see Jackie in a few minutes. What can you tell me?"

Bob cocked his head. "Well, I heard that she was digging into Tate Lieberman."

"Who's Tate Lieberman?"

"Exactly. Who's Tate Lieberman? No one knows who he is. The guy's like a ghost but he's one of the most powerful people in DC."

"He's in Congress?" asked Cadence, confused. "I'm drawing a blank." Soon after moving to DC, Cadence realized she had to get up to speed with how America's seat of power worked. Now she could just about name every member of both houses plus their state of origin. Hell, she could practically recite when they were elected and when they were up for reelection. But Tate Lieberman was a name she had never heard of.

"No. He's in PR."

"Public relations?"

Bob nodded. "He runs Berrins." He paused. "You have heard of Berrins haven't you?"

"Yes," Cadence said. "High end PR. Blue chip clients. Petro-chemical firms love them. They could convince us that the Gulf oil spill was a natural event."

"Exactly. But you know nothing about Tate Lieberman, right? And that's because he wants it that way. He likes to stay in the shadows. Check out the Berrins website and you won't find a team page. No bios. No smiling headshots. No names. They get the client's message out loud and clear all while staying invisible themselves."

"Why?"

"I can't help but wonder if that's what Tessa Reeves was trying to find out."

"Are you implying Tate Lieberman was threatened enough by a young reporter to have her killed?"

"This is DC, Cadence. If the powers that be want you to disappear, you disappear."

"Whatever happened to PR being all about air kisses, swanky launches and canapes?"

"That's your garden variety PR firm. It's a long way from what Lieberman does."

"What kind of thing does he do?"

Bob dusted a knee. "He's changing the game here in DC."

"What do you mean?"

"I've been in DC now for almost thirty years and this is how power works. If a company wants to get a congressman on board, they hire a lobbyist to whisper sweet nothings into his ear. Lobbyists. They were your in, if you could afford them. Now, it's all changing, thanks to the Tate Liebermans of this world."

"How so?"

"A lobbyist persuades a politician directly. He may appeal to his beliefs, he may co-opt him, bribe him or pressure him. It's a one-on-one relationship. The new PR way is different. Companies are now hiring these firms to win over the minds of the people who put that congressman in power. They put together TV commercials. They go to the cities and towns of that state and make ads that get thousands of people worked up about an issue. They make content and local newspapers run it. And they do this so well that the congressman has little choice but to toe the line or else he's not going to get reelected."

"Give me an example."

"Soda taxes. We all know that high soda consumption translates into bad health outcomes like obesity. On a community level, obesity puts a huge strain on our health system. And it's a plain fact that soda is the number one cause of obesity in the US. You'd think we could agree that being less dependent on soda would be a good thing."

"That seems logical."

"Logic's got nothing to do with it. When Tate Lieberman and his team produced a barrage of slick ads to drum up fear of massive price hikes, the soda tax was dead in the water. That was three years ago. My understanding is that he's now got Zellus as a major client."

"Okay. I'm not going to pretend I know who or what Zellus is."

"It's a pharmaceutical company. And having them as a client is making Tate Lieberman extremely wealthy and more powerful than ever. And from what I know, he'll do everything he can to safeguard what he wants to hide. And he's got a lot to hide."

"Corruption?"

"Well, yes. Moral corruption, I guess you could say. Apparently, he's a serial cheater, God help his wife Kelly."

"Sounds like a man with a lot to hide."

"Yes. And he's ruthless."

"You look like you're a bit fired up there, Bob. Are you tempted to put your press badge on again to bring Tate Lieberman's deeds to light?"

"Don't think that it hasn't crossed my mind," Bob laughed. "But if I were to do that, I'd do so with the utmost caution. In fact, he's the kind of guy I'd tell everyone to steer clear of. God knows what he'd be prepared to do to keep his sordid little secrets safe."

"You mean kill someone?"

"Maybe."

"Someone like Tessa Reeves?"

"Put it this way. It doesn't seem impossible that Tessa got too close for comfort."

There was a pause as Cadence took in all that Bob had said. "You know, Bob. Whenever I start to really love living in DC you come along and say something that ruins it. A few joyous minutes with you and I feel like I'm living in Gotham City."

"Well, think of it this way. Maybe one day you'll get to be its Batgirl."

"Yeah, right." Cadence checked her watch. "Geez, I've got to go see Jackie. Look what you've made me do. I haven't finished my breakfast."

She took a quick bite and sprang to her feet.

"I'm telling you. It's over-rated."

Bob was up and following Cadence out the door. She stopped and turned, finishing a mouthful.

"You know what's over-rated?" she said, holding a finger up in front of Bob's face.

Bob looked at her deadpan. "What?"

"Tofu."

"Tofu?"

"Yeah, tofu," said Cadence with a wry smile. "It's just a curd to me."

Bob shook his head with mock shame yet could not help but laugh.

"Good grief," he said. "If I wasn't fasting, you'd have just put me off my breakfast."

Chapter 3

Jackie Hardwick was never prone to lavish displays of emotion, but she practically glowed with pride at the sight of Cadence. Years ago, Jackie had forged a reputation in the DC courtrooms as something of a prosecutor's worst nightmare. She looked and dressed like a million dollars, but she always built an excellent rapport with the jury. She commanded the courtroom with confidence and poise. Her potent mix of charm, intelligence, and clear moral purpose allowed her to connect with anybody. To the jurors she was a peer, albeit always sharper, wiser and prettier. In time, she built an excellent reputation and started a law firm of her own. Along with her long-time friend Alan Henshaw, she ran a firm that was at or near the top of any law graduate's list. And she had the pleasure of hiring more than a few. None, though, meant more to her than Cadence.

In the near five years since she had hired Cadence, Jackie had witnessed her young protege deliver on the abundant promise she had shown in law school. She was now an associate at the firm and just like Jackie, was gaining a reputation as being one of DC's best trial lawyers.

Everything about Cadence's character was an asset in her profession. She was quick witted and quick tongued and had a great feel for the courtroom. She was tireless in her trial preparation, working round the clock to ensure no stone was left unturned. And the results spoke for themselves. Cadence had yet to lose a case and various news reports had touched on her brilliance. Jackie knew her protege was being targeted by other firms, but she looked after her young gun well. Not just in terms of salary and benefits but she felt sure that Cadence felt right at home at Hardwick and Henshaw. And if that ever changed, Cadence had assured her that Jackie would be the first to know.

After greeting Cadence, Jackie tapped away at her keyboard. "Sorry. Just a sec. I'm just messaging Alan to let him know you're here. He'll be joining us."

Alan Henshaw was the firm's other cofounder and its managing partner.

Cadence had brought with her a briefing she had prepared for a sexual assault case. The client was a substitute teacher by the name of Doug Nolan, accused of raping a fifteen-year-old student. The evidence was damning as the girl recorded him admitting to the crime but the teacher insisted he wanted to plead not guilty. "I thought we would be going through the Nolan case."

"We were, but that's changed." Jackie raised her eyebrows in a way that showed the decision was not hers.

"Why is that?"

Before Jackie could answer they heard a jovial voice over Cadence's shoulder. "Good morning, ladies."

Alan Henshaw brought a vibrant energy into the room. He always had a spring in his step and a spark in his eye. He took hold of a spare wing-backed chair and slid it next to Cadence. "This weather's too good to be inside an office."

This was rich coming from Alan Henshaw. He practically lived in his office, and despite his general conviviality, he did not mind letting his displeasure show if one of his staff left the office early. Long hours were the norm of any successful lawyer and Henshaw considered being entrenched behind his desk for most of his waking hours a badge of honor. He did like to sail, so it must be said he had some appreciation of the outdoors. All told, though, he never looked happier than when he was at work.

"Have I missed anything?" Alan asked Jackie.

Jackie shook her head. "No, we haven't started at all."

It was now clear that the purpose of this meeting was not what Cadence had expected. She braced herself to say nothing about the Nolan case, even though it had been her main focus for the past two weeks.

"Good," said Henshaw, shifting in his seat and running a hand down the length of his tie. Cadence could not help but savor the sandalwood scent of Henshaw's cologne. She, like most people who worked at the firm, knew his go-to fragrance was Chanel's Egoiste. He kept a bottle of the appropriately named cologne on his desk. "Would you like me to start things off, Jackie?"

Jackie glanced at Alan and opened her hands. "The floor's yours."

As much as Jackie and Alan were equal founders, being managing partner effectively put the boss's hat squarely on Alan's head. He liked to project a modesty and fairness about it but when push came to shove, he always made it clear who was in charge. Jackie was no wallflower and had no problem disagreeing with Alan when she saw fit to do so, but generally speaking she was happy he was the managing partner. It was not a position she coveted, mainly because its demands would draw her away from her true professional love: criminal law.

"Cadence, you may have read about the death of a young reporter named Tessa Reeves," Alan said.

The words that came out of Alan's mouth seemed like such a coincidence, she thought Bob must have spoken to Alan before he dropped in to see her.

"That's weird," she said. "I was just talking about her with Bob. But then again, it's far from weird. Just about everyone in DC would know her by name and the way she died."

"True. It's everywhere," said Alan, his eyes flicking away for a moment. Cadence thought she had said something wrong. Maybe she made it sound like she and Bob were sitting around wasting time trading gossip when there was work to be done and clients to bill by ten-minute increments.

It was only a few minutes past nine o'clock, Cadence reasoned. *Surely, he wouldn't have his nose out of joint about that.*

But Alan returned his eyes to her and smiled, his brain calculating something that pleased him. "I'm glad you're somewhat familiar with the case," he said.

"Are we involved?" Cadence asked, trying to guess where this conversation with Alan was headed. "I thought it was a suicide."

Alan shook his head. "Not yet. But we're about to be."

Cadence could not help but start thinking aloud. "And that means I get the case? Which means it's a murder case? The cops must have charged someone."

"You're right on both counts," he said. "Well on the matter of the charges, I can tell you that they are imminent."

"That changed quickly."

Alan coughed lightly and pressed his lips together. "Doesn't mean they've got it right, Cadence. In fact, it's my firm belief that they've got it dead wrong."

"What do you mean?"

Alan looked at his watch. "In exactly one hour's time, a Detective Hudson is going to be knocking on the door of someone I know. Not quite a friend but a very important business associate."

"How do you know this? Since when does the DCPD give an accused person such a polite heads up?"

"I got a call from the DA's office. They don't want to be seen as turning the arrest into a media circus."

"He's a client of Hardwick and Henshaw?"

"Yes, but we are one of three firms he uses for his business affairs. I want to get all his business, so I told him I would take good care of him on this matter."

Since Hardwick and Henshaw formed, the firm had been split between two areas of practice, reflecting the expertise of its two founders—business law and criminal law. While Alan had partners beneath him who handled most of the business law accounts, he naturally placed a great deal of importance on keeping the business law stream growing.

"Who are we talking about, exactly?" asked Cadence.

"His name is Tate Lieberman," said Alan, emphasizing the words clearly as he believed Cadence would never have heard of him. "He works in—"

"Tate Lieberman?" Cadence asked in mild shock. Given Alan's obvious bond with Lieberman, she had to refrain from spilling what Bob had told her. "He's a client of ours?"

"As I said, he is but I'd like us to be handling all the legal needs of his company. Up until yesterday, we've only ever talked about his business. But now it's personal. What I have made clear to him is that, besides excelling in business law, Hardwick and Henshaw has a peerless track record when it comes to criminal law. And while the bulk of the credit must go to Jackie, you have been key to that success, Cadence. And that's why you are now Mr. Lieberman's lawyer. You're going to get any charges dropped pronto, okay?"

There was a pause as Cadence tried to ignore her gut reaction. Until that morning she had never heard of Tate Lieberman but what she had learned only a few moments earlier made it clear he was not the kind of person she wanted to represent. Of course, she accepted that working in a law firm meant she did not get to pick and choose her clients. Nonetheless she immediately looked for an out.

"Alan, did Jackie tell you I've got the Nolan case? There are other associates who would be better at taking care of Mr. Lieberman."

Jackie stared at Cadence with her disappointment clearly showing. Alan cocked an eyebrow.

"This is not a request, Cadence," Alan said, as his cheeks flushed with irritation. "Let me explain something to you because I really don't think you're getting it. Criminal law does not keep this firm afloat, business law does. No disrespect to Jackie or anyone who works under her in the criminal stream of this firm, but my side of the firm, the corporate and business law side, is what keeps this firm thriving. It's what allows us to have the best offices in DC. It's what allows you to welcome your clients into an office most lawyers your age would kill for."

"I'm sorry, Alan. I meant no disrespect. I wasn't trying to get out of it."

"Don't take me for a fool, Cadence. By God, I hope you're more convincing in court."

Cadence sat up taller in her chair in response to the insult. The urge came to throw her stunning successes back in his face, to remind him of how every criminal law firm worth its salt in DC had come knocking on her door after her string of victories. Deep down she knew her response to Alan's request was immature. Now she had to pull her big girl pants on and do whatever the hell she was told.

"Alan, I apologize. I didn't mean to sound ungrateful that you've chosen me. Of course, I'll gladly do as you ask."

Cadence felt compelled to keep talking, so she could steer the conversation away from her and back to the case.

"You said the police will be charging Mr. Lieberman soon," she said, looking at her watch. "What can you tell me?"

Disarmed, Alan's countenance relaxed and he crossed his legs.

"It's got to be a mistake," he said. "Or a set-up. We can't rule that out."

"Why would anyone set him up for murder?"

Alan shrugged. "This is DC, sweetheart. We're all swimming with sharks here. But I'm telling you, Tate's a stand-up guy."

Cadence bit her tongue.

"Why are they arresting him?"

"The victim, a reporter, was working on a piece about his business activities. Apparently, he was in contact with her just before she died. He sent her threatening messages. They were seen arguing just before she died."

"Alan," said Jackie, "I'm just mindful of the time. The details can wait. Cadence, you need to get over there right away. Alan's already given him the legal advice he needs at the moment."

"To keep his mouth shut," said Cadence.

"Indeed," said Jackie. "So you get over there and stop him from making things worse. Make sure the cops run everything through you. Got it?"

"Yes," said Cadence, getting to her feet. "I'm on my way."

"Good," said Alan. "Don't let us down. We need you to get those charges dropped pronto."

Chapter 4

The Uber driver was a young man who liked to talk. On the way to Tate Lieberman's residence he told Cadence the rideshare gig was not all he had going on. He had two side hustles in play. Then he started on her name, complimenting her on it and asking its origin. She told him her mother was a musician. And that was all she wanted to say about her mother. But before she knew it, her mind was drifting way back to a time when the memories were good and filled with laughter. When her mother was a star in her eyes, before she got addicted and beyond cruel.

A shake of her head snapped her out of it. She wished she had told the driver a lie she sometimes used, that she was an Army brat and named after the call-and-response marching songs her drill sergeant dad was renowned for.

The driver let out a whistle as he pulled onto Quebec Street, craning his neck to admire the oak trees arched overhead. The massive houses were almost hidden by a green mass of trees, leaves, hedges and lawns, and each was tucked comfortably back from the street. It reeked of proper table manners, tacit neighborhood rules and the smug comfort of having such a verdant refuge so close to the capital.

The driver stopped. "Does it get any better than this?" he said.

He was not necessarily after an answer from Cadence. He was thinking aloud. He went on. "Can you imagine coming home to a place like this? Your friend must do pretty well for himself. What's he do? If you don't mind my asking."

"How do you know it's a he?" said Cadence, reaching for the door handle.

"Okay, what do they do?"

"If I told you I'd have to shoot you, Tony."

Tony laughed. "Yeah, I get it. No worries. I'll find out when I move in here. We're going to be neighbors, your friend and me. I'll have them over for barbecue on Sundays."

"Maybe you will," said Cadence cheerfully. "Enjoy the rest of your day."

Cadence got out and stood for a moment to take in the grand splendor of the Lieberman home.

It was a red brick colonial that resembled a stock children's drawing of a house: flat-faced and symmetrical with a black door in the center and four bay windows, two up, two down. It was when Cadence's eye was drawn higher that she saw the figure standing at the right-side window. Dressed in a blue suit, white shirt and red tie, Tate Lieberman stared grimly at her without moving. She gave him a small wave but got nothing back. She stepped onto the stone path and made her way to the door. She paused for a moment, waiting to hear if Lieberman was approaching. After a few moments of silence, she knew he was not exactly rushing down to greet her and she pressed the doorbell.

A woman's voice could be heard, and the door was opened by a middle-aged Hispanic woman dressed in uniform. She smiled at Cadence as she introduced herself and she gestured for

THE LAWYER'S HEART

Cadence to enter. That Lieberman allowed the hired help to let his lawyer in spoke volumes to Cadence. There and then she was willing to bet that every bad thing she had heard from Bob was true. As she stepped into the house, she saw Lieberman's back as he entered a room off to the side.

"This way please, Ms. Elliott," said the housekeeper.

The interior of the house was surprisingly bright. The morning sunlight bounced from white walls to whiter ceilings and over shining caramel oak floorboards.

Cadence was shown to a room that opened to the back of the house. Facing her was a large window that framed a portion of the leafy garden. Positioned at the window was a three-seat couch. In front of the couch, facing away from her were two armchairs. Tate Lieberman sat in one.

"Take a seat," Lieberman said without turning around.

As Cadence settled on the couch across from Lieberman, she was left in no doubt that she was the subject of her host's disapproval.

"Where's Jackie?"

The question threw Cadence. Surely Alan told Lieberman who was going to represent him. Clearly, Lieberman just wanted to ask to be difficult. That was the kind of man he was. For an instant, Cadence daydreamed of a world in which she got to choose her clients instead of being assigned them.

As she was about to fill Lieberman in on who she was, he held up a hand to silence her. As much as she was inclined to ignore him and keep talking, she recalled her conversation with Alan earlier. He had made it perfectly clear she was here not just to clear the charges against him but to win all of his business. Resolving this case would make them his preferred firm, or so

Alan believed. She was left with the impression that anything she did to upset Lieberman would ruin Alan's grand plan.

"I've been told you are a very good defense attorney. One of the best. That's a lot to live up to."

The praise took Cadence by surprise, but it put her a little more at ease. "Mr. Lieberman—"

"Just call me Tate," he said firmly.

From one look at Tate Lieberman, it was clear he knew he was a handsome man. He was a sixty-year-old who looked at least a decade younger. His well-groomed looks—clean-shaven, strong jaw and graying hair—formed a conventional image of success, a living *Forbes* magazine cover shot. His piercing blue eyes peered out from beneath a thick hedge of trimmed eyebrows. Combined with a hooked nose and taut mouth, Lieberman bore a stern look and he seemed to savor the power he projected. He reminded Cadence of an eagle.

"Tate. I need to—"

"You know, Cadence. I'm surprised. Alan did not tell me you were so pretty."

Lieberman spoke slowly, suggestively, and with a wry smile. There was no doubt that he had a full tank of confidence. Eagle was right. The guy was positively predatory. The glint in his eye told Cadence exactly what he was imagining. She felt as though she was, in his eyes at least, wearing nothing but lingerie. If this was a social visit, he would be coming onto her. Of that she had no doubt.

Cadence made a point of looking at her watch. "The police will be here in a few minutes to arrest you. We don't have much time. So we need to get started. Why do they blame you for Tessa Reeves' death?"

"They've put together a bunch of nonsense. Two plus two equals five, according to these idiots."

"What's their evidence?"

"They say I was the last person to speak to her. Someone claims that they saw us arguing not long before she died. They know I was not happy about a story Ms. Reeves was writing about me. So these geniuses think I killed her to make sure her story never saw the light of day."

"When you say they. Who are they?"

"The lead investigator is Detective Steve Hudson. Looks like a used car salesman. Probably about as honest as one, too."

"Can't say I know him, but I'll check him out. But what about these claims against you. Are you denying them?"

"Yes. Emphatically."

"I need more detail, Tate. And this is when I let you know that whatever you tell me falls under attorney-client privilege."

Lieberman waved a hand. "Yes. Yes. That's well and good but there's not much to tell other than I'm not the only person who would be worried about a story like that."

"Like what?"

"One that delves into the public relations business in DC. Rather like your attorney-client privilege, my business relationships are built on discretion."

"Except it's not legally binding."

"Some of it is. It's written into contracts."

"Okay, so who else would have something to lose?"

Lieberman shrugged. "Where do I start? I deal with politicians from both sides of the aisle. I deal with successful businessmen and multinational corporations. I help them to get things done, discreetly."

"I don't know yet if the police had other persons of interest. So I need the names of anyone you think might have wanted to kill Tessa Reeves."

"Tessa Reeves was insignificant. She could be removed just like that, if certain people wanted."

He snapped his fingers.

"What exactly did you know about Tessa's story that could resemble motive?"

"Nothing."

"Mr. Lieberman, you must have some idea. You communicated with her." Cadence did not wish to say that she understood he threatened her. "I'm your lawyer. I'm—"

"Not for long if you do your job properly. The cops have nothing. Whatever Ms. Reeves was pursuing is irrelevant. All you need to know is they can't prove I had anything to do with her death. Because I didn't."

At that moment, the doorbell rang.

"That would be Detective Hudson," said Cadence.

"From here on in I'm not saying a damned word. I'm leaving all the talking to you. You're on, Ms. Elliott. The floor is yours. It's time to prove that you are every bit as good as Alan tells me you are. Send these fools on their way."

Cadence would have been wasting her breath to tell Lieberman that it did not work that way. He was going to learn very quickly that his power had limits and that those limits could close in very fast and very tight. It was scary how quickly a knock on the door of a mansion could lead to the locked door of a jail cell.

Chapter 5

The inside of courtroom number 501 was as bustling and noisy as a city street at rush hour. Located in downtown DC, it was a world away from the leafy embrace of Quebec Street. No eye-soothing foliage here. This was a colorless, grimy place, empty of fresh air and full of angst.

Standing behind bars amid a motley crew of fellow defendants, all waiting for the judge to call their name, Tate Lieberman's dignity was strained. He propped himself upright with all the pride he could muster. An admirable effort for a man chained at the waist, wrists and ankles. When the judge called his name, a bailiff unlocked the cage, let him out and escorted him to the defense table.

The moment he had seen Cadence enter the courtroom his eyes had locked onto her and had never let go. If he was steely in the comfort of his four-bedroom home, he was positively fuming now. Cadence did not have to be a mind reader to know she was the target of his rage. Cadence Elliott, the supposedly brilliant lawyer who was sent to his aid, who was meant to wave her wand to make the police disappear, had failed spectacularly in this seemingly simple task.

Despite leaving all the talking to her, despite taking Alan Henshaw's reassurances to heart, Tate Lieberman was charged right in front of his lawyer. And while she waltzed back to her plush office to report to her superiors, he was stripped of his designer suit, silk tie, Gucci shoes and organic cotton shirt and given an orange jumpsuit that smelled like it came straight off the back of the last #48575.

Lieberman had spent the night in DC Jail, bunking with a jittery meth addict who talked under his breath, and through gritted teeth told Lieberman—pretty much right after they had traded names—that he had slit a man's throat and enjoyed watching him gurgle to death. Lieberman had stayed awake all night. The arraignment hearing could not come soon enough, not least because he would get to give his so-called brilliant lawyer another serve.

"I see Alan doesn't have the guts to be here. What are you going to do for me now? Stand by and watch while they lock me up for life?"

Cadence kept her breathing deep and steady. Yesterday had not gone well by any measure. She had sat beside Lieberman as Detective Hudson put question after question to her client. Of the few questions she allowed him to answer, Lieberman only succeeded in deepening the cops' suspicions. The evidence they had ranged from trivial—circumstantial at best—to almost damning. That they could not land a decisive blow did not deter them from the conviction that Lieberman had thrown the young reporter in front of a train.

"I'm your lawyer, Tate," she said evenly, not wanting to further provoke his indignity yet not wanting to allow him to walk all over her. "But that can be easily changed. Anytime you want me gone you say the word."

"I'm stuck with you, for now," hissed Lieberman as he sat.

Cadence could not lie—she would have been only too happy to walk if Lieberman gave the order. It was clear, though, that beneath his rage he understood it was best to stick with Cadence, that if he started playing musical chairs with his lawyers then who knows where he would end up.

As Judge Martha Cockburn went to speak into the microphone nothing came out. She tapped it and called for it to be fixed. In a second the court reporter and the bailiff were trying to sort it out. The delay only elevated the agitation of the crowd in the courtroom and Judge Cockburn occasionally brought the gavel down and shouted to quell the rising din. The word went around that matters would be delayed until a technician arrived to fix the PA system.

Since Lieberman was still treating this ordeal as a passing nuisance, Cadence had to wonder if he really grasped the depth of trouble he was in. Sure, being arrested and charged was a shocking and sobering experience but he was still sure that it could somehow be taken away. All Cadence had to do was find the right button to press and he could not understand why she had not done that yet. Cadence quietly blamed Alan for that. He should have set Lieberman straight.

Tessa Reeves' phone records showed that she and Lieberman had exchanged messages the night before she died. Lieberman conceded he sent the messages but denied that they had met. He also denied having any malice toward her, yet was shown an aggressive email he sent to both Tessa and Wade Hampton. He scolded them before threatening legal action if they published so much as a pixel about his company on *DC Watch*. He told the cops he was doing what any business owner would do.

Cadence had had to step in and stop Lieberman from ranting during the police questioning. He was adamant he was nowhere near the train station where Tessa was killed. Yet he provided only hazy details about his whereabouts and activities on the night she died. He said he was with a friend and they drank a bottle of scotch between them. Then he took a room at the Fairbanks Hotel as he often did when working late. But when the cops called his friend, he said he was quite sure that he did not spend the night in question with Tate Lieberman.

Some part of Cadence thought the cops had booked Lieberman just to flex their muscles and it would not surprise her if it were so. All the while they were interviewing her client, they seemed like cops who were short of answers and chock full of questions. It was too early to tell if the arrest was premature. Under normal circumstances, a rushed arrest that failed to secure a conviction was the last thing the DCPD wanted but perhaps the priority had been placed on getting a conviction fast and at all costs. And if that were so, Cadence did not have to look far to see who might be pushing hard for that outcome. He had just entered courtroom 501 and joined his team at the prosecutor's desk.

US Assistant Attorney Gerard Underhill was an ever-ambitious man with one eye fixed on the top prosecutor's job of US Attorney for the District. Cadence understood he planned to run next year, so a very public murder conviction might be just the way to boost his credentials.

Cadence stood as Underhill got to the prosecution table and set down his files. He turned and flashed a radiant smile as Cadence approached, then extended his hand. His hand was strong and soft. An application of hand cream was no doubt a part of his morning regimen, along with a shave and a liberal dose of cologne. To say Underhill was well-groomed was an understatement. Cadence was sure he spent more time in front of the mirror than most women she knew. She could just imagine Underhill's morning routine. He would not step out his front door without attending to each and every detail from head to toe.

Underhill was conventionally handsome and was graying only at the sides and back of his head. For all his fussiness and preening, Underhill was far from queer. He bore an old-fashioned masculinity, and an air of entitlement. Cadence could not help but think Underhill and Lieberman were two of a kind. In other circumstances, they would be friends or at least members of the same golf club. Working as a lawyer in DC, Cadence was getting used to being sandwiched between two egotistical alpha males.

"Good to see you again, Cadence," said Underhill. "It's a credit to you that you won the trust of Tate Lieberman. It's a big job having the fate of that man in your hands."

"Yes, I'm sure his stature isn't lost on you, Gerard."

"What's that supposed to mean?"

"It means, this case is being pushed hard and my guess is it's your shoulder against the wheel. I hope you've got your priorities right, Gerard. But from where I'm sitting, I'm not sure you do."

Underhill did not have to guess what Cadence was getting at.

"We have strong evidence that your client killed that poor girl, and I intend to see that he gets what he deserves."

"I bet you can't wait to get out in front of those cameras."

"That comes with the job," Underhill smirked. "But mark my words, I won't be resting until he pays for what he did. That's what this case is about. Good old-fashioned justice."

Cadence folded her arms and nodded. "You know, you're right, Gerard. It is about justice. You may have your arrest, but we are a long, long way from conviction. And the evidence you have won't cut it. I'll make sure of that."

Underhill sighed. "Maybe. Never let it be said that you don't relish a fight, even one that you are bound to lose. Good luck, Cadence."

"You too, Gerard. And don't worry. When I kick your butt in court, I'll be glad to make it up to you. You can count on my vote."

Underhill laughed. "I'll take it. Every vote counts."

Cadence returned to her desk wondering if she would be happy working with Underhill. He had given her a standing offer to leave Hardwick and Henshaw and join him at the DA's office. She had politely declined, of course. The idea of taking a significant pay cut did not appeal. More to the point was that her heart was with defending clients rather than prosecuting them. Each side of the law saw itself as the true champion of justice, but for Cadence the most fundamental nobility of the law lay in a citizen's right to a staunch defense. She was more inclined to protect one's liberty than to try and have it taken away.

"You two look chummy," said Lieberman bitterly.

Cadence stared at her client. "We are adversaries, not enemies. This is the law, not a blood feud. The fact that I can converse professionally with the opposition has nothing to do with how I conduct your case. Between you and me, he wants to bury me. He wants to bury me by burying you. It's a two-in-one deal for him. I've beaten him before and I know he wants payback. His masculine pride demands it."

"I understand," said Lieberman.

"I wasn't going to say it but I knew that to be true. But believe me when I say this, to Underhill this case is everything. It's professional. It's personal. And it's political. And that makes him extremely dangerous."

Lieberman was about to speak when Judge Cockburn cracked her gavel and spoke into the microphone. This time her voice filled the room.

In less than five minutes, the arraignment was over. After hearing from Underhill and Cadence, Judge Cockburn saw no good reason to keep Lieberman in custody and ordered him to be released on bail.

Lieberman showed no reaction at all to the decision. He rubbed his wrists after the cuffs came off and looked at the back door.

"We should head back to the office," Cadence said. "We need to go over this evidence."

Lieberman shook his head.

"No," he said. "I'm going back to my office. I've got work to do."

Chapter 6

A gush of hot air hit Cadence and Bob Rhodes as they stood at the end of the Blue Line platform at McPherson Square station. All along the edge of the platform white circular lights began to flash. The distant rumbling from the tunnel grew louder before the train burst from the tunnel to the tune of screeching metal.

"This is what Tessa would have heard in her last moments," said Cadence. It was more a thought bubble than something she directed at Bob. She shuddered as her spine went cold. It felt creepy to place herself in the same spot as Tessa Reeves just before she met her fate.

As the train rushed by before slowing to a stop, Cadence thought how hopeless someone must feel to end it all. What desperate courage—there was no other word for it—it must take to throw yourself in front of a train. Cadence was not making a judgment about the cause of Reeves' death. Whether she took her own life or was killed did not matter. Cadence just knew she had to keep an open mind. But if it was murder, she could not bear to think of the horror of Tessa Reeves' last moments.

They were standing at one end of the platform. Commuters got off the train and walked to the only escalator that served the platform. Bob left Cadence's side and walked up to the access point of the escalator. He turned and faced Cadence and made a few mental calculations. Beneath the escalator was a large black metal container about seven feet high and just as wide. This was the escalator controller cabinet.

"There were no witnesses," Bob said. "She must have been standing behind here as the train was approaching. No one on the platform could see her here."

"So no one on the platform could see what happened. Shame there's no security video," said Cadence pointing up to a camera positioned on the end wall.

"Why not?"

"There was an outage," she said. "All the station's surveillance cameras were down for three days."

Bob shook his head. "Why doesn't that surprise me?"

"So there's nothing at all relevant to the case. We can't even see who came into the station, let alone onto the platform. Useless."

"There must be some witnesses," said Bob.

"Well, the train driver swears that he saw a man in the shadows."

"You mean here? Behind the controller cabinet? Really?"

"Yes. Yes. And yes."

"Was he just standing there? Or did he look like he could have pushed a young woman in front of the train?"

Cadence shook her head. "He didn't go into that much detail in his statement. The poor guy was in shock."

Bob reflected on that for a moment. "Of course. He must be going through hell. But he says there was someone else on the platform with Tessa."

"That's right. The cops would have been desperate to get a positive ID. But all he said was that it was a man. That's about it. Nothing to describe his height, build, or clothes."

Cadence watched the train pull away as the last of the riders got on the escalator.

"Okay let's assume this wasn't a suicide," she said. "Why would she be standing here? As a single woman at night, this is the last place you'd want to be."

"Well, you've got to think she came here to meet someone," said Bob. "Someone who wanted to meet in secret, and this was the agreed upon meeting place."

"Which is perfect if you're a spy," said Cadence. "But is that the level we're on? That Tessa Reeves was delving into some kind of Watergate or international conspiracy?"

Cadence shook her head and began walking up the platform. About fifteen yards away she stopped and called out, "This is DC, Bob. Who knows where her investigation was leading? Who knows the type of bear she was poking?"

Cadence held up her phone. "I've got no reception here."

She then made her way back to Bob at the end of the platform, all the while looking at her phone screen. When she reached the wall, she turned to face Bob.

"Look. Three bars."

"So?"

"So maybe she wasn't meeting someone here. Maybe she had to make a call. Or take one."

Cadence walked into the nook behind the controller cabinet. She nodded.

"It's a bit quieter here," she said. "If you want to be on the phone and be heard and hear whoever you're talking to, this is about the only part of the platform where you could do it."

"What's her phone data say?"

"The cops say they aren't through trying to get her phone data. Underhill hasn't passed it on to me yet. All I know is that they found messages that incriminated Lieberman."

"But that may not be everything."

"That's right. She could have been using a self-destruct messaging app like Snapchat. There are a bunch of them. So there may be no data to retrieve. But the cops will definitely be able to get her screen activity."

"You can't just settle for what the cops find."

"No. I'll get an independent data expert to examine Tessa's phone, you can be sure of that. Come on. Let's go."

Chapter 7

She never moved from her car. She never got out to stretch her legs or to try and get closer. She could never risk being spotted. Only after a thorough scan of the environment would she allow herself to wind the window down, but only a little so that the privacy tint kept her face relatively hidden. That was when she heard his voice for the first time. Just a ten-year-old boy calling out to his buddies. A young boy unaware that his birth mother was a stone's throw away, relishing every second that she got to look at the child she never got to hold in her arms. A child she was certain was stolen from her.

By now Cadence was accustomed to controlling her most desperate urges. It would be so simple to walk up to Ben and introduce herself. And he would know without a doubt that what she told him was the truth. He had her eyes, her nose. His handsome face was the perfect complement of her features. He was going to be tall, like she was. The times she watched him play baseball she could tell he was a natural athlete. She wondered what other talents and interests he had.

She was desperate to know everything about him. It killed her, but she knew she had to stay where she was. Experience had taught her that to get too close would put her life at risk. She had been warned in no uncertain terms one night when cycling home. A car ran her off the road, and a man got out and pressed a knife into her cheek. He told her to stay away from the Cordoba family or he would come back to kill her. She was sure he was the type of man who would enjoy finishing the job. So being even within earshot of her son, Cadence's vigilance was on high alert.

The boy was dressed in his baseball uniform with a gym bag slung over his shoulder. He was with two friends and they were sharing something on one of their cell phones, pointing at the screen and laughing.

Is he a fan of TikTok? Who did he follow on YouTube? Does he read?

The questions were endless. There was a quiet hope that her son shared her love of books but in the end she did not mind. The day that they could be together was all that mattered. Not that she hoped to take him away to live with her. She was not so delusional to think that she could right the wrongs of the past with a custody battle. She knew what she was up against. The doctor who had cut the child from her womb and handed him straight to the adoptive mother had insisted the process was legal. Her drug-addled mother had signed the papers in the trailer they shared in Colorado Springs, she was told. It was all perfectly legal, she was told. All her attempts to see the records had amounted to nothing. She was completely shut out. According to the authorities, she had given her son away.

But Cadence knew otherwise and perhaps that was what she wanted to say most of all: that she had only agreed to consider adoption, and only after having the chance to hold her child. This was the verbal agreement she had with her mother. Cadence made her promise and she gave her word. Then her mother turned around and deceived Cadence. For nine months she had her baby boy inside her, then she was put to sleep and woke to find him gone.

Lost in thought, Cadence found herself gripping the steering wheel hard and talking to herself. Quiet words to the boy, speaking from her heart, hoping he would forgive her. Hoping he was yearning for her, that he had somehow divined that whatever family he had grown up with, there was a big part of him missing.

The last thing she wanted was to disrupt his life. She guessed deep down that she wanted him to believe that she was a good person. She kicked herself. Even she did not believe she was a good person.

Cadence shook her head to erase these thoughts. She breathed in and just tried to appreciate the here and now and be grateful that at last, she had found him. After all those years of desperately searching, she had found him. Now he was so close she could almost reach out and touch him. At the same time, he seemed as far away and as out of reach as ever.

His dark hair was cut short at the sides and parted on the side. She thought the girls his age must think he was dreamy. She smiled and blushed a little with pride. It gave her a great deal of satisfaction to see that he seemed happy and that his world was so full of potential.

Just then, one of Ben's friends slapped his shoulder with the back of his hand and nodded in Cadence's direction. Ben turned and looked straight at her. She was a hundred yards away at least but she was certain he was looking at her.

Dread filled her body. Had they made her? Had she gotten too close? Had Ben and his friends noticed that there was some mad stalker woman hanging around their games and sometimes near the gates of their school?

Ben's face squinted into a frown and he shook his head. Cadence froze. She dared not move, even though she wanted to slide down and hide behind the dashboard or pull a frantic U-turn and get the hell out of there.

Ben turned back to his friends and picked up some belongings off the ground. A black limousine swept past Cadence's car and pulled up in front of the boy. She knew the car. It belonged to Monica Cordoba, his mother.

Cadence breathed a sigh of relief. She figured that Ben's friend had spotted the limo and told him. That explained it: they were not looking at Cadence, after all.

Still the mortification of being found out had not entirely left her. It gave way to shame. For how long could she keep up this painful, stressful charade? For how long could she just continue with her life, acting like there was nothing more important to her than her legal career?

As always, though, she had no answer. She never knew what to do. Only that she had to keep her distance.

She leaned forward and turned the ignition key, bringing her BMW's engine to life. She looked in the rear-view mirror and put the car in reverse. She backed up a little and then put the car into drive.

She checked her side mirror before pulling out. She was not going to leave before the limo in case she was detected but she thought she would check the road anyway. That was when she noticed that Ben had not gotten into the car. He had opened the door and was bent forward talking to someone inside.

The opposite rear passenger door opened and out stepped Monica Cordoba.

Cadence's insides churned with apprehension as she wondered what was going on. She did not have to wonder for long, though. Monica's eyes were fixed straight on her and she could see she was not happy. Monica slammed the door shut and after checking for traffic, began marching towards Cadence, not once taking her eyes off her.

Now doubly mortified at being irrefutably outed, and unwilling to have it out with Monica in front of Ben, Cadence turned the steering wheel hard and stepped on the gas. She had to brake suddenly and back up again before she could get away, but when she finally escaped, she did so with the image of Monica Cordoba in her rear-view mirror pointing a finger at her and yelling at her—the content of which never reached Cadence's ears.

She drove on in a haze of shock and shame. *What does Ben know about her? What has Monica told him about her? What lies had she fed him? What in God's name have I done?*

Beneath it all perhaps was a truth that she had never wanted to accept—that her son knew about her and wanted absolutely nothing to do with her.

Which now begged the question, what the hell was she going to do now?

"Stupid woman," Cadence yelled at herself, slamming her hand onto the steering wheel. "You stupid, stupid woman."

Chapter 8

Cadence heard her name called and stepped up to the counter to take her coffee. The barista put a small cookie on top of her to-go cup and gave her a big smile.

"Just as you like it, C," he said and Cadence knew he was right. She did not drop in every morning of the week, but he knew her order. Not every Monday was a caffeine fix day for Cadence but after two restless nights' sleep and a workout that she had to push her sleep-deprived body through, she needed the pick-me-up more than ever. She thanked the barista and turned for the door, already mentally running through her to-do list for the day. She front-loaded her lists with the hardest or most unpleasant tasks. Yes, everything was ranked by degrees of importance and this morning the top of the list was a brief she had to present to Jackie and Alan.

Normally she only reported to Jackie but since Alan was clearly invested in the Lieberman case, he was not shy about pressing her directly for updates. In fact, she had spent much of her weekend responding to his questions via email.

The fact that she had not yet succeeded in getting the charges dropped riled Alan no end. She knew she needed something this morning to reassure him. But what was there to be done? The police were not on a fishing expedition. They obviously believed they had their man. They got sufficient evidence to file charges and now Cadence was getting down to the business of dismantling them before the case ever saw the inside of a courtroom.

The sun was bright and warm and there was but the gentlest of breezes. Still, she had seen better days. Much better.

"Ms. Elliott?"

The woman's voice came from behind the moment she had set foot on the pavement outside the cafe and headed for the office. The woman's voice was flat and even and it sent a rush of panic through Cadence's body. She spun around, ready for confrontation, only to find that the person facing her was not Monica Cordoba. It was a woman in her early thirties, dressed in a way that squeezed out every inch of her sex appeal. Her hair was pinned up and drop earrings hung from her ears. The make-up was not subtle, but it was done with style. The red floral dress that hugged her curves put her ample cleavage on full display. It was quite an eyeful, and Cadence could not help but raise her brow. What on earth did this vision of womanly splendor want with a lawyer at this hour of the morning?

"Yes," Cadence said. "And you are?"

"Phoebe. Phoebe Baker," the woman said. "I was wondering if I could have a few minutes of your time."

"What's it regarding?" Cadence asked, not minding that she sounded a little too much like a receptionist playing defense.

The woman stalled and was hesitant to respond. The amount of patience Cadence had for this woman was rapidly diminishing. She needed to get to the office.

"Is there somewhere private we can talk?"

THE LAWYER'S HEART

Great. No. There's not. Do you have any idea how busy I am? Cadence kept her true thoughts to herself and shook her head. "Sorry, I've got to get to work. I don't know who you are or how you found me, but I need a nutshell explanation from you right now or I'm walking. If you need a lawyer, by all means, contact my firm, but I can't help you right now. My dance card is full."

The woman nodded. "You're Tate's lawyer. Cadence Elliott. You work for the law firm Hardwick and Henshaw."

"That's right," Cadence said. Phoebe Baker's words had bought her some time, though it was hardly a secret that Cadence was defending Lieberman. The press was all over it. "Do you know Tate? Or are you a friend of Tessa's?"

Phoebe shook her head. "He told me he wasn't worried, that he was going to beat the charges," she said. "He told me he's got the best legal representation in all of DC."

"Is that right?" said Cadence, not hiding her surprise.

"Yes. But he didn't say anything about his lawyer being young and beautiful. Though it doesn't surprise me. I bet he sure likes you."

"Do you have something to tell me? Because I have to go."

"I wanted to tell you that he's innocent," she said, perfectly aware she was revealing that she and Tate Lieberman were more than just friends. "He had nothing to do with that poor girl's death."

"And you know this how?"

Phoebe held her face still and stared unblinkingly at Cadence, unwilling to be ashamed. "Because he was with me that night."

"Is that right?"

Cadence checked her watch and repressed the flush of annoyance at her client, whose sketchy alibi was a big part of both their problems. His fuzziness made him look guilty. That he did not see fit to provide his own lawyer with more details than he gave the police, annoyed her no end.

"So you can confirm his alibi?" Cadence asked, not mentioning that her client's alibi was so vague and weak, it must have played a key role in the police's decision to arrest him.

"I'm not sure. But I think so."

"Okay," Cadence said and tilted her head at the cafe. "Let's go inside and grab a quiet table. I can give you ten minutes."

Once they were seated, Phoebe leaned forward. "He can't know I've come to you. He explicitly told me to stay out of it, and to keep my mouth shut but I can't. Not now that he's been charged."

"Did he say why he wanted you to stay out of it?"

Phoebe shifted uncomfortably. "Because he doesn't want his wife Kelly to find out about us."

A look of disappointment came over Phoebe's face. "He's told you nothing about us, clearly," she said.

"Not a thing."

"He's petrified about what Kelly will do if she finds out. Obviously, Kelly doesn't know about me."

"You say you were with him that night. Where were you exactly?"

"The Fairbanks Hotel. Room 306. We were there from about nine until late."

"Neither of you ever left the room?"

Phoebe's answer was to shake her head with a distinct lack of conviction. Skeptical, Cadence scrutinized her face. So far, this was not sounding any more credible than Lieberman's feeble offering. The most positive aspect that Cadence could see was that she now knew why Lieberman had a reason to lie.

"Are you sure neither of you left the room, Phoebe? This is important."

The woman hesitated, unsure of how to reply. It was as though she had thought she would come and tell Cadence her piece and then leave, and that nothing she said would be held to account.

"What did Tate say?"

"I can't tell you what Tate said. He's my client and that's privileged information. What I can say is that I don't think what you just told me is true."

Phoebe bit her lip. She was all at sea and did not know which way to turn.

"Did he say that he went out for a while?"

Cadence shook her head. "I'm here right now to listen to what you have to say, Phoebe. Nothing more. Please answer the question."

"He did go out. For about two hours."

"What time did he leave and what time did he return?"

"He left at about ten and got back just after midnight."

Seeing it from the cops' point of view, that was plenty of time to go meet Tessa Reeves and kill her, Cadence thought ruefully.

"Did Tate say how Kelly would react if she found out he was cheating on her?"

Phoebe blushed and lowered her eyes with shame. "It's because I'm not the first. But he said if Kelly found out about me it would be the last straw. She said she would make him pay. Like, divorce him and take him for all she could get."

"He told you that?"

"Yes. She was not going to keep up appearances anymore."

"Well, thanks for coming to see me. Straight off the bat, I have to tell you that there's a good chance you'll be called as a witness in his trial. At this stage, I couldn't tell you whether you'll be called by me or the prosecution. I'll need to flesh this out with Tate."

Phoebe looked horrified. "What? No. I can't. I came to tell you these things in confidence. He's in trouble and I want to help him. I can't possibly testify. I won't. That will ruin him."

"Phoebe, the man is accused of homicide. If he's found guilty, he could spend the rest of his life in prison. And as his defense lawyer, I have to use every means at my disposal to keep that from happening. And if there's collateral damage in the form of Kelly's vengeance then I'm afraid we just have to let the cards fall where they may."

"I'm not going to testify," Phoebe said with a huff and getting to her feet. "You can't make me."

"Actually, Phoebe, that's not true. I can. And the prosecutor can and will if he finds out about you, which is bound to happen."

"How could he find out if I don't tell him? He would have to be told by you, me or Tate himself."

"Do you seriously think no staff member at the Fairbanks saw you together? Do you think the cops aren't going to go there asking questions? Someone's going to blab to the cops about your little secret. It's not a matter of if but when."

Cadence stood up and placed a hand on Phoebe's arm.

"Look, Phoebe," she said. "You did the right thing coming to me. You did the best possible thing for Tate. He may not be happy about it, but his case has improved because of what you've done."

"God. I feel sick."

The two women walked out of the cafe. Cadence offered a few more words of encouragement, but once Phoebe had left, she was conflicted. Something was nagging at her. She could not decide whether Phoebe Baker had come to her of her own volition or whether Lieberman had sent her. It did not seem out of character for Lieberman to manipulate his mistress into presenting Cadence with both an alibi and a reason for Lieberman to lie.

From one point of view, it could easily be seen as the devious act of a guilty man.

Chapter 9

Tate Lieberman had rejected Cadence's demands for an urgent meeting. He told her it would have to wait until the end of his workday. He was not in jail yet and he had a business to run, he pointed out with typical arrogance.

Cadence had contacted Lieberman right after her morning meeting with Jackie and Alan. Neither of them was comfortable with her progress on the case, but even Alan conceded Lieberman was his own worst enemy. He did not try to advise Cadence on criminal law procedure, which was not in his wheelhouse, but he could not help but convey how important it was for the firm that she keep Lieberman on the hook.

She decided against insisting that Lieberman meet her earlier. It was not only pointless, but it would also surely aggravate him enough to complain to Alan. She had to accept that her power had limits. She could not order her client to do anything.

Lieberman's secretary got back to Cadence later in the day to tell her to meet Lieberman at seven o'clock at his office. But as she was about to leave the office, he sent her a message.

"Change of plan," he wrote. "Meet me at Off the Record."

Off the Record was an upscale bar right across the street from the White House. A favorite meeting place for DC playmakers and insiders, the bar was renowned as a place to get discreet business done in plain sight. Lieberman clearly expected that his meeting with his lawyer would not go unnoticed. It was one way to show he could not be intimidated. Just business as usual, thought Cadence. Ever cognizant of keeping Lieberman's complaints about her to a minimum, she agreed to the change of venue.

On the way in a cab, she got a text message from Gerard Underhill, letting her know he had fresh evidence to share. He referred her to an email he had just sent through. Reading it, Cadence's frustration only grew. The police had witnesses that placed Lieberman and Tessa Reeves together at Jameson's, a gentlemen's club that prided itself on offering fine spirits and top-shelf dancers.

Cadence shook her head. The cops and Underhill knew more about her client's activities than she did. She wondered if there was some purpose in Lieberman's insistence on keeping her in the dark. Did he confide more in Alan? Was she being put through some weird test? Never before had she felt like such an underling as opposed to a defense attorney with a proven track record.

Cadence told herself to park the new information for the time being. First, she had to confront Lieberman about Phoebe Baker. She had to get this man to trust her. She needed to know precisely why he was being so vague about his alibi. Not from Phoebe Baker's lips. Not from Alan's. From his.

Off the Record was a cozy, crimson den of a place. The moment Cadence walked in, eying the padded booths and dark wooden beams, she felt the reassuring hushed vibe that regulars came back for. Tate Lieberman was seated in one of the booths. He was not looking out for her. His eyes were fixed on his phone.

"Ah, you're here," he said as she got to his table. "Sit yourself down and we'll get you a drink."

The odd thing was that Lieberman seemed to be in an upbeat mood. She had never seen him anywhere near the happiness end of the emotional spectrum.

"I'm okay," she said.

"Nonsense. Come on. I'm not suggesting we tie one on, but I don't want to drink alone."

"You're not alone and I don't need a drink. I'll just have water. Sparkling."

Lieberman caught the attention of a waiter and placed the order, getting another brandy for himself.

Cadence put her phone on the table and tapped on the audio recorder app. "For your benefit and mine, I'm going to record our conversation."

Lieberman shot her a look as though she was a party pooper. She could not help but wonder how many drinks he had polished off already. He picked up his glass and drained the remnants.

"Why didn't you tell me about Phoebe Baker?" she asked.

The cheer vanished from Lieberman's face in an instant and he glared at Cadence. "How did you find out about—?"

"About your mistress? She came and saw me this morning."

"That stupid bitch," Lieberman spat. "I told her to stay out of it. I told her to keep her goddamn trap shut."

"So you were in a hotel room with Phoebe Baker?"

"Yes."

"But that's not all, is it?"

"What do you mean?"

"You left the Fairbanks to meet Tessa Reeves, right?"

"That's right."

"Where did you meet her?"

Although she already knew, she just wanted to see if Lieberman could bring himself to be truthful with her.

"It was a club. It's called Jameson's. It's incredibly discreet so I have no idea how anybody would know I was there."

"So you were with Tessa the night she died?"

"Yes, but only briefly."

"That's not the point, Tate. The point is that you didn't tell me about it. You lied to me. You lied to the police. You're doing exactly what guilty men do."

"What's that?"

"They tell the truth only as a last resort. The cops see this every day. You fed a bullshit alibi to your lawyer, who is trying to keep you from going to prison. I find out you were with your mistress only because she told me herself. Likewise, someone else, the prosecutor no less, tells me you were with the woman you're accused of murdering just before her death."

"It's complicated," said Lieberman.

The waiter appeared with the drinks and set them on the table.

"What were you meeting her about?"

"She was not backing off," he said, taking another sip of brandy. "I'd given Wade Hampton a piece of my mind and he told me not to worry. He'd deal with her."

"He said that?"

Lieberman shook his head. "He didn't need to. It was understood. He was getting cold feet about the story, anyway. He's got one foot out the door from that place and he did not want a lengthy defamation suit to drag out his departure."

"If you had that assurance, why did you meet with her?"

"Because it seemed like Wade had no control over his reporter. She kept at it. Calling Berrins staffers and ex-staffers to get information about how I ran things. So I decided to engage with her."

"So you arranged to meet her at Jameson's?"

"Yes. She only had to mention my name at the door and she'd be shown to a private room."

"So the staff know you met her."

"The staff are extremely discreet. That's part of the member benefits."

"Discreet? Really? The cops already have them singing like canaries. No waterboarding needed. And just you wait until Gerard Underhill gets them on the stand."

Lieberman waved her off.

"But that wasn't it, was it?"

"What do you mean?"

"You messaged Tessa after she left Jameson's, didn't you?"

"Wrong. I did no such thing."

"It's on her phone, Tate. A text message from you saying you had forgotten to tell her something urgent and to wait for you at McPherson Square, the metro station nearest the club."

"That's preposterous."

"Is it? How many phones do you have, Tate?"

"Two."

"And you never use a burner phone for extra-curricular activities like contacting Phoebe Baker?"

"Don't be ridiculous."

"What are your credit card receipts going to show, Tate? Underhill will get his hands on them and there's nothing you can do to stop him. And is Phoebe going to commit perjury for you? Will she lie and say she never saw you use a burner phone?"

"The last I saw of Tessa Reeves was when she left the club. That's it."

"Look, Tate. As your lawyer, the very minimum I need from you is a detailed alibi, an account of every little thing that you did that night so I can go out and verify it."

Lieberman nodded.

Cadence picked up her cell phone to double check it had been recording.

"Turn that off."

"No."

"Turn it off. There's something I need to say that can't be recorded."

"Okay," said Cadence, tapping the pause button. She showed Lieberman the screen to assure him she had complied.

"I can't say I was with Phoebe."

"There's no avoiding it. She is a vital part of your alibi. But this is about your wife Kelly, isn't it?"

"Yes. What did Phoebe tell you?"

"Forget about what Phoebe told me. How about you do the telling for a change?"

"We've been married for fifteen years and for the most part it has been a happy marriage. Well, that's not true. Kelly and I have made a great team. She's been on my arm at every conference that mattered and has been pivotal in the success of my company. Our company, I should say, because no one really knows that she owns half. Her family has plenty of money and she helped me launch Berrins with a bang. But I have needs and have had several affairs over the years."

"How many?"

"I don't know. Half a dozen, maybe?"

"Half a dozen? And how many does Kelly know about?"

"Three. And after the last time she swore that if she caught me cheating again, she wouldn't just divorce me, but she would pull the rug out from under me and bring down Berrins."

"I'm not sure I blame her."

"No, I don't expect you would, being a woman."

"What you tell me remains between us. As I've told you, it's covered by attorney-client privilege. Why don't I turn this back on and you can tell me exactly what happened. We can decide later on what you state publicly, but I can tell you now that Kelly is going to find out about Phoebe—not from me, mind you—so it's going to be best coming from you."

Lieberman breathed in and nodded. "You're right. Okay. Turn it on again."

Lieberman tipped the last of his brandy down and ordered another. Cadence had not touched her water.

"I've been seeing Phoebe for almost a year," Lieberman said. "I tell Kelly I've got some meeting in town or I'm working late, and I book a room at the Fairbanks. It's not just to see Phoebe, I genuinely have to do that sometimes."

"I understand. Go on."

Lieberman proceeded to tell Cadence that Phoebe got to the room ahead of him, and that he arrived at eight. He said when he got there, they had a drink from the mini bar and then had sex. He said that Tessa had been in contact with him that day, asking questions about Zellus and Senator Ron Nagle, a Democrat from Massachusetts.

"What sort of questions?"

"None of your—" said Lieberman before checking himself. "I'm sorry, it's a reflex."

"I can tell. And I suppose you were no less clear about telling Tessa it was none of her business, right?"

"Right."

"What was she asking?"

"She had some information about connections between Berrins, Zellus and some politicians."

"What kind of information?"

"Now that's something I don't need to tell you and it's confidential from a business perspective. What I will say is that little bitch was right."

The anger rose in Lieberman. "Someone in my company must have talked to her. She had information that no one else could or should know."

"And that angered you?"

"You bet it did."

"Okay, so tell me about the meeting you had with Tessa. Who suggested it?"

"I did. She put me on the spot. She said she was going to run with the information that she had. I figured Wade Hampton would not be able to keep her in line."

"She was an investigative reporter. Doing her job," Cadence said.

"Whose side are you on?"

Cadence ignored the question. "Was this meeting you suggested designed to get her to drop the story?"

"Yes. You could say that."

"How were you going to convince her to drop the story? You had already threatened her. That didn't work. What was your plan B?"

Lieberman shot a knowing glance at Cadence. "I was going to throw her some information on congressman Jerome Hamlin. He's a Democrat from Nevada."

"I know who he is. He's served as the representative of Nevada's first congressional district for the past eight years. He's been the primary sponsor of three bills that have been enacted."

Lieberman's raised brow indicated he was impressed by Cadence's knowledge. "Yeah, but he's a weasel."

"Why would she go for that as a story?"

"Because if she really wants to do some cleaning up around this town, he's a good place to start. What that guy gets away with is appalling. If this young idiot wanted a story to appease her do-gooder social conscience, then he was more her kind of story than me."

Cadence raised an eyebrow. "Isn't Hamlin already under investigation?"

Lieberman nodded. "Yes. Defrauding a charity? But anyway, it didn't work. She wasn't interested."

"Where did that leave your story?"

"She said she was going ahead."

"She told you she was going to go ahead and publish?"

"Yes."

"When?"

"As soon as she could, I suppose."

"Did you threaten her?"

"No. I argued with her. That was it."

"But you'd already threatened her?"

"True but I did not do so at the club."

"So she just left the meeting and you did nothing and said nothing more to stop her."

"I just told her she had better have a good lawyer on standby because she was about to put herself and her publication out of business."

Cadence leaned forward and paused the audio recorder again. She took a moment to imagine what a jury would make of what she had just heard.

Lieberman studied Cadence silently, waiting for her to speak but he could not help but speak first. "I know what you're thinking," he said. "And the answer is no. I did not resolve to kill Tessa then. But good God I'd be lying if I said I didn't think about it, client to lawyer."

Cadence still had no idea about what Tate Lieberman was prepared to do and say to save himself.

"You have denied killing Tessa," she said. "But what you have just told me amounts to a powerful motive for killing her."

"I would never say that on the stand."

"We don't know if we're going to trial yet, Tate, but for argument's sake, never say never. You may think you have what it takes not to give Gerard Underhill what he wants but you don't. Sorry to put that to you but it's the truth. You're my client and I'm being brutally honest with you. Gerard Underhill would not have to spend days backgrounding you. He could cross-examine you cold and have you pinned in a second. You know why? Because in his own way he is just like you. He will detect your self-importance, your pride, your indignation at having to publicly defend yourself against a charge of first-degree murder, and he will eat you up for lunch. Mark my words,

Tate, the courtroom is a long way from your office or wherever it is you get to play boss, but it's Gerard Underhill's domain. So forgive me when I say that, as your lawyer, you are going to take the stand over my dead body."

Lieberman could not hide his shock at being spoken to this way. Clearly, it was a rare moment indeed when someone gave him an unvarnished piece of their mind.

"It's my decision whether to take the stand, not yours."

"Okay. You can do that but don't say I didn't warn you. Because if you want a one-way ticket to prison for the rest of your life then by all means let's get you up there. But unless you undergo a personality transplant between now and then, you are going to make the jury want to find you guilty. You act as though this is all beneath you. And I have no doubt the jury will think that you believe you're above them and they will not hesitate to bring you crashing back down to earth. In their eyes, you'll have the motive, the means and the hubris to think you can kill another human being and get away with it. They'll look at you as the next Robert Durst."

"Do you always talk to your clients this way?"

"I don't appreciate being lied to, Tate. I'm giving it to you straight because it's what you need to hear. You're in desperate need of a reality check, and I don't mind being the one to deliver it to you. But what I'd really like is for you to start helping me to help you. This is not just going to go away because you find it disagreeable and unfair."

Lieberman's countenance softened. He was practically slumped back in his chair. He nodded and stared at his brandy.

Cadence got to her feet. Her phone rang in her hand. She looked at the screen and saw it was Bob and cut it off.

"What am I going to tell Kelly?" he said, staring into the table.

Cadence stood upright supporting her briefcase on the top of the booth. "It has to be the truth. The worst possible option is to let her find out in court."

"Are you sure it will come out?"

"I'm positive."

Cadence lifted her bag and let her right arm take its weight.

"I'll be in touch," she said and turned and left.

On her way out of Off the Record, Cadence returned Bob's call.

"Hey Bob, what's up?"

"Senator Ron Nagle, that's what's up."

"How so?"

"It's come to my attention that Tessa Reeves' real target may not have been Tate Lieberman. I'm beginning to think she was after Nagle. She wanted to scalp a prominent politician and Lieberman was just a way to get to Nagle."

"Nagle knew what Tessa was working on. Hampton told me that. What are you saying? That Nagle killed Tessa?"

"Who knows? But we need to find out, right?"

"Yes, of course."

"Well, I know just the place to start."

"Where?"

"He's speaking at a gala event tomorrow night."

"Is that so?"

"Yes. Black tie. So find yourself a dazzling dress because we need to go."

Chapter 10

Bob held a pamphlet out for Cadence to take. "Here. Take a look at this."

"What is it?"

"This is what we're celebrating tonight. The wonder drug Narcadia."

"Narcadia?" Standing under a gigantic chandelier, Cadence's mind shut out the cheerful banter of the formally attired throng around her in order to absorb what she was reading. The eight-page glossy pamphlet featured colorful graphs and photos of gleaming white labs and clinics. Narcadia, the text told her, was a wonder drug in the world of drug rehabilitation. With the opioid crisis running amok in hundreds of cities and towns across America, finally there was the perfect solution for people to break their addiction, regain control of their lives and return to the loving embrace of their families. Like most people in the US, Cadence was alarmed by the pervasiveness of the opioid crisis. Coming from a home in which her mother was addicted to meth, she was well aware of the ravages that drug addiction could inflict upon families and communities. The pamphlet heralded Narcadia as a game changer and its power was being embraced by doctors throughout the land. In the space of just six months, Narcadia had become the fastest growing drug prescribed to people addicted to opiates. And the people who made it all happen were the good folks at Zellus.

A photo accompanying the text showed the six Zellus board of directors. On the page opposite were photos of the night's speakers: three board members and Senator Ron Nagle, who was giving the night's keynote address. After scanning Nagle's bio, Cadence lifted her eyes to Bob.

"So Ron Nagle is getting the ball rolling on this love-in," she said.

"That's right." Bob checked his watch. "He's due on stage in thirty minutes."

"I can't see him," said Cadence, casting her eyes around the room. "Ah, there he is." She took another look at the inside page of the pamphlet. "And if I'm not mistaken that's Zellus CEO Melvin Muller he's talking to."

"You want to wait until Nagle's given his speech?"

"No. Let's go see him now."

The pair made their way through the champagne-sipping crowd. Nagle turned to them as they got near, and assuming that they were keen to come and shake his hand and perhaps wish him well in his imminent reelection bid, he greeted them with a wide and white smile.

"Senator Nagle," said Cadence, meeting the politician's outstretched hand and overstretched smile. "Lovely to meet you."

"The pleasure is all mine," said Nagle like all his Christmases had come at once. "I'm sure we haven't met. I'd never forget such a striking beauty."

"No, we haven't met. My name is Cadence Elliott."

Melvin Muller took this as his cue to leave, and placing a hand on Nagle's shoulder, told the star of the function to break a leg.

"Cadence," said Nagle. "What a lovely name."

"And this is Bob Rhodes."

"Hello there, Bob. Now are you investors or are you just here for the free Veuve Clicquot like me?"

"Neither really, Senator. I'm a criminal defense attorney and Bob here is my investigator."

The joviality seeped out of Nagle's face. To his disappointment, he sensed the conversation was not going to be a light one.

"That's fascinating," he said flatly. "Bob and I have met before, haven't we, Bob? Geez, from the White House press corps to—what is it you call yourself now?—a private investigator. What happened?"

"Lots of good stuff," said Bob, letting the insult slide right off. "I've never been happier. I have the time to dig so much deeper on whatever, or whoever, I'm investigating."

"And what brings you here tonight? Are you investigating me?"

"I'm defending Tate Lieberman, Senator Nagle," said Cadence. "I want to talk to you about Tessa Reeves."

"Are you out of your mind, woman?" said Nagle, his lip twitching with anger. "I've got absolutely nothing to say to you. And who's Tessa Reeves other than an unfortunate hack? I thought she killed herself anyway. I can't understand why they've got Lieberman involved. But regardless, now is not the time. I have a speech I need to prepare for, so if you don't mind."

With a shake of his head, Nagle made to leave.

"An unfortunate hack?" said Cadence. "Does your contempt have anything to do with the fact that at the time of her death, Tessa Reeves was investigating your activities?"

"What are you suggesting? Get out of here or I will have security throw you out."

"Senator, we can either talk now or I can raise my voice and begin asking my questions loudly enough for this entire room to hear."

Nagle could see that Cadence was not joking. At this point, a young man stepped in between Nagle and Cadence.

"Sir, is everything okay here?"

"Who are you?" asked Cadence.

"Never mind who I am," said the younger man. "You need to give the Senator some space."

"I'm not holding him anywhere. Am I, Senator? Like I said, how about we go somewhere quiet so we don't have to talk over the noise of this crowd?"

Nagle gently pushed his man aside. "It's okay, Ryan," he said. "We're just going to the Johnson Room. I'll be back in five."

"Are you sure, sir?"

"Yes," said Nagle tersely.

With that, Nagle led them to a large wooden door off to the side of the main room.

"Okay, Ms. Elliott. Make it quick," said Nagle trying to wrest control of the situation.

"I take it you are aware that Tessa Reeves was working on a story to expose political malfeasance here in DC."

"I wasn't privy to what Tessa Reeves had on her to-do list. Everything I do is above board. What exactly is it that you want from me?"

"Did you ever speak with Tessa Reeves?"

"No. The first I ever heard of her was when she died. A colleague told me."

"Did she ever contact you?"

"I can't recall."

"She never called you? Emailed you?"

"I get a lot of calls. I get a lot of emails. Hundreds a day, in fact. Mostly from my constituents who would like me to keep working for their best interests."

"You had words with Tessa's editor, Wade Hampton, though."

"I've known Wade for a long time. I speak to him regularly. He's been part of the DC press corps for many years. My door is always open to Wade."

"Did you ask him to rein Tessa Reeves in?"

Nagle laughed. "Don't be ridiculous. I have no such say in what Wade Hampton decides to publish. We deal with each other in a very traditional way."

"What way is that?"

"Journalism and politics in this country have been joined at the hip since Lincoln was a boy," said Nagle. "It's a symbiotic exchange of information that is of mutual benefit. It helps us get our message out and it affords the press the prestige of being insiders. Surely, I don't have to tell you that, Bob."

"You put a good spin on it," said Bob, "but things can go sour very fast when there's information you don't want to get out."

"Look, I don't tell Wade Hampton what to publish and he doesn't tell me how to vote in Congress. My constituents do that."

"I suppose your constituents are all for you doing the bidding of Zellus Pharmaceuticals?" said Bob. "I've looked at the rollout of Narcadia around the country. And wherever you go, a Narcadia monopoly follows. With your help, Narcadia is one of the fastest growing drugs on the US market right now."

Nagle turned to Bob and gave him a disdainful smile. "You know what you two sound like? Naive undergrads. How long have you been working in DC, Ms. Elliott? Clearly not long enough not to sound like a guileless fool. I'm in bed with no one. I work for my people. And I support good work where I see it. You may not like it, but Zellus is doing remarkable work in the field. Groundbreaking stuff. And I am proud to support them."

"But—"

"I'm not finished. If you want to try and get dirt on me, good luck. All my enemies are trying to do the same. But they have failed. My life is a very public one and I have nothing to fear from any reporter in DC. As for you, Ms. Elliott, you need to be a lot more careful about who you choose to aggravate."

"Is that a threat?"

"Just a word of advice. You've somehow gatecrashed this event to confront me but if you want to go after Zellus, you'd better have all your ducks in a row because they will not stand for anyone trying to tarnish their reputation."

He smiled and patted Cadence's shoulder. "I'm the good guy here. I play nice. Ask anyone. But not everyone in DC does. Tessa Reeves was dispensable. Harsh but fair. And so are you. Don't you ever forget it."

"Typical politician. You threaten me yet claim that's not what your words mean."

"Allow me to give you some advice, then," said Nagle. "Don't go poking bears with sharp sticks. You're likely to get your head bitten clean off. That's all I'm saying. Now if you'll excuse me, I've got a speech to give."

Chapter 11

"Come see me as soon as you get in."

Jackie's midnight text was unusually curt. Clearly, she was unhappy about something.

Cadence got to the office at seven and walked around to Jackie's office, not expecting her direct boss to be there yet. Jackie was a seven-thirty starter. She was like clockwork. She would sometimes stay until the early morning hours, but no matter what, her start time was seven-thirty. Today, however, Jackie was not only at her desk, but she had company with whom she was in deep and earnest conversation—Alan Henshaw. The pair of them turned to Cadence as she approached. Neither face warmed to a smile.

"Come in and close the door," said Alan, as though it was his office. Cadence did so and took the wingback seat beside Alan. She did not know what was coming except that it was most certainly not going to be high praise.

"Guess who I got a call from last night?" demanded Alan.

"Ron Nagle."

"Exactly. That's *Senator* Ron Nagle. He told me you accosted him at a function last night."

"Accosted would be too strong a word."

"Really? He said you demanded that he submit to being questioned on the spot and threatened to make a spectacle of yourself if he did not acquiesce."

"I did not want to take no for an answer," said Cadence. "And he was being dismissive."

"Is that so? It wasn't because you gatecrashed the event and treated him like a murder suspect?"

"I've got a client to defend, Alan. I received some information that warranted immediate investigation. And if that investigation proves fruitful, it means that I have a better chance at getting my client off these charges. In other words, I was doing my job."

"Our client," said Alan with slow purpose.

"Excuse me?"

"He's our client. The firm's client. The firm founded by the other two people sitting here with you in this room. What makes you think that it's okay to go out as our employee and attack a Senator like that?"

"It was not an attack, Alan. You've entrusted me to defend Tate Lieberman. It's not the first time that you and Jackie have put your faith in me, and to a large extent you have been okay with me going about my work the way that I see fit."

Jackie coughed. "Cadence, you can't mistake our faith in you as carte blanche to conduct yourself any way that you please. In the past, I've had to remind you that in your capacity as a defense attorney, you are a representative of this firm. You are our proxy. And that means in the way you look, the way you conduct yourself with clients and members of the public."

That was true. Jackie had to rein Cadence in once or twice. But up until now, Cadence had thought that while she took such reprimands to heart, there was a tacit understanding that Cadence's grit was a quality that set her apart from the pack. Jackie had said as much when she hired her, when she had shown Cadence a pile of Ivy League applications that Cadence had beaten to get the job at Hardwick and Henshaw. She was an outsider. She was not from DC. She had not traipsed the lawns of Harvard or Stanford. She had worked her tail off at Sturm College of Law, in Denver. And in the years after she had been hired, Jackie had oftentimes remarked how Cadence's individuality was such a strength. She had put her faith in her young protege and had seen her flourish into an exceptional attorney. Sitting there now, Cadence was no yes-sir-nor-sir underling fresh out of law school. She was a successful trial lawyer with major wins under her belt.

She was surprised how calm she felt. "Alan. Jackie. I'm doing what I think is right to clear Tate Lieberman's name. I didn't think that I would have to justify approaching Senator Nagle as I did. Do you seriously think calling his office and waiting for him to return my call was the way to go?"

"Now look here, Cadence—"

"I could tell from the moment I introduced myself that he would never have given me the time of day freely."

"He was about to give a speech," said Alan. "He called me as soon as he had finished and told me about your intrusion. He was livid."

"I know he was," said Cadence. "That was clear from the outset. He knows something, Alan. He was threatened by what Tessa Reeves was investigating, and God knows what he would have done to stop her in her tracks."

"My God," said Alan. "He was going about his legitimate business. Are you telling us that you consider him to be a suspect?"

"Yes. I am. On the surface his partnership with Zellus is kosher. Ostensibly, it's legal and legitimate. But what was Tessa Reeves trying to get to the bottom of?"

"What are you talking about?"

"I have reason to believe that Tessa's probe into Tate's affairs was merely a gateway she hoped would lead to her real target—the manner in which Zellus is achieving a monopoly of supply for one of its drugs."

Alan shook his head in disbelief. "You've lost me. You are representing Tate Lieberman who, just to remind you, has been charged with murder. As I said from the outset, your job is to get those charges dropped so that this case against him doesn't see the light of day."

"And so you get more business out of him. Oh no, I get it, Alan. You've made that very clear."

"Cadence," chided Jackie. "There is no need to be insolent."

Cadence checked herself. "I apologize, Alan. And to you Jackie. But I feel that I am serving two masters here. One is the welfare of my client, and the other is the business prospects of the firm."

"For God's sake, grow up," said Alan. "What do you think we do here? This is a business, not a charity. As I've told you before, our business law stream keeps this firm afloat. It provides the lion's share of revenue, and I will not have that jeopardized by your determination to act like a free agent who's just winging it."

Cadence bit her tongue. Perhaps she should have gone about approaching Nagle in another way. Suddenly, she doubted her own methods.

"I want to assure you both that I am approaching this case strategically."

Alan threw his hands in the air. "Strategically? It seems to me that you are not sticking to your main objective, which is to get Lieberman off. There's no hard evidence against the man."

"I've briefed you both on what I'm doing. I don't have a plea offer from Underhill yet, but we all know that Lieberman will not be willing to plead guilty to anything. So that means going to trial is very likely. And when that day comes, I want to be armed to the teeth with ways to convince a jury to throw those charges out."

Cadence, legs crossed and leaning forward, spoke with the coolest of heads. She sensed Jackie had one foot in Alan's camp and one foot in hers. Although it was not right for her to have to explain herself to someone whose specialty was not criminal law, because Alan was the managing partner, it was he she had to appease.

"Alan, Gerard Underhill is only too happy for this to go to trial with the evidence he has. They have motive and means and a dire threat as precursors to murder. He's not going to let it go easily with a generous plea offer. He'll be only too happy to take this to trial. And both you and I know that he's right to feel he has the advantage because Tate Lieberman will not play well in court. He's lied to the police. He's lied to me. And he's arrogant enough to think he can get himself off by taking the stand and telling everyone what to do. He has a madness born of hubris."

"I agree," said Jackie. "That would be suicidal. You can't let him take the stand, if it comes to that."

"I'm trying, believe me. But I don't see how we don't end up in court."

"It cannot go to trial!" said Alan, his face flushed red. "Don't you get it? Get the judge to throw out Underhill's evidence. Do that and where's his case? As cocky as he may be, he knows he can't afford to fail at trial. It will set his hopes of making US Attorney back years."

"I will challenge the evidence."

Alan let out an exasperated sigh. "Why haven't you done so already instead of going down rabbit holes in the hope of exposing some kind of Watergate conspiracy? You're a lawyer, not a journalist."

"I need to investigate leads to do the best for my client. I didn't think I'd have to justify that."

It was clear that nothing short of Cadence's apologetic submission would defuse Alan's fury.

"Let me make it clear, Cadence," he said. "You foul this up and you're gone. If this goes to trial and you lose, then as far as I'm concerned you can find another job. Now get back to work."

Cadence sat for a moment and bit her tongue. She was only too happy to walk. She knew her value in the DC job market.

Alan's words did sting Cadence but what stung more was that Jackie offered nothing in her defense.

"With pleasure," she said, and she got up and returned to her desk. In her head she began flipping through all the firms who had expressed interest in stealing her away, and then there was Gerard Underhill himself.

Whatever happened, this would be her last case with Hardwick and Henshaw, win or lose.

Chapter 12

The bartender spun a white cocktail napkin in the air, caught it on the back of his hand and then flipped it onto the counter in front of Cadence. The gin and tonic he then planted on it in front of her with quick panache was her second. It was not going to be her last.

Following her meeting with Alan and Jackie, Cadence had worked straight through to nine at night. Then, torn between heading home alone and needing to process what had happened, she called her colleague Sophie, who suggested they go for a drink and a debrief on the morning's events.

"This is Beefeater," said the bartender, who suggested she try it instead of the Tanqueray she had ordered first. "It doesn't have the reputation of Tanqueray, but it doesn't need to. It's cheaper, but for a G&T, it's hard to beat, trust me."

The bartender was all set to go into more detail about the qualities that made Beefeater shine, but her friend joined Cadence at the bar and cut him short.

"I'll have what she's having," said Sophie Shields, Cadence's closest female friend at Hardwick and Henshaw. Sophie was the firm's first black hire and she worked harder than any paralegal in DC, as though she felt she needed to counter any sense that her position was an act of affirmative action.

As Cadence took a sip, Sophie leaned into her and placed a caring hand on her shoulder.

"So you took a beatdown from Alan," she said. "Maybe it's a first for you but he's been on everyone's case lately."

"He's more than on my case. It's like he wants to pound me into submission. I actually think it would make him happy if I snapped to attention and saluted him. He must know that the DA's not going to drop Lieberman's case easily. It just pisses him off and he takes it out on me. That's my take, anyway."

The bartender delivered Sophie's drink and Cadence told him to put it on her tab.

"Look, they put you on this case because you're the best trial lawyer at the firm," said Sophie. "If they thought there was no chance Lieberman would wind up in court, they could have given the case to someone else."

"Alan's made it clear my job is on the line. And he's always telling me to make sure it doesn't go to trial."

Sophie shook her head. "Of all people, he should know that it's not something that anyone can control. I guess trying to control you is the next best option. You know how Alan likes to feel he's got his big, strong hands on your levers."

The sudden laugh that escaped Cadence's mouth almost sent her drink across the bar. She wiped her mouth as she giggled with delight. "Oh my God. Can you imagine?"

Sophie laughed. "Come on. You know you'd love it. Those puffy old paws all over you. You running your fingers through the strands of that shiny dome of his."

Cadence crumpled over, enjoying a real belly laugh. "Oh, my God, girl. You crack me up. I needed that." She shook her head, smiling. "Thank you."

Sophie studied her friend's face. "You looked like you were in a dark place when I got here. What's going on?"

"I think I'm going to leave the firm," she said, her fingers toying with her glass. "There are a couple of other firms that I like the look of, and I know they pay well. Or maybe the DA's office would be a good move. I've got plenty of time to build up my salary and I've always thought a few years' experience as a prosecutor would be a great asset for a career in criminal defense."

"Has Gerard Underhill been after you again?"

"Not recently. I'm sure he'd love to beat me in this case first. Then, with his ego restored, I'd imagine he'd be happy to offer me the chance to work under the master prosecutor before he steps up to US Attorney."

"He is very, very good at what he does. But if you cost him another conviction, I doubt he'll want to hire you. He'd be too scared you'd show him up. Isn't that the golden rule of public service? Never hire anyone that might outshine you?"

"You may be right there."

Just then, Cadence's phone lit up and began to vibrate. Cadence started to pick it up off the bar.

"Let it go to voicemail," said Sophie. "It can wait."

"I'll just check," said Cadence, taking the device in her hand. She was surprised to see it was an unknown number calling. As much as she would have liked to let the call go through to voicemail, she always made a point of answering such calls. It might well be a telemarketing call but then it could just as easily be someone reaching out to her about the case. They might have new information and they might not be willing to leave a message or even call back. She could not take that chance.

"Hello, Cadence speaking," she said, turning her head down and blocking her left ear with her free hand.

"I have some information that will be of interest to you."

It was a woman's voice. She was outside. Cadence could hear traffic in the background.

"Who is this? What is this information about?"

"It's about your case," said the woman. "I'm a friend of Tate Lieberman. I can help you clear his name."

The voice was cold and flat, but the words got Cadence's pulse racing.

"Yes?"

"There are some things you need to know."

"What kind of things?"

"Not over the phone," said the woman. "You'll have to come and meet me. I'll be at the Lincoln Memorial at eleven thirty. I'll be watching and won't show myself unless I'm convinced you have come alone. Do you understand me?"

"Yes," said Cadence, looking at her watch. It was five past eleven.

"Be there or you'll never hear what I've got to tell you."

With that, the caller hung up. Cadence slowly returned her phone to the bar. She then grabbed her glass and took a big gulp. She got to her feet.

"What are you doing?" said Sophie.

"I have to go."

"What? Go where? You look like you saw a ghost. What's going on, Cadence?"

Cadence went to move away but Sophie grabbed her by the forearms. Cadence bowed her head. "I can't tell you, Sophie. I'd like to but I can't. But I have to go."

"You're not going alone," said Sophie.

Cadence did her best to brighten her mood. "Sophie, don't worry. Look, I'll see you at the office tomorrow bright and early, okay?"

"Don't give me that," said Sophie. "I don't have a good feeling about this. I'm coming with you."

"No, Sophie," Cadence said firmly. "You can't. You just can't."

The unexpected force of Cadence's order took Sophie by surprise.

"Who is it? What did they tell you?"

Cadence did not want to share the little detail she had. It would only make Sophie more protective.

"I'm sorry, Sophie. I can't say. I swear, I'll be fine. I'll see you tomorrow. Okay?"

The look on Sophie's face as Cadence left the bar made it clear that her friend was not buying it.

Chapter 13

Cadence got the driver to stop on Henry Bacon Drive and she got out and watched him go. Across the road, the Lincoln Memorial stood tall and bright, its marble columns and walls lit up grand and white like a wedding cake. Even at this hour the building appeared reassuringly open and exposed. There were a few people here and there, and seeing a break in the light traffic, Cadence crossed over the road, still feeling tipsy from the gin. The apprehension of what was to come had not fully overridden the alcohol's effects.

She scanned side to side as she climbed the steps, looking for the female caller. She saw not a soul. She looked back, thinking people must come here at all hours of the night to sit on the famous steps and take in the view down the Mall before they got their drunk asses home. At the bottom was a couple kissing. Their embrace broke, and they stood and walked away hand in hand.

By the time she reached the top landing, Cadence was uncomfortably certain no one else was around. She turned left and began walking the length of the landing, passing one great white column after another. When she reached the end, she looked down the side. No one. She then turned back and began walking toward the other end. That was when she saw a woman appear. She was too far away to identify but she flashed her phone at Cadence and waited facing her. As Cadence drew closer, the woman stepped out of view. Still uncertain who her contact was, Cadence pressed onward, keeping her steps light and near silent. She looked at her phone and brought up the voice recording app. She pressed record and then placed it in her coat pocket. Whatever happened tonight, she was going to make sure she went home with evidence to analyze. She did not want to rely on memory alone.

When she reached the corner, Cadence saw that the woman had disappeared. She must have shifted behind one of the side columns. She heard some movement and was convinced the woman was close.

"Hello?" she said.

Nothing.

"Are you there?" she said.

Cadence stopped and strained her ears for any sign from the woman. Still, there was no reply. A flush of annoyance ran through her. She was not in the mood for games.

Waiting in silence her ears picked up the sound of rain. It came down lightly at first but quickly got heavier and steady. She remembered that she had read a forecast earlier that day that predicted a front to come through overnight bringing rain for forty-eight hours at least. It was now a downpour. Great, she thought to herself. She was going to get soaked on the way home.

Her patience waning, she moved forward without any pretense of stealth. The sound of her rubber-soled flats on the stone rose above the rain. Her phone pinged with a text message.

Expecting it would be from the woman, Cadence took it out and saw it was from Sophie.

"Are you okay?" the message read.

Cadence's face broke into a smile as she read the message and sent a message back saying she was fine.

Absorbed by her phone, Cadence was fractionally slow in hearing the sudden movement that came from behind her. By the time she spun her head around to see what it was, the man was ten feet behind her. His arms were outstretched and in one hand she could see clearly that he was holding a knife.

Instantly, Cadence broke into a sprint. Thankfully her shoes gripped the marble, and she managed to stay just out of reach of the man as she set off. As she bolted for the next corner, she let out a scream, but it only came out as a gasp. She could hear the man behind her grunting with his effort to catch her. *If he gets me, I'm dead*, Cadence thought. She knew who it was. She was in no doubt it was the same man who threatened her with his knife in her face.

She cut in close to the edge when she reached the corner,. She put her hand on the wall to help fling herself around faster. Immediately, she saw to her desperate disappointment that there was no one else around. This was the back side of the memorial, and a bank of shrubbery shielded it from beyond. She could not see out and more to the point, no one could see in.

As she swung around the corner, she momentarily thought she had widened the gap between her and the knife man. But her left hand remained outstretched behind her for a fraction of a second too long. It was enough for the man to reach out and snatch her fingers. He did so by diving forward so that when Cadence felt the strong and sickening grip around her fingers, she tried to recoil her arm with horror. But his grip was too solid.

She was yanked back and twisted downward as the man lost his footing and fell. He hit the stone but never loosened his grip, so Cadence fell down with him. Even as she fell, he pulled at her so that she landed on top of him. A frantic horror consumed her as she tried to break free while his arms wrapped around her tighter and tighter.

She tried to scream again but with her exertions it came out as a loud grunt. She wriggled and kicked and somehow managed to land a heel hard on his shin. The kick clearly stung but it did nothing to deter him. The hand with the knife was pressed against her chest now, the blade pointing up to her chin.

Cadence began screaming and this time it came out loud and shrill. But in an instant, she was silenced by his gloved hand pressed hard over her mouth and nose. She could not breathe and her lungs were in painful need of more air.

Her eyes were now bulging in terror and all she could think of was what she had learned in the krav maga class. Where were her keys? Could she reach them?

Her right hand shot into her coat pocket, which was where, thanks to her krav maga instructor's advice, she kept her keys, as opposed to her handbag. Her attacker's arm was positioned just above that pocket, so as she kept wriggling and trying to roll free of him, she was able to reach in and grab the keys. Her instructor stressed that she should never try to place the keys between her fingers to use Wolverine style. The best bet, she remembered clearly, was to bunch them up in a fist and have the ends protrude above her hand. This formed a makeshift shiv that she could wield with some degree of power, if only she had the room to strike.

Clenching her as tightly as he could, the man began trying to maneuver them both to the edge of the landing by sliding on his back with her still held on top of him. Clearly, he intended to haul her into the bushes. If he succeeded, Cadence knew she was dead.

She relaxed her whole body and in that brief moment the man responded as she had hoped. He mistook her deception as a sign of exhaustion and so he relaxed his grip slightly in order to try rolling out from under her to get on top. As he rolled to the side, he let go to reposition his grip. In that instant, she twisted in his arms and shot her fist towards his face. He arched back to try and dodge the blow, but he was too slow. Cadence's keys dug into his skin and cut across his face with such speed and force that they sliced him from the middle of his left cheek to the bridge of his nose.

The man grunted loudly with pain and swore and instinctively brought his hands to his face.

Cadence rolled away and scrambled for a few yards on the stone before she could get to her feet.

The man dove forward to grab her legs, but he missed. But no sooner was she running again than he was once more in hot pursuit.

Exhausted yet thrust forward by the fiercest will to live, Cadence saw a break in the bushes and ran straight for it, her right side brushing against a great column as she began her leap. She landed in the soft garden bed, then cut through the bushes and leaped clear onto the lawn beyond.

The grass was slick with rain and she slipped and fell hard onto her back. The blow winded her and so hampered her effort to get back onto her feet.

Slowly, in the pouring rain, panting like a wild animal, Cadence rose. It immediately occurred to her that she no longer heard any sounds of his pursuit. She stood and faced the gap between the bushes.

At first, she thought the man had disappeared. Her heightened sense of alarm prompted her to look to each side to see if he was coming at her another way. But then, against the lights of the Lincoln Memorial, she saw some movement at the bottom of the bushes. It was him. He had not reached the grass. From what she could see, he appeared to be lying in the bushes. His body was flinching but he seemed unable to move.

She took a step toward him. And another. She did not know why he was not on his feet but she could see he was pinned down by something. His body was no longer flinching. All he was doing was groaning. Then his groaning stopped.

Cadence edged closer. Just a few yards away now, she could see clearly that the knife man was dead. He had somehow fallen headfirst into the bushes and landed on the low wrought iron fence that lined the garden bed. His head, impaled on one of the flower shaped spikes, was jutting sharply skywards. His dead eyes were open wide, the rain falling directly into them.

By the severe backward angle of his neck, Cadence deduced it was broken.

For a moment, Cadence took in the macabre sight as the rain soaked through her clothes.

Suddenly there was a noise from above and the woman appeared on the landing. Now there was no doubt who she was and why she had lured Cadence here.

It was Monica Cordoba.

Without a word between them Monica turned and left.

Moments later, Cadence did the same.

Chapter 14

Cadence heard a light tap at her open office door but did not lift her head to see who it was. Since arriving at work, she had sat down and had not moved from her chair. Her body was sore all over, and she knew that moving her quickly triggered a fierce pain in her neck.

"Just leave it here, thanks, Sophie," she said, expecting Sophie to have the brief that she had asked for. Naturally, this request had only come after she had addressed Sophie's questions about the night before. Cadence said the source's information was not as good as she had hoped but it might prove useful. Cadence made some comment about how people always believe that their information is critical to a case but all too often it proves to be underwhelming for the lawyer.

"Those people can be deluded," said Sophie. "Which means it was a total mistake that you went to meet them by yourself in the dead of night. God knows what might have happened."

"You're right," said Cadence. "But I'm here and at work and I need that brief, if you'd be so kind."

With that Cadence expected to be left alone with her work for a good while. But that tapping at her door was not Sophie.

"I've been called many things, but Sophie's not one of them," said Bob Rhodes. He stepped in. "I just thought I'd drop by with something I discovered about our friend Ron Nagle."

"Great," said Cadence.

"Well, don't sound too enthusiastic. I thought you'd be pleased."

Cadence straightened up in her chair. She was pleased to see Bob, her good friend and a man whose advice and opinion she rated highly. Until Bob appeared, she had tried to lose herself in work to stop thinking about last night's attack and the dead man staring grotesquely up at her. After scurrying away from the Lincoln Memorial, she did not call an Uber to take her home until she was well clear of the vicinity. This left her with the verifiable alibi that she was nowhere near the dead man when she called for a ride home.

"Actually, Bob," Cadence said, "you don't know how pleased I am to see you."

Cadence looked through the glass wall into the center of the Hardwick and Henshaw offices. "Get the door, would you?"

"What's up?" asked Bob when he had settled into his chair. "You look a little, er, frazzled."

"That's because I am."

"What's going on?"

Cadence took a deep breath before recounting the events at the Lincoln Memorial in detail. Bob was the only person familiar with the secret life of Cadence Elliott. She had told him everything, from how she was tricked into giving up her baby to the time the man with the knife run her off the road and threatened to kill her if she continued to look into the whereabouts of her child. Bob was the one who discovered that Monica Cordoba was infertile and that she had faked her pregnancy. He had agreed with Cadence that while her mother had apparently signed off on the adoption in her name that did not mean the adoption was legal. The viciousness with which Monica Cordoba had reacted to Cadence tracking down her son made it seem clear she had something to hide. Then again, she may have just been a powerful person protecting her adopted son from the intrusion of his birth mother. Cadence struggled with her own demons on that one. Was she a horrible person or did she have every reason to pursue the truth? Bob was adamant that she was entitled to answers, answers that her now dead mother could not provide.

When Cadence had finished recounting the attack, Bob raised his eyebrows and dug into his pocket for his phone.

"Are you okay?"

Cadence nodded. "Just twisted my ankle a little, that's all."

"Are you sure he died?"

"Yes."

Bob lowered his gaze to his phone and began swiping across the screen. When he found what he wanted, he leaned forward with his elbows resting on his knees. After a minute or so, he shook his head.

"The cops haven't ID'd him yet," he said. "They think he slipped. They think he was in some kind of fight. His hands were slick with blood. There's a photo of the blood stain on the column. They think he was trying to get away from someone who was chasing him, that he turned to jump off the landing onto the lawn, but his bloody hand slipped on the column and he broke his neck. They don't mention him being impaled. I suppose discretion got the better of them there."

"Well, they got most of it right," said Cadence.

"Except for the fact that he was the one doing the chasing."

"Exactly."

"Look, Cadence," Bob said, "it's no crying shame that this creep is dead. And while the cops say they're looking for witnesses and want to find the other person or people involved, they're not saying that this is a murder case. How did you get home?"

"Uber."

"From where?"

"I walked all the way to 12th Street."

"Good."

"I guess I'm wondering if Monica will make an anonymous call to send the cops my way."

"That's possible, I guess."

Bob kept scrolling through his phone. "Hang on. Here's something new. Just posted."

"What's that?"

"It's a *DC Watch* story. They've identified the guy. His name's Matteo Santino. Argentinian. Does that sound right to you?"

"I don't know," said Cadence, casting her mind back to what the man had said to her with the point of his knife digging into her cheek. *You've been asking the wrong people the wrong kind of questions. This is your first and last warning. Back the fuck off, you hear me?*

"I mean, I didn't exactly converse with the guy. He did not have a strong accent. It could have been Spanish, Portuguese or Eastern European for all I know. So he was Argentinian?"

"Yes."

"Like Ben's father, Simon Cordoba."

"Yes."

"So I guess we could assume that Mr. Cordoba wants me dead just as much as his wife does."

"I'd say that's right on the money."

Cadence shook her head and looked at Bob. "She's not going to report me to the cops, Bob."

"Why not?"

"Because she doesn't want to provoke me. She doesn't want me to go public with what she's done."

"So far all she's done is pretend to be pregnant," said Bob.

"True but I'm convinced she doesn't want anyone snooping around anything related to how she got hold of Ben. Not me, not anybody. And that tells me it wasn't kosher. Nothing about that adoption was routine. It could not have been legal."

"Maybe. But you have no way to prove it."

"I know. But she knows and I need to confront her. Or maybe I could go and try to have a conversation with her."

"What planet are you living on, Cadence? She tried to have you killed. That's how much she'd love to sit down and chat with you about all this."

"Who does she have to stand in my way? Her thug is dead now."

"Who's to say there won't be more? You know the Cordoba story. You know what they're capable of."

Ever since Cadence identified her son's adoptive parents, she and Bob had dug up everything they could about the Cordoba family. Simon was the youngest son of Eduardo Cordoba, a billionaire who for a time headed up Argentina's state-run oil and gas corporation, Petrosol. Tracing the family further back, they discovered that Simon's grandfather Arturo had helped organize ODESSA, an operation to smuggle Nazis out of post-war Europe into South America. Unlike his elder brother, who followed their father's footsteps into Petrosol, Simon left his homeland in his late twenties, and had been living in America for almost thirty years. It seemed, intentionally or not, that he was a black sheep. Eschewing the oil game, he began investing in renewable energy projects. And while that may make him sound soft and enlightened, he was far from a soft touch. In fact, Bob had discreetly conversed with several business associates of Simon Cordoba, and all had remarked on his sense of power. From their anecdotes, Bob and hence Cadence, had formed the impression that Simon was something of a Michael Corleone—a quiet-spoken man who could read people extremely well, a graceful host with an eloquent tongue but an absolute ruthless beast when it came to protecting his own business interests.

"For all we know, Simon may have ordered the hit on you, not Monica," said Bob. "We have absolutely no idea what their relationship is like. Marriages are not always grounded in love. Factors like greed, gain and fear underpin the unions of many power couples parading themselves around DC. For them, it's a pact."

Cadence nodded. She could not help but think of the Liebermans and how Kelly had endured so much in order to keep living the life to which she had become accustomed.

"Monica Cordoba has money to burn," said Bob. "She found one killer for hire. What's stopping her from finding another? Nothing. As we speak, she might be making moves to finish the job."

"Which is why I need to go to her now," said Cadence. "I mean, what can I do, Bob? It's not like I can walk in there and take Ben away."

"Is that what you want to do?"

"It is. It's what I've been desperate to do. But I know it's not right. For Ben, that is. I don't even know what I can really hope for. But now is the time to strike. Maybe I can reason with her."

Bob held up his hands to help his words sink emphatically into Cadence's mind. "Trust me," he said. "Reason is the last thing you should expect from Monica Cordoba. You don't know what response you'll provoke by confronting her. Listen, you need to let this blow over. Give it a month or two and then reassess. This is not urgent. Don't do it just yet. Wait till the investigation into this Santino guy's death blows over. Let her cool off. Then confront her. You need to step back and put all your energy into the Lieberman case."

"You're right."

"You bet I am. Your case is everything right now, even if it's the last thing you do for this firm."

A look of surprise came over Cadence's face.

"Come on," said Bob. "You don't think I know? But my two cents? Fine. Go wherever your heart desires but win this case first. If you don't give it your all you won't be able to live with yourself."

Cadence leaned back in her chair and let all the thoughts about the Cordobas seep from her mind. She felt much better for it.

"Right you are, Bob," she said. "Now, what have you got on Ron Nagle?"

"Well, I heard that his chief of staff is leaving him once the midterms are over."

"So?"

"So, it's my understanding that his replacement has already been found."

"Who?"

"Someone who currently works at *DC Watch*."

"Wade Hampton?"

"Who else?"

Chapter 15

At the front office of *DC Watch*, Cadence gave her name to the middle-aged woman behind the desk. The receptionist hit a button and stopped chewing her gum momentarily to speak.

"Mr. Hampton, there's a Ms. Elliott here to see you…

"Yes… Yes… No… I scheduled it for now. I wrote it down for you. Well, two minutes from now, to be precise. She's a little early…

"Certainly, Mr. Hampton."

With that the receptionist tapped a button to end the call and looked up at Cadence once more. "Go on in, hon. Just through that door and second on the right."

The main office area was an open-plan room no bigger than half a basketball court. Based on a quick scan, Cadence guessed there were fifteen desks in the room. She only counted six heads though. The office was drab with little effort made to improve its visual appeal. Between the beige walls and dirty, off-white ceilings with fluorescent lights were cubicle dividers coated in gray carpet. Sheets of paper of various sizes were pinned everywhere, some going yellow with age. Cadence could almost feel the dust enter her lungs. Although she saw no signs of movement, she could hear phones ringing and keyboards clattering away at a furious pace. Clearly, it was a place that lacked prettiness not purpose. Cadence briefly considered how a young reporter like Tessa Reeves might get excited about working here.

Wade Hampton's door was a slab of cheap laminate that was stained orange and coated in thin varnish. The nameplate on the door was white. At least it was once. Now dust and grime were turning the letters brown.

At the sight of his visitor, Hampton stood and came out from behind his desk.

"Hello, Cadence," he said. "Welcome to *DC Watch*. Please, take a seat."

As Cadence lowered herself into a well-worn office chair, Hampton closed the door behind her and resumed his position behind his desk. She felt like she was almost squatting, but before she could even begin to try getting her seat up to a more comfortable height, Hampton waved his hand.

"Don't bother," said Hampton. "It is what it is. Sorry. Part of the charm of the place."

He could see Cadence did not equate austerity with charm.

"We're a pretty no-frills operation here," he said. "We like it that way."

"No, I get it," said Cadence with a polite smile. She thought for a moment of her own office, which was the epitome of a modern thriving law office in which every detail was pleasing to the eye. The cost of the carpet at Hardwick and Henshaw alone could cover the expense of giving *DC Watch* a wholesale makeover. "There's a vibe about this place. A spirit."

Hampton's eyes gleamed. "You bet there is. But let's get to why you're here."

"Yes, Mr. Hampton—"

"Please. It's Wade."

"Wade, as you know I'm representing Tate Lieberman, the man charged with Tessa's murder."

"Yes, I'm very much aware of that," said Hampton, twisting his mouth wryly. It was clear that while he was being polite and civil, there was an impassive tone that suggested that he was not inclined to go overboard with his assistance. Not without a good excuse, anyway. He probably knew that Cadence did not need to give him any such excuse. She could get what she wanted with a subpoena. "So forgive me for saying that I'm wondering what the hell you're doing here. No offense, mind you."

"I totally understand why you might think it's perverse that I'm asking for your help. But I'll be totally straight with you."

"Please do."

"I believe Tate Lieberman is innocent," she said. "And I'd like to prove it. Now the best way for me to do that is to find evidence that someone else killed Tessa."

"Ah," Hampton smiled and shifted some papers on his desk. "The old S-O-D-D-I defense. Some other dude did it, right?"

"Right," said Cadence, smiling good-naturedly. She had no problem with the weeks of thought and preparation she had put into the Lieberman case being simplified to a flippant five-letter acronym.

"I spent two years covering courts," Hampton said. "Hated it. How they can call it a justice system is criminal. The whole game is rigged, as much if not more than any other sector in this town."

"A cynical journalist," said Cadence, playfully. "You don't see that much."

Hampton held his hands up. "Guilty as charged," he said. "But I've been around long enough to earn the right."

"But back to Tessa. Aside from murder, there may be evidence that points to another explanation, as you alluded to in that article you wrote after she died."

"You mean suicide?" said Hampton. He shook his head. "The cops may have taken it off the table, but I guess that doesn't mean it didn't happen that way. But as I wrote in my editorial, the police obviously think otherwise."

"Well, as far as I'm concerned, the jury is out, as they say," said Cadence.

"Okay, we've got the small talk out of the way. I'm not sure where I fit into whatever angle you're working. Unless you want to pin it on me."

"No, Wade. All I want is your cooperation."

"Cooperation? How, exactly?"

"I'd like access to Tessa's computer. I want to see her workspace. Her files. I'd like to go through everything."

"On the Lieberman story?"

Cadence shook her head. "That and more. I don't want to restrict it to just that story."

"Why not?"

"I'm not convinced Lieberman's PR firm was the be all and end all of Tessa's story."

"Really? What makes you so sure?"

"You could set me straight, couldn't you? Being her editor and all."

"There's some things that I'll keep between Tessa and me but I can honestly tell you I didn't know everything that that kid had up her sleeve. She shared what she wanted to share with me.

She could have been working on debunking the Deep State, for all I knew. Or verifying it. You never knew with her. But the answer's yes, you can have a look at her computer."

"Thank you."

"Don't mention it," said Hampton getting up and opening the door. "I'm just saving you from getting a subpoena."

"Wade, one more thing," said Cadence as she got to her feet. "Was there someone here who Tessa totally confided in?"

Hampton nodded. "Yes, Danielle Farrell. She's our junior reporter. At least she was. She's not here."

"Where is she?"

"She's on leave."

"When will she be back?"

Hampton looked at Cadence and held his answer back momentarily. He then shook his head. "I can't tell you that."

Cadence looked puzzled. "Is it some sort of secret? I'd really like to speak with her."

Hampton reached across Cadence and closed the door again. He stopped and lowered his voice. "Look, the truth is I don't know when she'll be back. As you might expect, she took Tessa's death particularly hard. A few days after the funeral, she told me wanted to take a break. She said she wasn't in the right headspace to continue working. I suggested she take some leave. She did that, then she called to say she needed more time."

"Is she coming back?"

Hampton shrugged again. "She hasn't returned my calls. I've actually had Irma draft an ad to fill her position. So I guess that tells you what I think."

"Where is she?"

"I have no idea. She's given me nothing. I couldn't even tell you if she's in the country. She could be on a beach in Cancun for all I know."

"Are there any family members or friends you can put me in touch with?"

Hampton shook his head. "I've got nothing but her DC address and social security number. I really wanted her to come back. She wrote a great piece about how crooks are using AirTags to track their victims."

"AirTags?"

"Yeah, you know those little round tracking devices made by Apple? You use them to keep track of stuff, like keys or your luggage when you travel."

"Yes, of course."

"Danielle wrote about how crooks are using them in all sorts of nefarious ways. And I wanted her to do a follow up. Now it looks like I'll have to get someone else to do it."

"What about her resume? Would you still have that on file?"

"I wouldn't count on it. But I'll get Irma to check."

Hampton's eyes flicked up to a clock on the wall behind Cadence. "Listen, I've got a conference call." He then opened the door and stuck his head out. "Irma!" He turned back to Cadence.

As they stepped out of Hampton's office, they could hear Irma reply that there was no need to shout, that there were modern devices called telephones that rendered such primitive forms of communication obsolete. There was a huff and clatter of jewelry before Irma, straightening up and adjusting her dress, came marching toward them.

Hampton did not bother to acknowledge Irma's objections but took hold of the door handle once more, leaned out and said, "Show Ms. Elliott here to Tessa's desk. Give her all access. You got a log-in she can use?"

"Yes, Mr. Hampton."

"And see if you can dig up Danielle's resume, will you? Cadence wants to see it."

As Irma nodded, Hampton returned to his desk.

"A please would be nice, occasionally," she muttered with a roll of her eyes to Cadence. "This way, sweetheart. I'll log you in myself."

"Thank you."

Chapter 16

Cadence followed in the wake of Irma's perfume. When they stopped at a cubicle on the far side of the room, Irma rolled out the chair and positioned herself in front of the keyboard. She brought the monitor to life and typed the login details.

"I've used a master account," she said. "It will give you access to Tessa's desktop, hard drive and the network folders. And, just so you know, whatever you do will be logged. So while you are free to read and to copy files, please confine your curiosity to Tessa's work. It's all read-only. Okay, hon?"

For a woman who looked like knitting was her favorite hobby, Irma exhibited a very modern comfort with technology. Cadence smiled as she looked on. Irma read her mind.

"I've been with this website since inception, sweetheart," she said. "I know my way around the network better than anybody. Poor Wade is still a print man. Types with two fingers and hammers the keyboard like it was a Remington. Just about all our virus attacks come from him opening emails he shouldn't."

"Old school, hey?"

"Please don't make it sound like a term of endearment, hon. It's not."

Irma got up. "I'll leave you to it and go see if I can find that resume."

"Thank you."

Once Irma had left, Cadence took a look around the cubicle. There were a few scraps of paper pinned to the wall and a small collection of postcards. She looked over her shoulder and then plucked off one of the postcards. It was from Miami. The message was short and sweet with a few hearts and kisses at the end. It was signed off with a signature that read "Faz." The next one was the same, except it was sent from Tampa. The short note was the typical expression of fun with the obligatory "wish you were here" type statement in there. The third was the same. This time from another Florida beach town. Again from Faz. The handwriting looked feminine and young—all sweet and rounded. Cadence took out her phone and took photos of each postcard.

Looking at the stamped dates, Cadence realized the postcards were unlikely to have been from the same trip.

She then replaced the postcards and turned her attention to Tessa Reeves' computer.

As she worked, she heard a male voice in the background on a call. She could not make out everything he was saying but he was speaking loud enough for everyone to hear. She tuned out his voice, took some earbuds from her handbag and began her scrutiny of Tessa's desktop.

Cadence's first mission was to find all the material Tessa had for her Lieberman story. Tessa's computer was like her desk—well organized and neat.

It did not take Cadence long to find where Tessa kept her story files. A shiver ran through her when she spotted a folder named "DC PHARMA." Within that were sub-folders containing research documents, screenshots, photos and notes. There was information on Lieberman, Zellus and Narcadia but it was all cursory, which Cadence thought was odd. She thought there would be dozens, if not hundreds, of documents a reporter would amass in the process of piecing together an investigative story.

It then occurred to her that, given Tessa's reputed guardedness, maybe she kept her most prized documents where other staff members could not access them.

A quick scan of the taskbar at the bottom of the screen showed Tessa had a Dropbox account. Cadence clicked on the icon but when she searched through the account, she saw nothing of interest. This struck Cadence as odd, as she would have expected Tessa to have saved some of her work on the cloud. Perhaps she backed it up to a portable hard drive. If so, where was it?

As Cadence kept looking through the Dropbox folders it seemed that there had been recent activity, as in after Tessa's death. The "date modified" for most of the folders told Cadence someone had gained access to Tessa's account. The material she had gathered to expose Tate Lieberman and Zellus was gone.

Cadence moved to Tessa's browser. There she found various folders of bookmarks. She pressed a thumb drive into the USB port and began saving all the bookmarks on it. As the files were being copied, she heard a man's voice over her shoulder.

"Excuse me. What are you doing?"

Cadence spun her head around to see a tall, overweight thirty-something man looking at her indignantly. Before she could answer, he spoke again. "Who are you? And who said you could use Tessa's computer?"

His schoolmaster tone worked. Cadence, already conscious of being an intruder, felt as though she had been busted smoking behind the school gym.

"Wade Hampton did," she said. "I'm a lawyer working on her case."

The man's face-broad and fleshy-changed in a flash, a big, congenial smile spread across it like a brand-new welcome mat. His hair was ruffled and his face was between shaves.

"I know you," he said. "You're Cadence Elliott, Tate Lieberman's lawyer."

Cadence tried not to show her surprise, but she could see he was pleased to meet her. "I'm Luke Everson. You might know me, or at least have read some of my stories."

His hand was out now. They shook and he then swept his hand through his thick, sandy red hair. Cadence did know the name. Everson wrote the story that identified the knife man as Matteo Santino. She switched into charm mode, hoping to subtly pry more information out of him.

"Of course I know you," she said. "I just read a story of yours the other day. The one about that poor man who died at the Lincoln Monument. It was you who found out who he was, not the police. Do I have that right?"

"Yes, yes you do."

"How on earth did you manage to do that?"

Everson had to apply some restraint to keep himself from beaming. "Trade secret, ma'am," he said with fake seriousness. "If I told you I'd have to kill you."

"But he was from Argentina, yes?"

"That's right. Not one of their most honorable exports. He was a nasty piece of work."

"How so?"

"In the olden days you'd call him a gun for hire, I guess."

As much as Cadence tried to keep it light, she was practically shaking at the memory of that hideous night. The dread had never really left her. "As in a hitman. In DC? And someone was chasing him?"

Everson's face twitched. "That wasn't in my story," he said warily. "But yes, the theory is that he had reached his use-by date."

"Goodness. It sounds like something out of *The Sopranos*."

"It was all quite odd, really."

"In what way?" Cadence forced herself to ask. Some part of her wanted to shut her ears and never hear of Matteo Santino again. Yet she had to keep playing the fascinated audience to Everson's story.

"His vocation was security, you could say, but it's my understanding he was the Man Friday for a very prominent family here in DC."

"Really? Who?" Cadence did not expect Everson to tell her, she just thought she would see if he would.

"No. I can't say. My lips are sealed."

"Fodder for your next article?"

"Ah, no way."

"Why not?"

Everson grabbed a chair opposite and rolled it over. "That would not be wise, for obvious reasons," he said, rather cryptically. "Now what about you? If you're defending the man charged with Tessa's murder, why did Wade let you scan Tessa's computer?"

"You'll have to ask him."

"I'm asking you."

Cadence tilted her head and smiled. "I can't read Wade's mind, can I?" It was time to change the subject. "Did you work closely with Tessa?"

"No, not really. We did our own thing."

There was a pause as Everson sat there slightly dissatisfied with how little Cadence had told him.

"I see," said Cadence. "Well, nice to meet you. I'd better get back to work."

"Me too," he said.

He stood up and went to leave.

"Oh, just a sec," said Cadence. "I don't suppose you know where Danielle is?"

"Danielle?"

"Yes."

"What do you want with her?"

"I just want to touch base. Do you know where she is?"

"On leave."

"Yes, but where?"

"No idea, sorry. I emailed her but got no reply. Wade wants me to do a follow-up on one of her stupid stories. She should be doing it."

"The AirTag one? Why is that stupid?"

"You don't know my main gig, do you?"

"It's not tracking down mysterious foreign killers?"

"Well, that's part of it. I write The Cloakroom. It's a column."

Cadence shook her head. Everson failed to hide his disappointment, as though she was totally unaware that The Cloakroom was compulsory reading.

"It's the most read column here at *DC Watch*. You don't know what you're missing."

"Clearly, I don't. Well, good luck."

"Hey, if you do find Danielle, can you let me know? I need to talk to her too."

"About AirTags?"

"Yes," he said drearily. "About AirTags."

As Everson trundled off, Irma and her perfume returned. "Here you go, hon," she said, handing Cadence a one-page printout. "Not a lot there but it's something."

"Thank you, Irma."

Cadence ran her eyes over the one-page document. They fell on Danielle's education notes. They said she had attended Hillsborough High School.

Cadence looked it up. It was just as she thought. Danielle Farrell was from Tampa and those postcards suggested she still had family there.

Wade Hampton might not have known where to look for his junior reporter. But Cadence did.

Chapter 17

"That's her," said Bob Rhodes, handing Cadence his binoculars. Sitting in the passenger seat of their rental car, Cadence trained the glasses on a young woman crossing the road from the beach fifty yards ahead of them.

"You sure?" she asked. The girl had a towel wrapped around her waist and wore a baseball cap and large sunglasses. The thumb of one hand was hooked into the straps of her tote bag while the other held her phone, which she studied as she walked toward them.

"Positive," said Bob. "In about thirty feet she'll turn into that Starbucks there."

Bob had traveled to Florida five days ahead of Cadence. After staking out her family home in Tampa and seeing no sign of her, he did a property search under Danielle's father's name, which led him to a condo in Fort Lauderdale. After telling Cadence he was sure Danielle was keeping a low profile in her dad's investment property, she got on the next flight.

Cadence had drilled down on everything she could find about Danielle. She had a good eye as a photographer, being credited with some striking pictures for Tessa's suicide story as well as her own AirTags piece.

Danielle disappeared into the Starbucks just as Bob predicted.

"First rule of hiding out," Bob said. "Never follow a routine. She missed the memo on that. So I can tell you with full confidence that she won't stay inside."

"Okay. What's her drink?"

"Dunno. I haven't actually been in there with her. I just know she gets her mocha-choco-latte grande or whatever to go. Always."

Cadence handed the binoculars back to Bob and grabbed the door handle. "Okay, I'll go wait outside and catch her when she leaves."

Cadence got out of the car and looked up and down the street, making sure that they were the only people conducting surveillance. The last thing she wanted was to expose Danielle to the very people she was hiding from. It occurred to her that approaching Danielle on the street may not be such a good idea. She decided to enter the Starbucks to see if she could win Danielle's confidence, fast but subtly.

To her surprise there was no sign of Danielle inside. She looked for restroom signs but there were none. She then saw there was a rear exit. She went and pushed the door open and stepped outside. She found herself in a small alley. Each end led back to streets that ran away from the beach. Cadence pulled out her cell phone and called Bob.

"Bob, did you see her?" she asked when he answered.

"No, why?"

"Because there's a back exit. She's gone."

Cadence picked a direction and broke into a jog. "I'm heading north. She can't have gone too far." As Cadence hung up, she wondered if Danielle had spotted them and made her escape. Then again, maybe she just changed up her routine.

At the end of the alley, Cadence stepped out into bright sunshine. She looked both ways but caught no sight of Danielle. It was anyone's guess which way she had gone.

Cadence took her phone and tapped on Bob's number and put the phone to her ear.

"Why are you following me?" came a voice from behind her.

Cadence spun around and lowered her phone as Bob answered. She hit the end-call button with her thumb. She was face to face with Danielle Farrell.

The young woman was about half a foot shorter than Cadence. Her hair was tied back under her baseball hat. The sunglasses covered her eyes but by her body's composure Cadence surmised that Danielle was not at all scared. In fact, she seemed in complete control, as though she could make herself disappear with the snap of her fingers.

"I'm really sorry, Danielle."

"So you know my name. Who are you?"

"I'm Cadence Elliott. I'm a lawyer and I'm trying to find out what happened to Tessa."

"You're a lawyer trying to find out who killed Tessa? Really?"

By Danielle's tone of voice and expression Cadence knew that this was a test. Danielle knew exactly who she was.

"I'm a criminal defense attorney defending—"

"Tate Lieberman. Yes, I know. So what do you want? And how did you find me?"

"Wade said that you were the only person that Tessa really trusted. I know she was working on more than Tate Lieberman. I know she wanted to expose something about Zellus. I don't know what yet. So I don't think my client's guilty. And if he's not guilty but takes the fall, then Tessa's killer will still be out there. And my guess is that you know that. And you know that you could be next on the list."

Cadence took Danielle's silence as an invitation to keep talking.

"Look, there's still talk in the press about how Tessa might have killed herself or that it was some random act of violence, like the subway shovers in New York. I think she was murdered to stop her exposing the nefarious deeds of some very powerful people."

Danielle nodded, almost imperceptibly. Cadence saw her bottom lip start to tremble. She stepped closer. She knew her ability to win Danielle's trust was hanging by a thread. To that end, she kept talking. "I know that Tate Lieberman is a very powerful man with secrets to hide. I know Tessa was doing a story on him, but I think he was a gateway into a bigger story."

Danielle looked around. "What do you want from me?"

"Someone removed all the files from Tessa's Dropbox account. I have my suspicions about who did it, but I wanted to ask you for your opinion on who would do such a thing. I want to know what's been going on at *DC Watch* because I don't think I'm getting the whole picture."

"You went there?"

"Yes," Cadence said. "I spoke to Wade and he let me take a look at Tessa's computer."

"He shouldn't have done that."

"I think he wanted to appear to be helpful."

"You would have only seen what he wanted you to see."

"I thought as much."

"He'd have already swept her computer and all her files and everything she had stored on the network."

"So I was right. He somehow got access to Tessa's Dropbox and emptied it."

Danielle shook her head. "No," she said. "That was me."

"You? Really?"

Danielle looked around. "Look, I'm not comfortable doing this here. Is he with you?"

Danielle lifted her head for Cadence to look behind her. Bob was approaching them with polite caution.

"Yes," said Cadence. "That's Bob. He's my investigator."

"Not exclusively hers," smiled Bob. "Bob Rhodes."

Danielle's jaw dropped. "Not *the* Bob Rhodes?"

Bob's head recoiled a fraction with surprise. "I'm betting there's more than one."

"You're not the journalist Bob Rhodes?" asked Danielle. "You look like him. I've seen photos. You won the Arthur E. Rowse Award in 2008."

"Yep. You got me there."

"You exposed the political interference at PBS."

"Got me again."

"It's an honor to meet you, Bob. What Tessa would have given to meet you."

"I'm flattered," said Bob. "But enough about me."

Danielle snapped out of her hero worship. "Yes. Are you guys sure you weren't being followed?"

"I'm positive," said Bob. "But I think we should continue our talk somewhere more private."

"Danielle," said Cadence, "the more I find out about this case, the more I think Tate Lieberman, who I'll admit isn't the nicest person in the world, did not kill Tessa. Something tells me you agree too. I can only stress that yes, I'm defending my client but the best chance of doing that is to find out who really killed Tessa. I was hoping you'd help me do that."

Danielle nodded. "Okay. Follow me."

Chapter 18

The condo was well furnished, clean and orderly. Dad may have paid for the place, but Danielle knew how to take care of herself. Cadence could not help but note the stark contrast with the *DC Watch* office and wonder how Danielle coped. The living room opened onto a balcony with ocean views. Danielle said the place was one of her father's investment properties.

"I don't understand," said Cadence. "Wade said he has no idea where you are."

"I don't want him to know where I am."

"Seems to me he didn't try too hard to find you."

"I think he'd be happy to see me go," said Danielle. "He wasn't keen on Tessa's work. And he would not have liked me picking up her baton and forging on."

"Danielle, who are you hiding from?"

Danielle shrugged. "I wish I could tell you. But the same people who killed Tessa will not think twice about killing me."

"Why would they do that?"

"Because I did some of the research. I made calls. I did preliminary interviews. And I took photos."

"You were helping her investigate Zellus, is that right?"

"Yes."

"What was the focus of the story exactly?"

"She wanted to look at how Zellus is undermining state legislatures to secure monopolies for one of its drugs."

"You mean Narcadia?"

"Yes. Zellus has been targeting various states that have acute opioid addiction problems. They want them to have no choice but to use Narcadia as the prescribed recovery drug. They co-opt congressmen and senators to pull the right strings to get certain state laws passed or denied or modified to suit. That's the politics side. On the PR side, companies like Tate Lieberman's Berrins produce slick advertising campaigns that convince the general public that Narcadia is a wonder drug."

"And Tessa's story would threaten this plan?"

"Illegal plan, you mean. It's perverting the course of democracy. It's like the soda industry. When states tried to introduce a soda tax, how did the industry stop it? They did not lobby congressmen; they went to the grassroots organizations. They ran ads using scare tactics by telling people they would have to pay so much more for soda. Heaven forbid. Never mind the health costs."

"Do you know of anyone in particular who was concerned?"

"Yes. Ron Nagle."

"What happened?"

"Well, after Tessa died, he came in and spoke to Wade. After Ron left, Wade came out and went through all of Tessa's stuff and he got onto her computer. But he never got the Dropbox files."

"So what was in these files exactly?"

"Details about various congressmen and senators who were doing the bidding of Zellus. They meddled in state legislatures and in return received lavish holidays, houses and shares."

"You have proof of this?"

"Yes."

"And Wade doesn't know the extent of it?"

"No. He's just in the game for the ad dollars. He's not like you, Bob. He is very concerned about ruffling the feathers of DC's power brokers."

"The irony," said Bob. "Why am I not surprised? But what does he know about your involvement?"

"He thinks I just got Tessa coffee. I was her gopher. But that's what we wanted him to think. It was Tessa's idea. She wanted him to believe I was peripheral to the research, like I really wasn't too involved. But I was. She involved me in everything. She said that when the story was ready to go, she was going to give me a byline. I objected but she was for real."

"So who was on this list?"

Danielle proceeded to rattle off a string of names of congressmen from both sides of the House. The first name she mentioned, though, was Ron Nagle.

Chapter 19

From her seat at the bar, Cadence overheard Luke Everson order a pint of Fullers London Pride. When the bartender presented him with a thick glass of rich amber ale, Everson regarded it with relish. He took a sip with one hand while tapping his card to pay with the other. Still sipping, his eyes then momentarily flicked over to the television positioned at Cadence's end of the bar. For a moment, she thought he must have caught sight of her but she was wrong. Having found nothing of interest on the screen, Everson carried his drink over to a chesterfield booth with a window overlooking D Street.

He was dressed in a navy jacket, light blue shirt that was in need of an iron and cream chinos that were slightly frayed at the heels. He looked like he felt right at home at The Gladstone Arms, DC's most British bar. Cadence found the dark wood and antique fittings of the bar to be comforting, a feeling only enhanced by the waft of roasted meat coming from the kitchen. She was hungry and perused the menu while she waited for Everson, but the list of pies, bangers and mash and curries did not whet her appetite. It all seemed like the kind of food that went hand in hand with heavy drinking. She decided she could wait until she got home to eat and ordered a glass of lemonade in a tumbler with a slice of lemon and a straw. When she approached Everson, she at least wanted to give the appearance that she was drinking.

She stirred the ice in her glass as she watched Everson for a few minutes. It was almost a shame to disturb his privacy, she thought. He looked like he had found his happy place. Still, she would not keep him long. She got to her feet.

"Luke?" she said, smiling as she reached his booth.

Everson looked up at Cadence and returned the smile. It was not every day, clearly, that such a visually appealing woman approached him. "Cadence. What are you doing here?"

"Well, the truth is I came to see you."

The words might otherwise have pleased Everson but given what he knew about Cadence, he became wary. He could not help but let his smile fade. "Is that so?" he said with a degree of suspicion. "How did you know I was here? Did you follow me?"

Cadence nodded. "Yes. I did. If you'll let me sit down, I'll tell you why."

By Everson's look of surprise it was clear he was intrigued by Cadence's words. He gestured to the seat opposite. "Okay. By all means. Take a seat."

No sooner had he said these words and Cadence had acted upon them that he seemed to think it prudent that he add some sort of caveat. "We need to keep it quick," he said with a glance at his watch. "I'm meeting a friend."

"I understand," said Cadence, sitting down and placing her handbag on the table. "Totally. This won't take long, I promise."

Everson looked unconvinced, like a dentist had just told him it would not hurt a bit. He was now staring at Cadence, slightly dejected that there was nothing flirtatious or amorous about Cadence's intentions. It was all business.

"I don't know why you didn't come to the office to talk about Tessa, which I presume is what you're here to do."

"You're right. I do want to talk about Tessa but I wanted to talk to you discreetly."

"What's that supposed to mean?"

"It means I don't particularly want Wade to know that I've come to you."

"You're asking me to keep this between us?"

"Yes. Is that okay?"

Everson leaned forward on his elbows. "That depends on what we're talking about, Cadence. It's time to stop beating about the bush, wouldn't you say?"

"Yes. I think Tessa was killed because there were people who feared what she was going to make public."

"That's pretty much clear now. It's why Tate Lieberman has been charged. Makes sense to me."

Cadence paused momentarily, unsure what to make of Everson's words.

"So you think Lieberman is guilty?" she asked.

Everson shrugged his shoulders. "I'm not a cop but why else would they have charged him. If there's one person you don't want to get on the wrong side of in DC it's Tate Lieberman. I think the DA—what's his name? Gerard Underhill?—he's a brave man going through with it but I guess it only indicates the strength of the case they have against him. But that's just me reading it from afar."

Cadence decided she needed to keep the conversation agreeable, so she refrained from challenging Everson's viewpoint. "Well, nothing's been proven in a court of law yet, Luke, but we'll soon see."

"So it's going to trial?"

"Looks that way. Listen, it's funny you mention Gerard Underhill because there was something about him that I wanted to ask you."

"Really? Like what? What did he say exactly?"

"He seems to know some details about the story or stories that Tessa was working on. The way he mentioned it to me, he made it sound like Lieberman had a strong motive to silence Tessa."

"Didn't you discuss that with Wade? I thought that was why you were in our office."

"We discussed it briefly but I don't believe that Wade was being entirely open with me."

"Why should he be? You're defending Tessa's killer."

"Alleged killer."

"Okay," Everson said thoughtfully and took up his glass for a long draw of beer. He kept his eyes on Cadence as he drank and then set the glass back down on a coaster. "So you're not convinced you'll get much more out of Wade, or else you think you can't trust what he does tell you. So you come to me, why? What is it you want from me?"

"Did Tessa have Wade's full support for the kinds of stories she wanted to write?"

"Of course she did. He's a good editor."

Everson's reply was left hanging. As a defense of Hampton's qualifications, it was not a strong endorsement.

"You don't seem to mean what you say."

"Look, like every reporter, I guess, I just don't think our commander in chief is as pure of heart and mind when it comes to the pointy end of journalism."

"You mean he lacks the courage to rock the boat? Or the will?"

"Both."

"That's not what he told me. He said he was one hundred percent behind Tessa and her work. He said he was nothing but encouraging about Tessa's ambitions, but she was a bit wild and raw or—"

"Idealistic?"

"Something like that."

"Look, it's no secret that Wade's put himself out to pasture, journalistically speaking. He'll never admit it, but everyone knows. He's just a dollar man now, taking care of advertisers, doing just enough to keep the spirit of *DC Watch* alive but never going too far out on a limb."

"He's got one foot out the door?"

"Yes."

"Were you impacted by his supposed lack of courage?"

"Yes. He was holding off on one of my stories to allow Tessa to publish hers but now he killed it."

Everson took a large draw of beer, downing a few gulps and leaving just an inch at the bottom of the glass. Cadence took a sip from her drink.

"Did that upset you?"

Everson's eyes widened with indignity, and he shook his head. "No, of course not. That's just the way things go."

"Can I ask what your story was about?"

"No, you cannot."

"But was it related to Lieberman in some way?"

Everson shook his head. "I think that's obvious, isn't it?" He then drained his glass and looked eager to head back to the bar to get another. "But the truth is it's not the first time Wade's pulled one of my stories. Losing his nerve has become a character trait. A habit. Are we done now?"

"Can I just ask a couple more questions?"

"Hold on. I meant to ask, did you have any luck finding Danielle?"

"No, I didn't, I'm afraid."

"That's unfortunate."

"And because I can't speak with her, I wanted to ask you a couple more things about the office."

"Like what?"

"Like, was Wade cozy with any politicians in particular?"

"Are you kidding? He has to be cozy with them to do the job. Without contacts, *DC Watch* would have nothing to publish. I would have thought that was obvious."

"Yes, I get that. But I'm particularly interested in Ron Nagle."

There was a look of surprise on Everson's face. "Why would you be interested in Senator Nagle?"

"I heard Nagle would come into the office to express his disagreement with a story."

Everson's eyes narrowed. "Sounds to me like you're trying to make a generic statement about something quite specific. You have made contact with Danielle, haven't you?"

"No, Luke, I haven't."

"Look, I need to speak with her. So if you'll help me, I'll help you. Okay?"

"Why do you need to speak with her?"

"Because Wade wants me to take on Tessa's story."

"Really? Not just the AirTags follow-up?"

"He's dumping it all on me. I need to get access to the research."

"I thought you said Wade did not have the will to publish a controversial piece?"

"I did, but who knows what he's planning. Part of me thinks he's glad about all this. I know it's not lost on him that Tessa's death is sending a lot of eyeballs *DC Watch*'s way. I think he'll want to milk it for all it's worth. You know, increase its value, fatten it up before he sells it."

"Are you being serious?"

"I was being facetious but, in all honesty, I don't think it's far from the truth."

Everson shot a glance at the bar. "Look, I came here to relax and meet a friend, so can we wrap this up?"

"Yes, of course. Just one more thing."

"What's that?"

"Look, if this case goes to trial, I'd like to call you as a witness."

"What?"

"Do you want to help Tessa?"

"I don't see how that would be helping Tessa. It's just helping you."

"Either way, I'd like to call you as a witness for the defense."

"Tell you what. There's a whole bunch of files that have gone missing and I think Danielle has them. And I'm not convinced you don't know where she is. So, I'll cut you a deal. You get me those files and I'll take the stand."

Cadence shook her head.

"No dice. I told you I haven't been able to find Danielle and that's God's truth. I don't want to be adversarial about it, but I don't need to ask you to testify. It would just be to present insights into the culture of *DC Watch*. I struck out with Danielle and was hoping you could help, that's all."

"Tell you what. I'll get you your next beer while you think about it."

Everson paused for a moment, dug into his coat pocket and pulled out a packet of gum. He popped two pellets into his mouth and began chewing with a smile. "Okay," he said. "I'll think about it. I'm drinking Fullers London Pride."

Cadence took her purse out of her handbag and went to the bar. After a few minutes, she returned, placing a pint of ale on the table in front of Everson.

"So, Luke. I can count on you, right?"

Everson nodded, shifted his gum to the side of his mouth and lifted the glass to his lips. He took a big gulp and exhaled.

"Is that a yes?" asked Cadence.

"It's a yes."

Chapter 20

As her feet drummed out an even beat on the gray cobblestone, Cadence began to feel the tension in her body and mind melt away. For some people, exercise was a means to an end, a way to get the body that social media tells them they should aspire to. Cadence loved to feel fit, but more important to her were the benefits of exercise for her mental health. She was an expert at hiding her anxiety from others. Her colleagues and friends knew her as a beautiful and driven young woman. They admired her devotion and grit. They marveled at her ability to focus and apply herself. And the few who were allowed close to her—like Jackie, Bob and Sophie—saw the gentleness of her heart and the sense of humor she so rarely shared.

Vexing thoughts about her son gnawed at her constantly. This had been going on for years, filling up just about every mental space between work and daily functions. It was not a self-righteous feeling of being horribly wronged. She could not consider what had happened without thinking she was to blame. She could never long for a connection with her son without feeling he was better off without her. She could not imagine the tender moment when she told him that she never wanted to let him go without thinking it was something he should never have to hear.

Deep down, though, she always got hung up on the fact that the decision to adopt was taken away from her. No matter what papers her mother Tina had signed, no matter how much the Cordobas had paid her.

Cadence had gotten on with her life, but she always felt part of her was missing. When, late on a Saturday afternoon, Cadence found herself once again dwelling on what she should do, she changed into her jogging gear and drove down to the Georgetown Waterfront Park. A five-mile jog would pound her mind into relative ease, doing her mental health a world of good.

It was Bob Rhodes who had introduced her to this run. She lucked out and found a parking space on 31st Street, crossed K Street underneath the Whitehurst Freeway and headed for the path that ran alongside the Potomac.

She would head up to the Key Bridge, cross over, then head east until she reached the Theodore Roosevelt bridge before crossing that and returning west. She disliked running with earbuds stuck in her ears. She preferred the ambient sounds around her. She wanted to experience her surroundings with all her senses. The thrum of the cars on the elevated freeway, the ducks on the river, the jets and helicopters flying overhead, the machinery humming in the streets and the voices of passersby. It was the symphony of Washington, DC, and to her there was no better soundtrack for running through the famous historic district of Georgetown.

As she crossed the Key Bridge she smiled as she saw there was a brilliant sunset in the making. Her timing was perfect, she realized. By the time she was back to her starting point she would be doing her cool-down stretches at one of DC's best sunset vantage points, taking in the Rosslyn Skyline across the river.

During her run, not all cares were swept from her mind, and the memory of that nightmare at the Lincoln Memorial came to her once more.

The words of Luke Everson also came back to her again and again. He had said, or at least hinted, that there was a link between his gossip story that had been put on hold and the dead Argentinian. She knew his gossip story was held back because it related to Tessa's, so it most likely had something to do with Tate. What did Wade object to about his story? And where did Ron Nagle fit in?

As Cadence neared the end of her run, she picked up the pace, stretching out her stride as she built to a sprint. At the completion of her lap, she stopped and bent over to catch her breath. She stood back up, breathing fast and deep and shook her arms and legs.

She walked to the railing and looked west at the setting sun. The amber sky was crosshatched with contrails that extended overhead. It was beautiful graffiti on a divine sunset. Cadence took out her ear buds, placed them in her ears and then selected a Spotify playlist. She stretched her hamstrings and thighs before finally standing still, her hands on the railing, taking in the spectacular view.

By the time Cadence headed for her car, the streetlights were illuminating the growing darkening. She had no plans for the evening other than to go over the Lieberman files with a glass of white wine and a slice of gourmet pizza.

Coldplay's *The Scientist* was playing as she neared K Street, her car within eyeshot. She looked both ways, and when there was a break in the traffic she began to cross.

The song was loud enough to mute the sound of screeching tires that came from her right, about a hundred yards away. She crossed the first lane safely enough but when she was stepping over the dividing lines a black car came into her peripheral vision. She snapped her head to the right, and seeing the driver was giving the car a full dose of throttle, she stopped and then took a step back.

"Idiot," she muttered to herself as she waited for the car to pass. But when the car suddenly changed lanes, drifting into the middle, she thought it best to get herself further out of harm's way. She took two steps back.

In the fading light, she figured the driver might not be able to see her, assuming he was looking where he was going. The driver might well be on his phone or texting—basically, doing anything other than driving with his hands at ten and two and his eyes on the road ahead. And she had to assume it was a he. How many women drive like that? Like they're trying to impress someone?

A horn blast sounded from behind her as a car rushed by. She had unwittingly stepped into its lane.

Shocked and disoriented by the passing car and the horn, Cadence instinctively stepped forward again onto the middle line. The black car was now just about ten feet away and she was sure it was drifting towards her. Actually, she was now convinced it was aimed straight at her.

In a moment that seemed to span seconds yet in reality was a mere fraction of one, Cadence tried to identify the driver through the tinted glass but was unable to. She spun around and dived as far as she could back into the lane behind her. Luckily, she landed in an unoccupied lane, but her elbows smacked hard into the road.

As she hit the ground, she could feel and hear the black car speed past just inches from her feet. She tucked them as the car flew sped by, its tires screeching, its engine growling.

Cadence saw the car's brake lights come on and for a second, she thought he would turn and come back for her. She sprang to her feet and darted across the road. She did not go straight to her car, which was less a getaway than a trap. If the black car came back before she got started and pulled out, he could pin her between the cars in front and behind.

She ducked into the doorway of a nearby shop and waited, her chest heaving, her heart racing at what felt like a thousand beats per minute.

A second later, she heard the screech of tires again and the sound of the engine faded into the night.

She got in her car and pulled out. She felt as though she was in no state to drive but she was not inclined to stop until she got home.

Along the way, her fear had turned to anger. Bob had told her to give Monica Cordoba a wide berth until the death of her hitman blew over. She had wanted to confront her right away. Now it seemed that waiting was poor advice. She should have done it right after Santino attacked her. All she had done was give Monica more time to plan her next move and now it was clear her intent had not changed. She wanted Cadence dead. Yet she could not do it herself, so she had hired some other henchman to do the job for her. More than ever, Cadence wanted to confront this woman head on.

Enough time had passed since the knife man's death. She had watched the story evolve in the news. The police were still looking for witnesses.

Fearing Monica Cordoba be damned.

She had waited long enough.

The time had come to confront her once and for all.

Chapter 21

The limousine pulled up in front of the Cordoba residence, a hulking, two-story home on California Street in Kalorama Heights. Amid the flat face of the off-white building was a tall black door and towering windows.

This was the first time Cadence had seen the Cordoba home. She had had their address for months but had stayed away, restricting the times she watched Ben to when he was with his friends outside school or the sports field. She kept her car well behind the limo knowing that if she was found out the reaction would be swift and violent. She needed to find a moment to get Monica alone. The last thing she wanted was to have a standoff in front of Ben.

Cadence saw Ben exit the vehicle and make his way up the path to the front door.

The limo began moving. Cadence was unable to see if Monica was in the car but since Ben had turned to wave goodbye, she figured Monica was in the back seat. She eased her BMW out and began tailing the limo.

A few minutes later, the limo pulled outside The Line, a boutique hotel in Adams Morgan.

Cadence swung her car into an open space and watched Monica Cordoba exit the vehicle and make her way up the steps to the entrance. The driver was at her heels carrying two large designer shopping bags. Halfway up the steps, Monica slipped and the driver was swift to take her by the elbow and steady her. For a second, Cadence wondered whether Monica was drunk.

Soon after they had entered the building the driver emerged. He trotted down the steps, returned to the limo and drove off.

Cadence's gut was twitching with nerves. She had no idea what Monica Cordoba was doing here but she was now sure she was alone. Even if she had to confront Monica in front of her friends, Cadence was prepared to do that. She figured that Monica would not want anyone to hear that she had tried to have her killed.

Cadence did not need much time. She could convey what she wanted to say in a few seconds. But her message could no longer wait.

Stepping out of the heat and into the cool air-conditioned interior was refreshing and soothing. Cadence scanned the foyer and saw no sign of Monica. She made her way over to the bar scanning everywhere.

There were a few people in the bar but no sign of Monica. When Cadence returned to the foyer, she saw Monica exit the women's bathroom before positioning herself in front of the elevators and pressing the button.

Cadence stepped back, succumbing to a reflex to hide herself and avoid a confrontation. But then her defiance kicked in and she stepped toward the elevators. A bell sounded and Monica Cordoba stepped in.

"Hold the elevator, please!" called Cadence.

Monica did no such thing. Cadence got a hand between the closing doors, swiping through the red sensor beams to get them to reopen.

When Cadence stepped into the elevator, she saw Monica standing at the back with her sunglasses on and her eyes fixed onto her phone.

"Didn't you hear me?" said Cadence.

"Sorry," said Monica, still looking down. "I wasn't paying attention."

Cadence paused and found it odd that Monica still had her eyes down. It was as though she was pretending to be invisible. The doors closed but the elevator did not move. Cadence turned and saw no button had been pressed.

"Which floor?"

"Oh, three. I thought I—"

It was at that moment that Monica looked up and realized to her horror that she was alone in an elevator with her nemesis. And at the very same moment, Cadence realized that something was not right with Monica. As the elevator started with a gentle shudder, she lost her balance. And there was a slur to the words that had come out of her mouth. Cadence's suspicion that Monica was drunk seemed accurate.

"What the hell do you think you're doing?" said Monica.

"I don't want any trouble, Monica," said Cadence, "but it's high time you and I talked. I've got a few things to say, and I've got some questions and I'm not going anywhere until we address them."

The elevator came to a halt on the third floor and the doors opened. Monica did not move, resting her back against the wall.

"This is your floor, isn't it?" Cadence said. "I just want five minutes. That's it. We can do this now or so help me God I will come to your home and we can have it out in front of Ben."

"You're a maniac," said Monica, glaring at Cadence over her sunglasses. "Get away from me."

Before Cadence could get any words out, Monica pushed her back off the wall and went to step past Cadence, but she overbalanced and lurched forward. If Cadence had not grabbed her, she would have fallen on her face.

"What's wrong with you? Are you drunk?" Cadence said as she braced her legs to keep Monica from falling. This was not what she had expected—to be so physically close to this woman.

"I'm no such thing," Monica said indignantly but drowsily. Again, the unthinkable happened to Cadence—she felt pity for this woman.

"You need to sit down," she said. "Which room are you in?"

"Let go of me," Monica demanded, as Cadence led her out of the elevator. "You conniving bitch."

Inclined to reply in kind, Cadence bit her tongue. If Monica was not drunk, she must have ingested some kind of drug.

"I'll get you to your room," Cadence said. "What number is it?"

"None of your goddamn business," Monica burst out. It was then Cadence saw Monica had the key card in her hand. She snatched it from Monica's fingers. "Hey, give that back."

Cadence put an arm around Monica. "I'm helping you to your room. You need to sit down."

There was no reply from Monica other than an indecipherable murmur. She did not fight off Cadence's support, knowing it was the only thing keeping her from falling on her face.

Cadence saw the key card was in a folder with the room number written on it. She found the room a few doors down from the elevator. She pushed the key card in the slot with one hand while holding Monica's shoulder, then shoved the door open.

The room was a mess. Monica shrugged Cadence's arm away and stumbled forward. She reached the bed, let her bags fall to the ground and sat down. The relief to be off her feet was clear. As if by instinct, Monica reached for something on the bedside table. It was a yellow plastic bottle of pills. She shook out two and was about to pop them into her mouth when Cadence stepped forward and seized her hand. Before Monica could clench her fist, the pills were plucked out of her palm.

"You've had enough, don't you think?"

"Give me those," Monica said, swiping at Cadence's hand but missing.

Cadence picked up the bottle. The pills were Vicodin, a highly addictive opioid painkiller. "What are you doing? Are you trying to kill yourself? Is this your idea of being—"

Cadence cut herself off and reprimanded herself for almost blurting out the "bad mother" charge.

"What did you say?" Monica was sitting up, her blood hot and her back straight. She would have gotten to her feet if she could. "You know nothing about me."

Cadence stepped back. "I know more than you think. I know that you're infertile and that you faked your pregnancy. I know that you ordered Dr. Osbourne to take my baby before my due date. I know you bribed my mother to sign away my parental rights to my son. And I know you want me dead."

Monica stared ruefully at Cadence. "How do you know all of that about me?" Apparently, being accused of attempting murderer was nothing compared to having her privacy invaded. "No one knows that except—"

"Dr. Osbourne."

"I can't believe he told you. Stupid, spineless man. I knew I couldn't trust him."

Something occurred to Cadence. "Your husband doesn't know, does he? He doesn't know the child is not his. You tricked him. You pretended to be pregnant."

The blood drained from Monica's face. She shook her head ruefully. "If you say anything, so help me God I'll—"

"You'll do what? Send another thug after me to kill me? This is why I've come to see you. I want this to stop. I wanted to see if I could reason with you."

"Liar. You only want to torture me," Monica shouted.

"No. I want you not to fear me," said Cadence. "And I want to know the truth about what happened. I'm not foolish enough to think I can take Ben away from you. I just want to know the truth. You took advantage of me. You and Dr. Osbourne. That nurse, Janet Albright. And, of course, my mother. You treated me like garbage. And until I see the papers, I'm convinced you stole my baby."

A sense of resignation came over Monica in her drugged state.

"I need the bathroom," she said and pushed herself up from the bed. Cadence stood back and watched. Monica staggered to the bathroom and was gone for five minutes, giving Cadence ample opportunity to take a good look around.

"You're living here," Cadence said when Monica returned. "Alone."

"No shit, Sherlock," said Monica, bending over and picking up her handbag. She took out a pack of cigarettes, tapped it, spilled out two cigarettes on the floor and popped one in her mouth. "We separated two months ago."

They both remained silent for a few moments, Monica puffing listlessly on her cigarette. She looked beaten and weary. "What do you want? I don't know why I ask that. You won't be happy until you destroy me."

"I want you to stop trying to kill me," said Cadence.

"You killed Matteo," said Monica.

"Is that so? Then why didn't you go to the police?"

Whatever the response was that Monica formulated in her head, it failed to come out. She just shook her head listlessly.

"You didn't go to the police because you knew that I'd tell them you've tried to have me killed twice," said Cadence. "And now it's three times."

Monica shook her head. "What? I only—"

"First you sent that thug of yours Santino to threaten me with a knife to my face," said Cadence. "Then you lured me into a trap at the Lincoln Memorial so he could kill me. And then you had someone else try to run me over in Georgetown."

"That's a lie. Just like everything else you say. We did you all a favor by taking Ben. We gave him a life he never could have had with you. Even your drug-addled mother was honest enough to see that."

"No," said Cadence. "All she saw was the money."

"Who do you think you're fooling? She couldn't give him away fast enough. And she was right. She did you a favor and you still refuse to see it. You'd still be living in a trailer park just like your mother. You should be grateful."

"You are a vile woman. To think that is the family my son is growing up in."

Monica tried to spring up and launch herself at Cadence, but she fell flat on her face.

Cadence walked toward the door. "I came here angry. Then I felt sorry for you. And now, I don't care. You are not going to get away with what you have done."

"You're not going to take him. You can't."

"Well, we'll just have to see what your husband thinks."

Cadence put her hand on the door handle.

"Please don't tell him," said Monica, crying. "Look, I'm not well. You can see that. I almost died last year from taking too many of those damned pills. It will be the end of me. And Ben will be devastated. I'm his mother. You may not like it but it's the truth."

Cadence opened the door and walked out.

"If he finds out you're after Ben," Monica shouted, "he'll kill you, mark my words. You're as good as dead."

Chapter 22

Throughout her Monday morning routine, Cadence could not get the weekend's events out of her head. She got up at five thirty. She went to the gym. She went back home and showered and dressed for work. She got herself some juice and toast. She got coffee. She got to the office by seven thirty. None of it was rushed physically but her mind was constantly working overtime.

She had no idea what to do next. She had pangs of sympathy for Monica Cordoba yet could not forget that this was a woman who had tried to have her killed twice. Cadence was lucky to be alive. No, she vowed, she could not let compassion get the better of her. She now had a new objective. She needed to get close to Simon Cordoba without getting herself killed.

By the time she got settled behind her desk, she forced all those thoughts aside and got her mind into the Lieberman case.

At five minutes before eight, she received an email from ADA Gerard Underhill. The contents of the email were so alarming that all other thoughts were expelled from her mind. She read the email twice, making sure she got every point.

It was Underhill's final plea deal offer, and it did not make for pleasant reading. But that was not what got Cadence's blood pressure up. Underhill had informed Cadence that there was a new witness for the prosecution. It was a member of the staff at Jameson's who had come forward to say he saw Lieberman follow Tessa Reeves from outside the club.

Cadence picked up her phone to speak to Underhill. As she did, though, Tate Lieberman appeared at the door holding a phone to his ear.

"Good, you're here already," he said. "Hopefully we can get this done in twenty minutes, right?"

Cadence was not sure if Lieberman was addressing her or the person he had on the line. He lifted his eyes from his phone to Cadence. It was her after all that he was talking to.

"Oh, so you were talking to me?" she said. "How about a good morning? And no, we're going to need a lot more than twenty minutes. That won't cut it. In fact, as far as I'm concerned, this is going to be an as-long-as-it-takes kind of meeting."

"Not possible," said Lieberman. "I'm fully booked."

"You need to clear your calendar," Cadence said. "If you can think of something more important to do than work on how to keep you out of jail for the rest of your life then I'm happy to hear it. Because everything just got harder."

The tone of Cadence's voice stopped Lieberman in his tracks.

"What are you talking about?"

"Sit down."

He sat.

"According to Gerard Underhill's latest witness, you were seen following Tessa Reeves after you left Jameson's. This would be just after you were seen arguing with her and just before she died."

"Ah, no—that's not right."

"Tate. This witness is a staff member of the club. They're willing to testify that this is what they saw. And if there is one witness saying this then there will be others."

"Look I—"

"Why didn't you tell me? Why am I learning more about what you did that night from the man who wants to put you away for murder?"

"I'm telling you I did not follow Tessa," said Lieberman. "And I've told you that I didn't kill that stupid girl."

"Just because you say something is true, Tate, does not make it so. That may work in your company where your staff obey your every command, where they hang off your every word. It won't stack up in a court of law. We are going to get shredded by Underhill."

"I see."

"I'm not sure you do. He's just sent through his final plea deal offer."

"What is it?"

"If you plead guilty to second-degree murder or manslaughter, he will be happy with fifteen years."

"Fifteen years? You've got to be joking."

"I'm not joking and he's only leaving it on the table for today. I need to give him our response by this time tomorrow or there's no deal."

"And then?"

"Then we go to trial and if you lose, you'll get life."

"But we won't lose, will we?"

"Are you kidding? You seem to be doing everything you can to stop me from keeping a hold on your freedom. You're not honest with me. And whatever truth you tell me is only a selection. If you want me to defend your life with the weakest defense possible then you're going about it the right way. Do you understand?"

"There's no way I'm taking the deal."

"Look, maybe I can go back to Underhill and get the term cut down to ten years with a non-parole of five. What are you now? Fifty-six? You could be out before you turn sixty-two."

"Are you out of your mind?"

"Far from it. You are running out of options, Tate."

"I'm innocent, Cadence. I didn't kill that girl. Yes, I had an argument with her, but she left and that was the last time I saw her."

Cadence held up her hands. "Okay. We need to figure this out. But first, you need to know that there was more from Underhill this morning."

"What?"

"Phoebe is going to be a prosecution witness."

Lieberman tensed up with fury and looking for something to hit, slammed his right fist into his left palm. "That bitch."

"Tate, you need to calm down," said Cadence. "We need to go over everything again in fine detail. I don't want you to leave anything out. And you're not leaving till I'm satisfied you've given me everything."

Lieberman looked at his watch. "But I've got—"

"Whatever you've got is not more important than this."

"Okay, where do we start?"

"We start with the night of the murder. And then there are some other matters we need to discuss."

"Other matters. Like what?"

"Like what you've said to Kelly. And what we're going to tell Underhill."

"I told her everything. I told her about Phoebe."

"Well, I'm glad," said Cadence. "I want to know exactly what you said to your wife."

"Why?"

"Why? Because Kelly may well be the key to preserving your freedom, if not your marriage."

Chapter 23

"Good. You're here," said Cadence as she ran into Bob on her way to the bathroom. There was a faint sense of relief in her voice. Too much for her own liking. It showed her mind had slipped momentarily out of work mode the moment she spotted her friend. There was only one person in Cadence's life she could unpack the contents of her eventful weekend with, and that was Bob. She snapped herself out of it. "I've booked the conference room."

Bob had planned to deliver a quip in reply since Cadence's words had made him feel like a first responder. "Is everything okay?"

"We can talk in there," she said. "I've just had three hours with Lieberman going through his alibi."

"A bit late in the day for that, isn't it? Shouldn't you have the alibi from the get-go?"

"Normally, yes," said Cadence. "But Lieberman's got a double life. Maybe a triple one, who knows? He thinks it's smart to keep his cards close to his chest. Even with his defense attorney."

Bob held up a pile of documents he was carrying in his right hand. "I've been through Tessa's research and added a bit of my own. Got some interesting stuff that I think will help."

"Great."

"You want me to go down and grab some coffee? Food?"

Cadence checked her watch. She was hungry but she felt mentally sharper because of it. "Coffee would be great."

"Okay. See you in ten."

Cadence had gotten herself comfortable in the conference room and had laid out all the case files on the Lieberman case when Alan Henshaw appeared at the door. His face was not exactly cheerful. But at least it was not angry.

"I just got off the phone with Tate. He says you gave him a real onceover this morning."

Cadence did not know whether that was a complaint or a compliment. Right now, she did not care. "Well, he needed it. I hope you're not asking me to apologize."

The tone in Cadence's voice gave Alan the clearest message that she was not in the mood to be taken to task about anything. But that was not what he had dropped by to say.

"Not at all. Good work. He has to learn to trust you if he's going to shake this thing. He said there was a plea deal. I assume—"

"He's never going to plead guilty, Alan," said Cadence. "We're going to trial."

"You're not going to put him on the stand, are you?"

"That's not my decision. If he insists on taking the stand he can. I've advised him against it and will continue to do so in the strongest terms possible, but as you know it's anyone's guess if he'll listen to me or not."

"I think he'll listen to you," said Alan with a reassuring nod. "I think he'll behave."

"Really?"

"Yes," said Alan. "I'll leave you to it."

Cadence did not know what to make of Alan's content demeanor. As usual, it made her think he knew something she did not. What had Lieberman told him? Had Alan landed Lieberman as a business client already? But what business would there be if Lieberman was found guilty? Cadence shook her head. She could not let her thoughts go down the rabbit hole of Alan Henshaw's business strategy. She needed to play the cards in front of her and try to win this case. What happened after that was out of her hands.

"One flat white, no sugar," said Bob, striding in with two coffees before closing the door behind him with his elbow.

Cadence was going over the case files spread across the table.

"Okay, let's start with Underhill," she said as they took their seats at the table. "I don't think he's going to do anything but lay the cards out for the jury. What's he got? By way of hard evidence not a lot. What he does have is motive, circumstantial evidence and a growing list of damning testimony."

"Such as?"

"Oh, I haven't told you. The news of the day today is that, contrary to what my client Tate Lieberman had told me up to this point, he was seen following Tessa Reeves just before she died."

"What?"

"He arranged to meet her at Jameson's. They argued. She left and he soon followed."

Cadence leaned back in her chair, her eyes on the files in front of her, her mind deep in thought. "How did it go with the files Danielle removed from Tessa's Dropbox? Oh, and did you check out the bookmarks from Tessa's computer I sent you?"

"Yes, I checked it all out," said Bob. "It seems pretty clear that Lieberman wasn't Tessa Reeves' main target."

Bob began setting out some papers into three separate piles on the table, placing them in a particular order. "There were three main areas she was focused on. She had pulled news stories off websites and made them into Google docs. Plus there are emails, interview transcripts, information from company websites, business reports and Senate hearings. She saved everything here by the looks of it."

"Senate hearings?

"Yes, I'll get to that. See this pile here?" Bob pointed to the one on his left. "That's the material that Tessa had on Tate."

Bob then picked up a document. "But it can all be summarized by this document here."

"What's that?"

"It's a draft copy of Tessa's story on the questionable business practices of Tate Lieberman. Here," Bob said, handing the printout to Cadence. I've highlighted most of the first three paragraphs. They encapsulate what she unearthed about Berrins and point to what was to come."

Cadence scanned over the first few paragraphs. "Washington, DC, has long been the global epicenter of both democracy and capitalism," she read. "It's where power, money and politics intersect on a scale like nowhere else on earth. How Americans get to live their lives is decided here. But it's never been just our elected representatives pulling the strings. There are relatively invisible hands of interest groups—the corporations and industries who demand a seat at the democracy table. Most people know and accept that they have an influence. A whole distinct industry has developed made up of people whose job it is to get politicians to put their interests above those of their voter base. When it comes to legislation that affects business, they are the voices our elected officials listen to too often. This is nothing new. In fact, it's steeped in our country's history. The fact that lobbyists have the ear of the government gets no one hot and bothered. But times have changed. The power of the lobbyists is waning. Corporations are taking a more circuitous route to get what they want, and it's revolutionizing how American politics works.

"Increasingly, the way to get a politician to do what you want is to target their voter base directly. Today, the prize catch for industry is not the politician's ear but the politician's livelihood. The new agents wielding this power are public relations companies. They now hire more journalism graduates than news organizations, and their power dwarfs that of even the most seasoned lobbyist. PR campaigns are rolling out across the country with one aim: to change how average citizens think about an issue so that their senators and other representatives have little choice but to oblige.

"Leading the charge in this new power play is Tate Lieberman and his PR company, Berrins. But as *DC Watch* will show in this series, there are bigger players involved who will do anything to get their way. And those politicians whose ears the lobbyists sought to bend? They are becoming little more than PR tools themselves, conscripted to the cause through payments, bribes and worse. This is democracy for sale, pure and simple, a flagrant perversion of the democratic principles this country was founded on. Even worse than that, it's criminal."

Cadence lifted her eyes from the page and looked at Bob. "Whoa. Sounds like quite a story. My first question is, who was acting criminally. My second one is, did she have any proof?"

"I'll get to that," said Bob before pointing at the other two piles. "But I'm thinking it relates to one or both of these other subjects Tessa was zooming in on for the second and third parts of her series."

"And they are?"

"Senator Ron Nagle and Zellus Pharmaceuticals."

Bob proceeded to tell Cadence that Tessa had gathered a lot of information on how Nagle had essentially become a paid agent for Zellus and other companies. He was essentially a politician for hire. Not by just anyone. He had a small list of clients or paymasters. In his home state of Massachusetts, he had, according to two anonymous state legislators, intervened to block a bill that would result in imposing a sugar tax. The returns from that tax would be put directly into obesity treatments. These two legislators said what Nagle had done may not have been technically illegal, but it was highly unethical. A big soda company hired a DC PR company, one of Lieberman's rivals, to produce slick television ads that warned consumers that the price of soda would go up drastically if the bill was introduced. The bill failed, just barely.

Nagle had even more success with helping to make Narcadia the number one rehab drug in the US, even though it cost double the alternatives. That translated into hundreds of millions of dollars in profit for Zellus, and it also bought Ron Nagle a beach house on the North Carolina coast.

At one point, while Cadence was listening to Bob, she lifted a finger and gestured for him to keep going, that she was still listening as she grabbed her laptop and began tapping away at the keyboard. She then examined the results of her search as she listened to Bob's summary. When he finished, she pointed at her screen.

"What's that?" said Bob.

"Nagle's website. He's in campaign mode. Got the midterms coming up. And according to this report he has the most campaign funds of just about anybody in history. This article says he'll need it. He's desperate to grow his support base and will no doubt be operating a big and slick marketing campaign to ensure his reelection. He has threatened to sue several people who accused him of being a big pharma patsy."

"But the question is how far would he go to hold onto his power?" said Cadence. "I have to say, I'm impressed with Tessa's tenacity. How did she get all this stuff?"

Bob tapped the conference room table. "I'm glad you asked because I was thinking the same thing. As I went through all this material I was wondering if someone was helping her."

"As in a deep throat kind of character? A whistleblower."

"Yes, exactly," said Bob. "And then I came across these."

As he was talking, Bob was rifling through one of the piles. He then produced a three-page document and handed it to Cadence.

"What's this?" she asked. "Emails?"

"Yep. Mostly," said Bob. "It's an email chain between Tessa and someone using an anonymous, untraceable email account."

"And this person fed Tessa information?"

"If I'm reading it right, he or she may have put the idea of the story into Tessa's head."

"A mystery white knight championing the public's best interest."

"Something like that, I guess. But here's the kicker. Look at the last page."

Cadence flipped the sheets over to get to the last page.

"Read it," said Bob.

As Cadence read her jaw slackened. She pored over every word on the page. When she got to the end, she looked up at Bob, dumbfounded.

"Oh my God," she said. "Unbelievable."

"Narcadia is believed to have caused no less than a dozen deaths in Boston. Massachusetts Governor Cary Daniels has received a report, but Nagle has told him to bury it. Tessa's contact said they would provide her with an audio tape of Nagle making these threats."

"And we don't know who the source is?"

"Nope," said Bob. "And we probably never will."

Cadence raised her eyebrows and leaned back into her chair. "Well, then I'm just going to have to find a way to get Nagle to tell us all about it."

"How?"

"When he takes the stand."

PART II

Chapter 24

Cadence stood outside the courtroom door tapping her knees against her briefcase. For the third time since she had arrived, she checked her watch. She had asked Lieberman to meet her at eight-thirty. She liked being early, but she did not expect Lieberman to play ball. He was not entirely firm with his agreement. He had said more than once that he did not wish to spend a minute more in that courtroom than he absolutely had to. Expecting Lieberman to arrive at nine, she was pleasantly surprised to see him appear fifteen minutes earlier. What surprised her even more was that Kelly Lieberman was right by his side.

Kelly Lieberman had long amber hair that fell down to her shoulders. Despite the years, her beauty had been well preserved. Where once she would have been described as strikingly pretty, she was now strikingly handsome. Looking at her trim figure, enveloped in a tailored houndstooth skirt and jacket, Cadence had to ask herself what the hell do men want? A woman Kelly's age could not look any more beautiful and yet her husband was so sadly prone to hooking up with younger women.

Lieberman had reported to Cadence that Kelly had taken the news about his mistress Phoebe Baker surprisingly well. Understandably, she was angry about his foolish and habitual weakness for such affairs and tore him to shreds. She told him there and then that their marriage was indeed over.

He told Cadence that he could not believe what followed. She said she would play the devoted wife and stand by him until the trial ended. She said she would do whatever she could to help him and that she hoped that he would not end up in jail. But whether he was found guilty or not guilty, the day the trial finished was the end date of their marriage. He would have to vacate the house immediately. She was done with him and from that day on she would be getting on with her own life. She would owe him nothing. She would take her half of the property. She would not ask for more, but she would have nothing more to do with his company. She would withdraw her money and if that happened to ruin Berrins then it was not her problem. Whatever his fate would be was not her concern.

Lieberman had related this exchange to Cadence over the phone. The tone of his voice was like nothing she had heard from him before. He was touched but baffled. He could not understand why she chose not to destroy him.

Grateful as he was, he felt there must be something he did not know, something that she was not telling him. When he had asked, she waved a hand and said that she saw things differently now. Some part of her was grateful that his affair was out in the open. It showed her what a farce their marriage was. It struck her that she had been acting a role as Lieberman's wife, keeping up appearances while never trusting her husband's excuses for not coming home. It was a relief to call an end to the sham once and for all.

"Good morning, Kelly," said Cadence, freeing her right hand from her briefcase and extending it to Kelly. "I'm so glad you could come."

Cadence had had just one phone call with Kelly. It was short and to the point. When Cadence began asking just how public Kelly was prepared to be when it came to supporting her husband, she cut her short. "I've been doing that all my life, dear. I'm very good at supporting my husband even when he has behaved like an ass. I'll be there to support him in court every day. I did love my husband, Cadence, longer than I ever should have. He's capable of many hurtful things but I don't think he's capable of murder."

Looking at the Liebermans, Cadence thought what a perfect couple they appeared to be. It saddened her to know the truth of the lies and deceit that would soon bring their marriage to an end. She could not help but be impressed with Kelly's grace under pressure. She was all class, no doubt about it.

As Cadence spoke with the Liebermans, a group of photographers came forward and began shooting photos. Kelly hooked her arm into his husband's and together they faced the cameras stoically. Cadence noticed Kelly went so far as to pat her husband's forearm with her free hand while presenting a confident smile to the press. No doubt about it. Cadence had hoped Kelly would play ball, but under the circumstances never would she have expected Kelly to do so with such convincing enthusiasm. The only images the press was going to get of her were of humility, defiance and faith in her husband's innocence.

The questions had barely started before Cadence put an end to the press conference and ushered the Liebermans through the courtroom door. As she did so, Gerard Underhill appeared so the press turned on him. He was only too happy to stand there and answer every question thrown at him. Cadence did not wait to hear everything he said. All she heard as she stepped inside was Underhill's booming voice saying, "Today is the day that we get justice for Tessa Reeves."

Inside the courtroom, Cadence led Lieberman to the defense table while Kelly took a seat in the gallery directly behind them. Cadence knew this courtroom like the back of her hand and was happy with Kelly's choice. She leaned over the railing to tell Kelly quietly that she should choose the same seat every day so every member of the jury could get a good look at her. Cadence had told Kelly that the jury would be watching her almost as closely as they watched her husband so her every movement, reaction and facial expression mattered. Even as she delivered this advice, Cadence felt that Kelly knew it already.

The courtroom door was flung open and in came Underhill and his team, closely followed by several reporters and photographers and members of the public. Within five minutes, the courtroom was packed.

Cadence alternated between going over her opening statement notes and exchanging words with Lieberman. His demeanor was proud and slightly indignant, a quality that Cadence had tried to iron out of him without much success. He was not happy to be on trial. And as far as she was concerned that was fine. Innocent people must rightly feel shocked and outraged to stand accused of murder. But what was not okay was for the client to project a supercilious air, as though the whole process was beneath them. In spirit, if not in deed, this was contempt of court, and it was surefire way to offend both judge and jury.

"All rise," cried the bailiff. "The Honorable Superior Court Judge Samuel Gates presiding."

The onlookers had barely warmed their seats before the judge's arrival had them standing.

"Good morning, everyone," said Judge Gates. "Please sit yourselves down."

Gates was a thin black man of sixty-three who looked at the world through thick-framed oblong glasses. His face was lean and long and his long, lofty gray eyebrows gave him an expression of being ever aloof. He moved with such quick vigor you would think he had another forty years of work in him.

Judge Gates confirmed the presence of all the relevant parties and read the case before giving the gallery a heads up.

"Here are some things to know about me, okay?" he said. "The first is, I won't tolerate undue noise and outcries in my courtroom. Anyone who can't contain themselves will be expelled from the courtroom. Do I make myself understood?"

There was grave silence and widespread nodding. Convinced his message had hit home, Judge Gates asked the bailiff to let the jury in.

As the twelve jurors and four alternates entered the courtroom, once they had taken their seats and made themselves comfortable, each took their first opportunity to check out Lieberman. This was typical. They knew they were adjudicating a murder trial and their most urgent curiosity was to see what this man looked like who had been charged with murder.

Cadence was happy with what they saw in Tate Lieberman. She did not have to tell him to dress well. He did that every day of his working life. But she had impressed upon him to always remain calm, to never react and to never lock eyes with a juror. On this last point, some clients felt that eyeballing a juror might allow for them to connect and hence gain some leverage of sympathy. Cadence rejected this theory outright. As she told every client, seeking out sympathy in this manner risked being judged as manipulative. Do not look at them, was her advice. Look at the judge all you want. By all means run your eye over the jury box every now and then but always with a blank expression. And never, ever make eye contact with a juror.

As far as Cadence was concerned, the accused should be an inert figure in a trial such as this. He or she should be a small target, if not invisible. Let the jury look at you. And they will. Never look smug. Never look angry. It was the directive of a teacher to children. Sit still, pay attention and keep your mouth shut.

Cadence turned to see what Lieberman was presenting to the jury for the first time and was glad to see, as he sat up straight and stretched his jaw out, that his burning indignation was well hidden. Still, the jaw was a little too proud. She leaned towards him to say something but as she did so a hand landed on Lieberman's shoulder.

"Humility, Tate," whispered Kelly, who had leaned over the railing and positioned her head just behind her husband's. Immediately, his jaw eased and he bowed his head. Cadence resumed her position and stole a glance at the jury, whose collective eye had been drawn to the beautiful, elegant woman seated behind the accused. She shuddered to think what would have happened if Kelly had decided to use the case to exact revenge on her cheating husband.

"Mr. Underhill, Ms. Elliott, are we ready to proceed with opening statements?" Judge Gates's eyes switched between Cadence and her counterpart. Both of them nodded and confirmed verbally that they were indeed ready.

"Mr. Underhill. The floor is yours."

Chapter 25

Cadence could predict just about every move Underhill made in the courtroom. She knew his mannerisms, his character and his ticks. Following the judge's invitation, Underhill tapped the sides of the files on the table in front of him, got to his feet and buttoned his suit jacket. As usual, he was wearing a three-piece suit. She imagined he had a huge closet full of them. Today's was dark gray, his silk tie and matching pocket square were as blue as the Mediterranean shallows, his black oxfords polished to a mirror sheen. When seated she noted his socks were crimson red. Underhill had told her once that on the first day of trial he liked to wear red, white and blue in honor of the country whose justice he was serving and preserving. In a subtle way, he said. Today the white came in the form of a crisp and crease-free ivory shirt.

"Ladies and gentlemen of the jury," he began after reaching the lectern, nodding to the judge and then turning to his right. "My name is Gerard Underhill, Assistant US Attorney."

"Just a few minutes ago, I stood outside this courtroom and told the media that today marks the first step in winning justice for a bright, brave and gifted young woman named Tessa Reeves. This trial cannot do the impossible. It cannot bring Tessa back to life and return her to the arms of her loved ones who mourn her deeply. I wish we could do that, but we are not here to perform miracles. What we can do here is examine the earthly facts of this case, to study everything that we know to be true and to conclude that, even though we cannot undo Tessa's murder, then at least we can hold her murderer responsible.

"And make no mistake, the evidence tells us she died not by her own hand, but by someone else's. She did not throw herself in front of a train. No, the evidence will show that it was the accused who threw her to her death.

"Tessa Reeves was a rising star in the field of investigative journalism, the star recruit for the political news website *DC Watch*. As you will hear from her boss and her colleagues, Tessa Reeves pushed the envelope when it came to reporting. Not in the sense of ethics, but in her sense of purpose. In a city where it pays to be careful not to step on powerful toes, she was fearless. She had a reputation for exposing injustice and criminality where she saw it. And what she unearthed and threatened to bring to light, cost Tessa Reeves her life.

"You see, Tessa was intent on exposing the deeds of people who operated on the wrong side of the moral line and on the wrong side of the law. When she died she was researching a story on a company called Berrins, a public relations company founded by the accused, Tate Lieberman.

"Tessa conducted multiple interviews, cross-referenced the material she acquired and double-checked her facts. And the conclusion she came to was that certain businesses in America were hoodwinking the general public. And they did so by hiring Berrins, aka the accused Tate Lieberman.

"Now is not the time to detail the information Tessa had gathered on Tate Lieberman's activities. But it was certainly her intention to make that information known to the public. Unfortunately, that never happened. She was killed before her story could be published.

"So why am I talking about an expose on the accused, Tate Lieberman? Because he did not want Tessa's story to see the light of day. He knew what she wanted to do. He knew that she would expose him, and he knew that if he didn't stop her, her story might well ruin both his reputation and his company.

"I know this because this is what the accused told her himself. When he caught wind of her story, he sent her threatening messages. He sent searing emails to her and her boss. He told her that if she went ahead with her story, she would be finished. He told her that if her story went live, it would be her last. Mark my words, he said, it will be the last story you ever write.

"Less than forty-eight hours later, Tessa Reeves was dead.

"Let's look at what happened in the hours before her death. At six o'clock she was at her desk, working hard as usual. At about six-thirty, she received another text message from Tate Lieberman. Unlike his previous correspondence, this missive was somewhat conciliatory. He apologized for his behavior, and he suggested they meet face to face to discuss a formal interview. He suggested they meet that very night at Jameson's, a members-only gentlemen's club replete with exotic dancers and discretion about what happens behind its doors.

"Tessa Reeves went to the club and sat with Lieberman. At some point, witnesses say, the two of them argued, after which Tessa left the club for the nearby metro station. Ten minutes later, Tate Lieberman followed in her footsteps. He had arrived by taxi but he left on foot.

"Twenty minutes later, Tessa Reeves was hurled in front of a train.

"A question you might be rightly asking is that if Tessa left the club ten minutes before the accused, how could he know where she was?

"Well, the answer lies in a small piece of smart technology known as an AirTag. The detectives investigating the case found such a device in Tessa Reeves' handbag. Whoever planted it on her could track her every move. Whoever planted that device knew exactly where she was.

"What was the accused doing as he left the club? We have an eyewitness who says he was walking with his eyes glued to his phone.

"Of course, when detectives checked the defendant's phone, they discovered it had been wiped of all its data. In the time between Tessa Reeves' death and his interviews with police investigators, the defendant decided to erase his digital footprint. He told police this was part of a weekly regimen to protect his data security.

"Did the police believe him? No. They were so convinced that he was lying that they arrested him and charged him with murder.

"So we have motive, means and intent, members of the jury. As you will see in the coming days, the evidence that has been painstakingly gathered by experts points to one conclusion. And that conclusion is that Tate Lieberman killed Tessa Reeves in order to silence her. He was scared of what she would reveal to the public, and he decided to take drastic measures to make sure that didn't happen.

"I ask you to be the light of justice that Tessa Reeves hoped to be. Once you have seen all the evidence, I'm sure you will be left with one conclusion and one conclusion only—that Tate Lieberman murdered Tessa Reeves in cold blood. And to that end, you must find him guilty. While we may never see the truth revealed that Tessa Reeves wanted to show us, you can deliver justice in her name and return a guilty verdict for this man who took her life. Thank you."

The courtroom was silent as Underhill made his way back to his table. He took his seat, picked up a pen and began to scribble something down. His fawning team members leaned in and offered their congratulations in hushed tones. He pushed the note he had written to the person on his right, his second chair. Cadence watched as the woman read the note and barely stopped herself from smirking.

Cadence was disgusted. If she was not mistaken, Underhill and his colleagues were already practically high fiving, convinced that they had a case they could not lose. Their arrogance was galling. Her eyes flicked to the jury box, where she saw the barely suppressed glee of the Underhill team had not gone unnoticed by a few members of the jury.

She got to her feet. Unlike Underhill, she went to the lectern empty handed. No crib notes, no supporting documents. No nothing. She knew exactly what she was going to say and the sight of Underhill and his team gloating only sharpened her focus.

"Members of the jury," she said, "I want to thank you for your service. I know this phrase is typically used for the men and women of our armed forces, but you too are performing a task in the name of your country. That is, you're representing not only your entire community but the country as a whole in the task of finding justice in this case. You have had to take leave from work. You have had to make arrangements to ensure your kids are in good hands during your absence. You have had to put everything else aside to make this trial your main purpose in life. And for that I both thank you and commend you. Lord knows this is a very serious matter that cannot be taken lightly. This trial will not be a procession, a reel of information that demands little of you. It will test you in every way—mentally, physically and spiritually. A man's life is in your hands, literally."

As she said these last words, Cadence slowly turned and looked at Underhill and his team.

"Members of the jury, you have heard from the prosecutor that all evidence points to my client being guilty of Tessa Reeves' murder. This is not a suggestion that Mr. Underhill has made. To his way of thinking, it's a statement of fact. Here we have x and here we have y, so we end up with z.

"I must remind you that the certainty with which Mr. Underhill presents his argument is little more than a show of his confidence. The story he told to you is not the truth, it is a theory. And in a court of law, we do not convict citizens accused of murder on the strength of a theory. We do not send people to prison for the rest of their lives on the strength of suggestion. Convictions or verdicts must be based on facts. And I put it to you that the prosecution has in their possession little by way of fact.

"I could stand here and give you a number of other theories using the evidence that was used to bring this matter to trial. But I don't want to waste your time.

"Tate Lieberman is a man with a lot to lose. That is to say he's a highly successful man. Through hard work and enterprise, he turned the public relations company that he founded into a thriving business that earns over a hundred million dollars a year.

"Now, it is true that Tessa Reeves was preparing to write an investigative story about my client's company, Berrins. He was anxious about that. He was not happy about that. He was accustomed to carrying out his business quietly and went out of his way not to draw attention to himself.

"It is a fact that Mr. Lieberman made contact with Tessa Reeves to express his displeasure about what she was planning to publish. Does that mean he killed her? No. And there is no evidence to prove that he killed her.

"It is a fact that Mr. Lieberman threatened Tessa Reeves during his efforts to stop her from going ahead with her story. Does that mean he killed her? No. No evidence exists that proves he killed her.

"It is a fact that Mr. Lieberman met with Tessa Reeves and argued with her for about an hour before she died. Does that mean he killed her? No. Because again, there is no evidence that he killed her.

"Many people have differing points of view. More so in DC than practically anywhere in the world. This is true of politics and business and everywhere that those two industries intertwine. Competition and intrigue form the fabric of this great city. Conflicting interests. Competing agendas. Fierce rivalries. Mr. Lieberman has risen up through this tough environment and thrived. He is rightfully proud of his company and naturally protective of it. Yet the prosecution would have you believe he was willing to throw it all away to stop an unfavorable article from seeing the light of day.

"Mr. Lieberman left the club soon after Reeves and headed in the same direction as her. Does that mean he killed her? No. Because again there is no direct evidence that he killed her. What he did after he left the club was walk back to his hotel, which was the same direction as the station where Tessa Reeves died.

"Members of the jury, I must stress the most important aspect of this trial. It is not up to me to prove that Mr. Lieberman is innocent. The prosecution must convince you that he is guilty. If you are not convinced beyond all reasonable doubt that he is guilty, then you must find him not guilty. The evidence the prosecution has cannot dispel doubt from your mind. I'm sure you will believe this when it comes to considering your verdict. And in this case, there can only be one fair verdict and that is not guilty."

Chapter 26

Cadence may have done well to capitalize on Team Underhill's hubris, but a trial is a marathon, and they were only a few steps in. She was going to need a lot more convincing to post a win for Tate Lieberman.

Opening statements done, Underhill got down to business. He was going to make that slight embarrassment history as soon as he possibly could. That hint of a flaw was about to be obliterated. He got to his feet and called his first witness. Detective Steve Hudson.

Hudson slid his lean six-foot frame through the gate and gave Underhill a quick nod as he passed by the prosecutor's table. His stride was smooth and confident. He straightened out his tie as he took his seat and once his oath was done, cast a squinted eye over the packed courtroom before him. He looked like nothing could rattle him, but that comes with the territory of being a seasoned homicide investigator. He had seen it all, and then some. All eyes that fell upon him could see that.

Hudson's straw-colored hair was combed back, and his narrow face was clean-shaved except for a thin, well-groomed moustache. Evidently particular about his appearance, he did not just let his mustache grow—he shaped it with a razor from the top, Clark Gable style. Cadence thought all that was missing was a toothpick in the corner of his mouth and one of those bolo ties that cowboys wear. Hudson wore a slim red tie and white shirt under his buttoned blue suit jacket. He was no pretender. As Underhill was about to let the court know, this detective was a proven manhunter.

By way of a few get-to-know-you questions, Underhill unpacked Hudson's professional history. After graduating from the Boston Police Academy, he spent ten years in various positions before joining the Criminal Investigation Division. Underhill drew out a string of Hudson's achievements as a homicide detective but since they were all in Boston, none of the jurors showed any recognition of his cases. Hudson said he relocated to DC for family reasons—his wife wanted to be close to her gravely ill mother. As it happened, there was a detective position available at the DCPD and he relocated three weeks ahead of his wife.

Following a fifteen-minute presentation of Hudson's crime-fighting CV, Underhill started on the case at hand.

"Detective Hudson, can you please tell us when you started on this case?"

"Sure," Hudson said and lifted his hand to scratch the side of his nose—an almost perfect dorsal fin shape, save for the sharp deviation it made at the bridge. Whatever bent Hudson's septum out of shape, it happened recently. His index finger was scratching lightly at the fringe of a scab next to the bend. His action brought attention to his nose and the jury was close enough to see the skin was still faintly bruised at the bridge.

"I'm off duty and asleep but in my job you're never really off-duty," he said. "About one-thirty I get the call. We had two suspected homicides at once. Detectives Monroe and Keating had been dispatched to a siege that ended up a double-fatality, a murder suicide. So I was told to get myself to McPherson Square Station as quick as I could."

"Could you describe the crime scene for us?"

Hudson sucked in a breath and leaned back in the chair. "Yes, I can. All I could do was look when I got there. Forensics owned the crime scene until they said otherwise. They had to take photos, bag the evidence, check for prints. All that sort of thing. I just eyeballed the place. They'd closed the platform, obviously. The train was still there. They had moved it forward, so it was clear of the victim's body."

Prompted by Underhill's questions, Hudson revealed how he was surprised when he had lifted the sheet covering Tessa Reeves' body. He said there were severe impact injuries but her entire body was intact. She had fallen underneath the train with no part of her body crossing the track. He said he had seen dismembered bodies on Boston's subway system. By the way he said it, he clearly considered this to be a small mercy for Tessa Reeves and her loved ones. He said there were about half a dozen deaths a year on the T system in Boston. Mostly suicides, he added.

"Did it look like a suicide, Detective Hudson?"

Hudson shook his head. "Who can say? The girl ended up under a train. How she got there was anyone's guess at that point."

"But you said it was a crime scene."

"The most common reason people end up that way is suicide. But it's standard practice to rope off the scene so we could rule out anything suspicious."

"Was there anything suspicious?"

"Yeah. Pretty quickly we were inclined to treat it as a murder."

"Why was that?"

"The driver told officers he saw a man behind the victim and that he believed she was pushed."

"Objection, Your Honor. It has not been established that Tessa Reeves was pushed to her death."

Whether it was accurate or not, Cadence had to keep the suicide theory in play.

"Your Honor," said Underhill, "Detective Hudson is, if nothing else, an expert witness whose opinion carries significant weight."

"That may be so, counselor," said Judge Gates, "but the objection is sustained. It has yet to be proven before this court that Tessa Reeves was murdered."

Underhill bowed his head briefly before returning his gaze to his witness. "Okay, I'll rephrase. Detective Hudson, did the train driver's words prompt you to treat this case as a murder?"

"Yes, most definitely. I spoke with him directly once I'd heard what he said."

"This was at the scene?"

"Yes. I spoke to him on the platform."

"What did he tell you?"

"He said the girl screamed and that she looked terrified. He said that the way she fell forward, it was not a voluntary movement."

"What do you mean by that? Voluntary movement?"

"The driver said it looked for all the world like Tessa Reeves did not jump in front of the train willingly."

"I see. Was the train driver able to describe the man to you?"

"Not in great detail, no. It happened so fast."

"When did the defendant become a person of interest?"

"It wasn't our immediate line of inquiry," said Hudson. "It took a few days and a bunch of evidence to connect him to the crime."

"What led you to believe that Tate Lieberman killed Tessa Reeves?"

Cadence wanted to object but sat on her hands. Underhill had found a way to state to the jury that "Tate Lieberman killed Tessa Reeves," and he would have been congratulating himself on getting away with it. With no solid grounds to object, she kept silent.

Hudson began describing the path his investigation had taken. It started with the driver but there were a couple of pieces of evidence at the scene that not only made murder the most likely explanation for Tessa Reeves' death but that made it clear she knew her killer. Reeves' phone records had led them to speak with Lieberman as one of many people she had called over the forty-eight hours before her death. Among the phone records was a threatening text message he had sent.

"Detective Hudson, you said the defendant sent a threatening text to the victim."

"That's right."

Underhill held up a document in his right hand. "In my hand here are printouts of all the text messages found on Tessa Reeves cell phone. Your Honor, may I approach the witness?"

"You may," said Judge Gates with a nod.

Underhill bowed his head as he entered the well of the courtroom—the floor space between the judge's bench and the lawyers' tables—showing Judge Gates the proper deference. There was a reason that lawyers had to ask a judge's permission to approach a witness. It was not just to keep lawyers from intimidating witnesses; it was for the judge's peace of mind. Though they share the same profession, judges can often see lawyers as their most natural enemy. The well ensures the bailiff has time to save a judge from an attack by a disgruntled lawyer.

Underhill handed Hudson the paperwork and returned to the podium.

"Detective Hudson," he said. "Could you please read the highlighted text message from the defendant?"

"Sure. It reads, 'You run that story and it's going to be your last. Do not underestimate me.'"

"Thank you. When was that message sent to Tessa Reeves?"

"The day before she died."

"I see," said Underhill. "And so I take it you sought to speak with the defendant about this message?"

"Yes, we did. My partner, Detective Ely Kramer, and myself went and questioned Mr. Lieberman about the message."

"What did he tell you?"

"He told me it was nothing," said Hudson. "He was just letting off some steam. He did not like the fact that Tessa Reeves was planning to write an article about his business affairs."

"Did he tell you this?"

"We found out what Ms. Reeves was planning to write. We went and spoke with her editor. I can't give you the exact details of the article, but I can say that it would have brought to light certain things about Mr. Lieberman's PR company that were not flattering. In fact, it suggested Mr. Lieberman's PR firm operated outside the rule of law."

"How did the defendant respond when you told him this?"

"He appeared surprised that we knew so much about the story," said Hudson. "But he did not deny sending the messages. He conceded that he knew what Tessa was up to and admitted he was not happy about it."

"What else did he tell you?"

"He told us that he did not want to see his reputation sullied by this story. He said it was a hatchet job and that he regretted letting his emotions get the better of him."

"How did he explain the threat he sent Ms. Reeves?"

"He said it was not serious."

"Did you believe him?"

"No."

"But you did not charge the defendant then, did you?"

"No, we did not."

"When did you charge him?"

"When we became convinced that he killed her."

"What made you so sure?"

Detective Hudson coughed lightly then faced the jury. "Because we think he stalked her and lured her to her death."

A murmur swelled in the gallery. Judge Gates raised his gavel. "Silence in the courtroom," he said firmly and whacked his gavel down. At the sound of the wooden hammer, all noise ceased. "I will not hesitate to clear this courtroom if this trial cannot proceed in an orderly fashion, and by that I mean in a quiet and dignified manner. This is not a stage show. Please keep your thoughts to yourselves."

Underhill had stood waiting in silence for Judge Gates to finish his admonition. When the judge indicated Underhill was free to resume, he stepped to the side of the lectern and cleared his throat.

"Can I ask you to repeat what you just said, Detective Hudson?"

"I said we got a warrant for Mr. Lieberman's arrest after we were convinced that he stalked Tessa Reeves and lured her to her death."

"Could you please tell the court how you came to that conclusion?"

"It was the combination of a few pieces of evidence that convinced us. The first was the exchanges between the defendant and the victim in the days and hours leading up to her death. The defendant threatened to kill her. Then he attempted to get on her good side."

"How so?"

"He proposed that they meet at Jameson's. At this meeting, Mr. Lieberman offered Ms. Reeves a deal. He said if she dropped her story on him he would give her information on another person of interest who he said was crooked."

"How do you know this is what they spoke about at that meeting?"

"Straight from the horse's mouth. The defendant told us."

"What was the outcome of this meeting?"

"Tessa Reeves refused to back off," said Hudson. "She was not interested in the story he offered her. We have witnesses who say they heard Tessa and Mr. Lieberman argue. He admitted he was not happy that she planned to go ahead with her story. She left the club and went to catch a train home. But he stalked her."

"Objection," called Cadence.

"Your Honor," said Underhill. "Detective Hudson is merely stating the reasons why he charged the defendant with Tessa Reeves' murder."

"I agree," said Judge Gates. "Overruled."

Cadence sat down.

"What's he going to say next?" Lieberman hissed at Cadence. "That I confessed?"

Cadence stared Lieberman down. "Tate, I know this is hard, but you need to stop talking now and stay calm."

"Calm?" he said, pushing the word out though tightly pressed lips. His eyes were wide and his chest heaving. He then lowered his head, knowing Cadence was right, and took a few deep breaths.

Cadence leaned closer to him. "Remember, Tate. I get a shot at this guy. And let me tell you, I don't miss."

Cadence was not quite sure where this flash of bravado sprang from. She only half believed her own words. She just had to get Lieberman to cool off as quickly as possible before the jury caught sight of his rage.

Her inner self was not so sure she would dismantle Detective Hudson on the stand. All she knew, all she had faith in, was that this trial was a two-way street. The legal pad in front of her was already covered in notes she had made while listening to Underhill's examination of Hudson. If she was not able to take Hudson apart altogether, she felt sure she could send him on his way with a few pieces missing.

She was relieved to see Lieberman get a hold of himself. He reached for the cup of water in front of him and took a sip, his eyes focused on the ceiling as he sipped. He replaced the cup, wiped his mouth and turned his eyes to Hudson. He was the picture of serenity.

Underhill had taken a moment to confer with his colleague. He stepped back to the podium, starting his next question before he got there.

"Detective Hudson, what makes you believe the defendant stalked Tessa Reeves?"

"The AirTag we found in the victim's bag," said Hudson.

"Do you mean this?" Underhill held up a clear plastic bag with a small white disc inside. "Exhibit 245, Your Honor."

"Yes, that's exactly what I mean."

"What is an AirTag exactly?"

"It's a tracking device that prevents users from losing their belongings like keys, wallets and bags. You attach them to frequently used items that often get misplaced, lost or stolen. It's a transmitter that you can track with your phone."

Underhill lifted the bag again. "How did this particular tracker become evidence in this case?"

"It was found hidden in Tessa Reeves' handbag."

"How do you mean hidden?"

"Someone had made a small cut in the handbag's lining and slipped it in."

"What does this mean, Detective Hudson?"

"It means that whoever put that tracker in Ms. Reeves' handbag could follow her. Stalk her. They could let her move out of sight and they would still know exactly where she was."

"And she would have had no idea she was being tracked?"

"No. Her killer followed her into the train station."

"So Tessa Reeves left the club and went to the metro station to catch a ride home."

"That's right but she never made it."

"Thank you, Detective Hudson. No further questions, Your Honor."

"Your witness, Ms. Elliott," said Judge Gates.

Cadence sprang to her feet. Underhill had the jury eating out of his hand. If she did not find a way to tarnish the reputation of this distinguished detective, this case might be lost before it had barely begun.

Chapter 27

Detective Hudson's eyes followed Cadence as she got to the lectern and laid out a few documents on its flat top. All through Underhill's examination, Cadence had made notes to modify her strategy for her cross-examination. Hudson was sharp, there was no doubt about it, and she was not about to kid herself that she could trip him up easily. But that was not exactly what she intended to do. She had no qualms about discrediting witnesses, eviscerating their credibility in full view of the jury, the gallery and the public beyond.

And she did think there was some discrediting potential when it came to Hudson. Something about his police work did not add up. What that was exactly she did not know. She had to find a clear and credible way to make the jury doubt him.

"Detective Hudson," she began, "you are obviously confident that you have your man. The prosecution has placed all its faith in your investigative work."

"What is this? Trial law 101," sniffed Hudson. "We wouldn't be here in court at all today if I hadn't given the DA a case that he could prove."

"No, this is no law school class, Detective Hudson," said Cadence coolly. "It is real life, with a man's life at stake. To start, I'd like to touch on your conviction rate for homicide cases, since Mr. Underhill was kind enough to detail each one for the benefit of the court. Eleven so far, and all but one of those in Boston, is that right?"

"That's right. This is my second in DC."

"Let's not count this one in your favor just yet, Detective. There's a lot of due process we need to get through. But I did want to ask: where does this case rank in terms of your confidence that you got the right man?"

"They're all the same. I don't make up my mind until the evidence tells me what to think."

"And you have no doubt that Mr. Lieberman killed Tessa Reeves, right?"

"Yes."

"We all now know about the unpleasant message my client sent Tessa about her story."

"It was more than unpleasant. It was as close to a death threat as you can get. I've seen men jailed for not much more than that."

"I don't doubt it, Detective Hudson. But despite this threat, of her own volition, Tessa Reeves went to meet Mr. Lieberman at the club."

"Is that a question?"

"Let's make it one. Why don't we make it several? Firstly, did Tessa Reeves go and meet with Mr. Lieberman at Jameson's by herself?"

"I don't know for sure. I wasn't there."

"Come on, Detective. You interviewed staff members who told you they saw her at the club. Did they say she had company?"

"No."

"So I think we can take it as a given that she went alone. Did she remain sitting with Mr. Lieberman after they argued?"

"I wasn't there."

"Detective, your investigation doesn't rest on what your own eyes and ears have seen and heard, does it? Did any witness tell you that Tessa Reeves left immediately after she argued with Mr. Lieberman?"

"No."

"Okay. So they talked some more. This is what the witness said they saw, is it not?"

"I believe so."

"So she didn't storm off in a huff. She did not flee in fear of her own safety. They talked for a while. They agreed to disagree, we can assume, right?"

"You might assume that. There may be other explanations. Who knows what they were saying?"

"But isn't that the point, Detective. The content of their conversation is just speculation, isn't it?"

Hudson sat silent and motionless save for his jaw muscle balling up as he clamped his teeth tightly. "The defendant knows."

"I'll continue, shall I? Detective Hudson, did anyone see Mr. Lieberman put this tracking device in Ms. Reeves' handbag?"

Hudson shook his head. "No."

"Did anyone see Mr. Lieberman pull out a knife or some sort of blade to cut a hole in Ms. Reeves' handbag and place a secret tracker in it?"

"Just because no one saw it doesn't mean it didn't happen."

"But as it stands this is just a theory of yours, is it not? You do not have any proof whatsoever that Mr. Lieberman placed a tracker in Tessa Reeves' handbag, do you?"

"The case is not built on that alone."

"Your Honor, I'd like the witness to answer the question."

"She's right, Detective Hudson. You need to give her an answer."

"No."

"Just so we're clear, there's no evidence to prove that Mr. Lieberman planted that tracker, is there?"

"No."

Cadence took a deep breath but did so through her nose to make it less obvious. She was not just nervous. She was excited. And worried. She knew her next question may not be good for her client, but it was necessary.

"Mr. Hudson, whoever planted that tracker must have tracked it, right? Did you find any evidence that my client tracked Ms. Reeves that night or at any time?"

"We will never know because your client scrubbed his phone before we could get a look at it."

This was an act that made Lieberman look somewhat guilty, so Cadence had to drive home the possibility that it implied no guilt at all.

"Detective Hudson, there could be any number of reasons why someone scrubs his cell phone, right?"

"If you say so."

"Are you saying anyone who scrubs their cell phone is a murderer?"

"Of course not."

"Detective Hudson, did Mr. Lieberman tell you why he got rid of his phone data?"

"Not initially. When we first checked his phone, he said he had no idea why there was no record of recent calls or text messages."

"But he told you eventually, didn't he?"

"Yes, he did. He said his wife thought he was having an affair, so if there was nothing to see there was nothing to explain. I didn't buy it, but I'm sure you swallowed every word."

As Hudson spoke the last phrase he grinned lasciviously as though he had conjured up a sexual image of Cadence. He was somewhat surprised to see her hold his gaze with a confident smile. He had just stooped to a moral low and the whole courtroom knew it. She may not have completely discredited Detective Hudson but a couple of chinks in that armor of his were there for the jury to see in plain sight.

Cadence let the detective's words hang there for a while. She then stepped to the side of the podium, standing a little closer to the jury. All the while she kept her eyes locked on the witness. The courtroom was dead quiet. There was now a sexual subtext to this exchange, and all ears were cocked to hear what came next from Cadence's lips.

"So you have no evidence that my client planted this tracking device. You have no evidence that he followed her…"

"Yes, I do. As you should know from the witness statements, the doorman said the defendant left the club five minutes after Tessa Reeves and walked in the same direction while he was checking his phone."

"Yes, I'm well aware that that's what they said. But did they say they saw him enter the station?"

Hudson did not want to be quick with his reply, as though he had options. But he only had one. "No."

"Okay, so we are clear on that. No one saw him enter the station. He told you where he was going, didn't he, Detective Hudson?"

"You mean he told me after he decided to change his alibi? Yes, he obviously was scared that his alibi was suspiciously weak, so he gave us another one."

"I'm not surprised that you find the fact that my client changed his alibi highly suspicious. But there was something that he did not want to admit at first, isn't that right?"

"I think we can agree on that. But then we have to disagree on what he told us next."

"He told you that what he was hiding was the fact that he was having an affair. Isn't that right?"

"Yes."

"He told you he was staying at the Fairbanks Hotel with his mistress and that's where he was going after the club, right?"

"Right."

"And his hotel was in the same direction as the station, right?

"Yes."

"And the hotel staff did confirm that he got to the hotel about thirty minutes later, right?"

"Yes, which meant he was walking very slowly, if not crawling, or he took a detour to kill Tessa Reeves."

"Is that rooted in speculation or evidence?"

"We have to connect the dots at some point. And they point to your client throwing Tessa Reeves in front of a train."

"I must agree with you in part, Detective Hudson. You have connected the dots but only to produce the image you want, isn't that right?"

"What a load of crap."

"Nothing further, Your Honor," said Cadence. She swept up her documents and marched back to the defense table. Detective Hudson watched her, his mouth slightly ajar. It was like she was a felon he could only watch disappear in the distance, diluting his power with every step she took further away.

"Thank you, counselor," said Judge Gates. "That will be all for today. We'll resume proceedings at nine o'clock sharp tomorrow."

Gates tapped his gavel lightly, stood and made for the door.

Chapter 28

Underhill's first witness of the day was the forensic expert Dr. Simon Holloway, a small man in a gray suit, white shirt and black tie. With his short-back-and-sides haircut and thick-rimmed glasses, he looked like an extra from *Mad Men*. After he had taken the oath, he dug a finger into his collar and stretched his neck. With his head raised, his glasses caught the ceiling lights and flashed them across the courtroom. Like most people, he seemed to find the witness stand about as comfortable as the dentist's chair.

"Dr. Holloway," Underhill began, "you were one of the first people at the scene of Tessa Reeves' death, weren't you?"

Dr. Holloway cleared his throat politely before leaning forward. "Yes. That's right."

If Underhill had hoped Dr. Holloway might expand on the question a little he would have been disappointed. "Could you tell us in more detail how you got there? You were called in, right?"

"Ah, yes. Of course. I understand I was called right after the first responders got there. In tragedies like this it is normal to treat the area as a crime scene. It's often very hard to know at first if the person had committed suicide or not, so the authorities like to cordon off the area. Then I go in, or someone like me, and we start taking a closer look."

"When did you start treating this as a murder rather than a suicide?"

"I approach things from a very scientific point of view. I don't make judgements before I have seen the evidence. And whether it was a suicide or not, I went about my job the same way. That is, methodically."

"Yes, I understand. But did you know that the police were treating it as suspicious?"

"Yes, I did."

"Did you find evidence to support the idea that Tessa Reeves was murdered?"

"Yes," said Dr. Holloway as he shifted in his chair. He clearly was not used to being questioned, and even though Underhill must have given him thorough preparation, it still seemed like he was being asked every question for the first time and that every question took him somewhat by surprise. It was evident from the start that Dr. Holloway was not Underhill's idea of a dream witness. He would have loved his forensic expert to deliver answers that had jurors riveted with fascinating detail. Instead, half the jury looked bored already.

Underhill paused, hoping Dr. Holloway would take the cue and know it was up to him to fill the void.

"There were a few indications that the victim did not throw herself in front of the train."

"Just to be clear, you mean indications that someone pushed her?"

"Ah, yes. The first indication was where her body impacted with the train. As you can imagine, there is not an exact manner in which every person jumps in front of a train to end their lives."

"Go on," said Underhill as though he feared his witness would stop there.

"But there is a general pattern, if you can call it that, for women in particular."

"What is that?"

"They tend to take that final step with some trepidation. They do not leap to their deaths with gusto. Men sometimes do, but women almost never."

"And why was this important in your evaluation of what happened to Tessa Reeves?"

"Well, when I examined the point of impact, it was quite high, almost level with the height of the platform. And the point of contact was almost right in the center of the train. So it was clear that she left the platform with some velocity."

"Like she had taken a running jump?"

"Yes, although, as I said, this was highly unlikely for a woman. It seemed obvious to me that she was not even pushed. She was thrown."

The murmur that broke out quickly faded in memory of Judge Gates's warning from the day before. Still, there was a distinct rustling of paper as journalists filled their pads with scribbled notes to capture the shocking revelation.

"So you have no doubt that Tessa Reeves was murdered, Dr. Holloway?"

"No, I do not."

"No further questions, Your Honor."

As soon as Underhill left the lectern, Cadence replaced him. She was bristling with energy and confidence. At least that was how she made sure she looked on the outside. Inside, she knew she had to walk a fine line between being challenging and aggressive. No matter how she might get her way with this witness, the manner in which she did it mattered. If the jury saw her as unfeeling and ruthless, it would tacitly indicate a lack of sympathy for the victim Tessa Reeves and her loved ones. Sure, that should not matter a damn in a court of law where evidence must be exposed to the utmost scrutiny. But a court of law was operated by flesh-and-blood people who were emotional, critical, skeptical, judgmental and sentimental in every possible way. Cadence knew she did not have to walk on eggshells, but she did have to resist the urge to crush them.

"Hello, Dr. Holloway," she said. "You maintain that Tessa Reeves was pushed into the path of that train, don't you?"

"Yes, I do."

"There can be no other explanation for what happened?"

"As I said, her trajectory indicates she was pushed."

"Yes, so you claim. Would you say that she must have been pushed very hard?"

"Yes, I believe that to be the case."

"Would you say a violent shove sent her to her death?"

"Yes, that's exactly what I think."

"Did you examine her body?"

"Yes, I did."

"Which part of her body impacted with the train?"

"Her right side."

"So, if your theory holds true, she must have been pushed from behind?"

Cadence pulled up a photo of McPherson Square station. The image showed a train arriving at the platform.

"Dr. Holloway. This is a photo of the crime scene. It was taken weeks after Tessa Reeves' death. What I'm interested in here is the physics involved. I'm sure you can help me here."

"Yes, I can. I measured everything."

"That's good," Cadence said. "Can you please tell us how far it is from the edge of the platform to the center of the train."

"Well, the width of the car is ten feet, one and three-quarter inches."

"We can say ten feet?"

"Yes. The side of the car sits almost flush with the platform's edge when it pulls in. In fact, the shape of the car's side gives it a slight overhang over the platform so that there is next to no gap."

"This is for passenger safety, so no one can fall through the gap."

"That's correct."

"So that means Tessa Reeves had to jump five feet if she hit the center of the train, right?"

"Yes."

"That must have been one hell of a push. Did you see any marks or bruises on her body other than those that could be attributed to her impact with the train?"

"No. It was amazing, really. The rest of her body was free of scrapes or bruises."

"But you do agree that for her to get that far in front of the train, she would have to be pushed very, very hard."

"Yes."

"Pushed violently, in other words, right?"

Dr. Holloway hesitated, careful not to give a reply without due consideration. He sensed that Cadence, as pleasant as she was being, was trying to prove him wrong. He shifted in his seat. "Those are your words. It was a strong push, I believe."

"Did you find any marks on her body that indicated she was involved in a struggle before she died?"

"No, I did not."

"No marks to indicate she had been grabbed and flung?"

"No."

"Dr. Holloway, do you know the average distance an average woman can jump from a standing position?"

Dr. Holloway blinked at Cadence and shook his head. "That's not exactly something I can tell you off the top of my head."

"It's five feet," said Cadence.

"Objection," called Underhill as he got to his feet, just as Cadence expected. "Ms. Elliott is testifying."

"Sustained," said Judge Gates before turning to the court reporter. "Strike that from the record."

It did not matter. The jury could not unhear what Cadence had said.

"Dr. Holloway, isn't it possible that Tessa Reeves, of her own volition, took a few steps and jumped in front of the train?"

"As I've said, this is not the typical pattern when it comes to suicides."

"But not every suicide fits a pattern, surely, Dr. Holloway."

"Well, no."

"One last question, Dr. Holloway. I assume you checked Tessa Reeves' clothing and body for DNA?"

"Yes, I did."

"And what did you find?"

"There were three traces we picked up. We have not matched them to date."

"But you did test them against my client's DNA, didn't you?"

"Yes."

"And did you find any trace of my client's DNA on Tessa Reeves' body, clothing or belongings?"

"No, I did not."

"But let's be clear, since there were no signs of struggle on Tessa Reeves body, it is quite possible that she played the only role in her death, isn't that right?"

"It's not what I have concluded."

"Your conclusions are based on your interpretation of the evidence, aren't they?"

"Yes."

"So other conclusions can also be drawn, correct?"

"Yes."

"So it is possible that no one pushed Tessa Reeves to her death, right?"

"Yes."

"Thank you. I have no more questions for the witness, Your Honor," said Cadence.

CHAPTER 29

The train engineer was a shy man named Garrick York. When Gerard Underhill called him forward and hence made York the most conspicuous person in the room, the witness did all he could to disappear before the courtroom's eyes. He walked hunched over, bowing his head so his eyes had to look up to lead the way. He touched the gate of the bar lightly, as though not wanting to rudely impose himself upon it. Heavily overweight, he walked to the stand with an exaggerated gait, almost tiptoeing, so strong was his desire to avoid making a disturbance. He squeezed himself around to the witness chair. He read the oath quietly, locking his eyes on the judge. He then faced forward. That was when the entire courtroom got a look at the toll that tragedy had wrought. His brow was shiny with sweat, his expression was forlorn, and there were dark rings around his eyes.

"Mr. York, can I ask you how much you weigh?"

The whole courtroom murmured with surprise and offense at Underhill's question. Garrick York was the least surprised. He knew what was coming.

"Two-forty-two," York said and pulled out a handkerchief to mop the sweat off his face.

"And how much did you weigh the night of Tessa Reeves' death?"

"One-forty-seven," said York. "Ever since the accident, I've sort of gone downhill on that front. A lot of fronts, really. I don't get out much, let's put it that way."

"Have you struggled to cope since this tragedy?"

"Yes, sir. Very much so. It robbed me of my sleep, my self-esteem, my livelihood and my future. Everything."

Underhill had York recount the accident from his perspective. He said his approach to the station was completely normal. When the platform appeared at the end of the tunnel he readied to decelerate. He began slowing the train about twenty yards short of the platform. He said that suddenly he heard a scream and then a young woman, who he came to know was Tessa Reeves, came flying into the path of his train. He said there was nothing he could do. He watched the woman hit the train with a dreadful sound and the screaming stopped and she disappeared from view.

York's account was interrupted several times by Underhill who asked him to speak up.

Having gotten those details out of the way, Underhill zeroed in on what else the driver saw.

"Mr. York, did you see anyone else on the platform where she had been standing?"

"Yes, I did. I saw a man."

"Did you get a good look at that man?"

"No, not really. Everything happened in a flash. I was in shock. I sounded the horn and hit the emergency brakes at the same time. So I wasn't really looking at him. But I saw him.

It was dark. He was wearing a long coat with his hands in his pockets."

"How would you describe the man's build, his physique?"

"He was average height. Short hair. There was some light on his face, so I know he was not a young man."

Gerard Underhill turned and nodded to one of his assistants who used a remote control to bring up an image on the courtroom monitor.

"Mr. York, the police showed you this image, didn't they?"

"Yes."

"For the record, this is a still from security video taken outside the entrance to the Fairbanks Hotel. From the time stamp we can see it's just 15 minutes after Tessa Reeves was fatally struck by the train. Mr. York, did the police ask you if you recognized this man?"

"Yes."

"And what was your reply?"

"I said, 'That's him.'"

The flurry of hushed exchanges in the gallery came and went quickly under Judge Gates' stern gaze.

"Did they ask you more than once?"

"Yes. Several times."

"And did your answer change?"

"No. I believed I was looking at the killer."

Underhill gave a satisfied bow. "I have no more questions for the witness, Your Honor."

Judge Gates nodded. "Your witness, Ms. Elliott."

"Mr. York," Cadence began but as soon as she said the words, she bowed her head. It appeared that she had lost her train of thought. What actually happened was that her mind decided to present her with a clear way forward. Her initial plan was to gently lead York into unsure territory, where she could flip him by presenting him with the points where the account he had just given differed from his police statement. But she was going to take a different, more direct approach. She lifted her head and locked eyes on York.

"Mr. York, I think we might take up where Mr. Underhill left off. This photo that was just shown, which I am not about to dispute, is of my client outside his hotel at the time stamped on the image."

"Objection," said Underhill before standing up to address Judge Gates. "Testifying. Your Honor, if there was a question in there I must have missed it."

"Sustained," said Judge Gates. "Would you care to rephrase, counselor?"

"Yes, Your Honor. Mr. York, you said the man you saw was not young. You said he was of average height. How could you tell, exactly, in that brief moment that you experienced this shocking event?"

"I'm sorry. I'm not sure I understand."

"How did you gauge the height of the man you saw that night?"

York shook his head, befuddled. "I don't know. How does anyone tell? I know he wasn't short. And I know he wasn't tall. He was average height."

"Okay. Average height of American males is five feet nine inches. Is that about the height of the man you saw?"

"Yes. Thereabouts."

"Are you sure about that?"

"Yes."

Cadence turned to Tate Lieberman. "Mr. Lieberman, would you kindly stand?"

Lieberman got to his feet. At six feet two inches tall, no one in the courtroom would say he was average height.

"Mr. York," said Cadence, "would you describe the defendant as being average in height?"

Garrick York's face was white and his lips dry. He shook his head. "I would not say that. No."

"Would you describe him as tall?"

"Yes."

"Please sit down, Mr. Lieberman," said Cadence before turning back to the witness. "Mr. York, you were shown photos of the defendant and you said you were certain that he was the man you saw."

"I said it looked a lot like him."

"The transcript of your police interview has you saying very clearly that you were happy to ID Tate Lieberman as the man you saw that night as you emerged from the tunnel, isn't that right?"

"Yes."

"Would you say the same today here in court?"

York tilted his head and shook it. "I just can't say that with total certainty. I cannot. That is to say, I think it could be him. I mean—"

"Really? You *think* it could be? Is that what you said, Mr. York?"

"I'm trying to help. I'm trying to help with this whole thing."

"I believe you, Mr. York. I really do. But more specifically, I believe you wanted to help the police, isn't that right?"

"Well, they did tell me that they had arrested someone. It seemed more a formality for me to take a look at the photos for them."

"So what you're telling me, Mr. York, is that you ID'd my client because you wanted to help the nice police officers. Is that right?"

"They said they had the guy in custody. A real asshole, they said. Oh my God, I'm sorry I cursed."

"And you thought it was only right to help them pin that young girl's murder on the defendant, isn't that right?"

"I'm sorry, it's unfair I know, but they seemed so sure about it."

"I get it," said Cadence. "You thought you were doing the right thing."

York dabbed his eyes with his handkerchief. "This whole thing has been a nightmare."

"I'm sure it has been, Mr. York. But can I ask one more thing of you?"

York sat up straighter and nodded. "Yep. Go ahead."

"I want you to look at the defendant."

York did as she asked.

"Take a nice long look."

Cadence counted to ten in her head. All that time, York kept his eyes on Tate Lieberman.

"Mr. York, can you tell me with absolute certainty that the defendant was the man you saw that night on the platform?"

York, with tears welling in his eyes, shook his head. "No," he said but so quietly he may well have just mouthed the word.

"I'm sorry, Mr. York, you'll need to speak up."

"No," he said firmly.

"No further questions," said Cadence. As she stepped away from the podium, she could hear York saying over and over again, "I'm sorry."

As she passed Underhill, he was having a furious conversation with his team. She imagined there was one key question he was asking: were the cops so confident of all the other evidence that they did not put Lieberman in a line-up?

"Do you wish to redirect, Mr. Underhill?" asked Judge Gates.

Underhill abruptly ended his team talk and sprang to his feet.

"Yes, Your Honor," he said, making his way to the lectern.

"Mr. York, it's clear and understandable that this tragedy has taken a terrible toll on you. I think we should clarify something. Are you sure you saw a man at the end of the platform positioned behind the victim?"

"Yes, I'm certain of that."

"Can you describe him?"

"No, that's what I'm saying. I know I've been unhelpful and have caused some confusion, but I do apologize."

"Thank you, Mr. York," said Cadence. "Now, since you can't give a meaningful description of that man, it's fair to say that it could have been just about anybody, right?"

"Ah, yes."

"Which prompts me to ask you if it's possible that it could have been the defendant?"

York nodded. All he wanted to do was get off the stand and go disappear into a hole. "Yes, I suppose that's true. I can't say for certain that it wasn't him."

"Thank you, Mr. York."

Chapter 30

After checking his watch and taking a sip of water, Judge Gates looked at Underhill.

"Call your next witness, please, Mr. Underhill," he said.

Within a few minutes Jason Banks was spilling what he knew under Gerard Underhill's guidance. The prosecutor established that Banks, a young black man with the build of a linebacker, had worked the door of Jameson's for almost two years. He testified that when he greeted Tate Lieberman that night, Lieberman asked to be seated at one of the back booths. He said that these were the most private since they were obscured from just about anywhere inside. It was the place to be if you did not want to be disturbed or seen.

"Mr. Banks, did the defendant say why he wanted privacy?" Underhill asked.

"Yes, he said he was expecting someone. A woman. He didn't say her name, but he said she would ask for him at the door."

"And you were instructed to let her in?"

"Yes. It's a private club. Members only. He had to sign her in. Well, that was what he was supposed to do."

"Was it a club rule that members have to sign guests in?"

"Yes, but you know. There are workarounds." At these words Banks held up a hand and rubbed his fingers together.

"Did the defendant give you some money to sidestep the signing in rule."

"That's right. Fifty bucks."

"Did he say why he didn't want to sign Ms. Reeves in?"

"No. And I didn't ask."

"I see," said Underhill. "Mr. Banks, are staff members at the club asked to conduct themselves with the utmost discretion?"

"You could put it that way."

"How would you put it?"

"The members count on us to keep our mouths shut. Our bosses count on it. Loose lips cost pay slips, you could say."

"What do your bosses think about you testifying about what you saw that night?"

"They're not my bosses no more."

"Did they fire you?"

"They let me go. They couldn't find a way to give me any more shifts."

"Did you expect that testifying would cost you your job?"

"Yes, I did. But I had to say what I saw and what I heard. That's all that counts in the end."

"Well, I for one am most grateful that you came forward. Now, when Tessa Reeves arrived what did you do?"

"I took her straight to Mr. Lieberman, just like he asked me to. And then I returned to the door."

"Did you see them talking together?"

"Yes, I took a bathroom break about fifteen minutes later. But they were not talking. They were arguing about something. It looked like it might escalate, so I went over. I asked if everything was okay, and the heat died down. Mr. Lieberman said everything was fine, that they just had a misunderstanding. So I went to the bathroom and when I came back they were just talking again, so I went back to the door."

"Then what happened?"

"The girl, I mean Ms. Reeves, left the club."

"Did she walk away?"

"Yes."

"In which direction?"

"McPherson Square station."

"And what about the defendant?"

"He left about ten minutes later."

"What was he doing when he left?"

"He just walked right by me looking at his phone."

"What? He didn't say goodnight?"

"No."

"Didn't acknowledge you at all?"

"No, he was pretty focused on his phone."

"And when he stepped outside?"

"He looked up, which to me looked like he was getting his bearings. Then he walked off."

"In which direction?"

"Same as Ms. Reeves."

Underhill thanked Banks and sat down. Cadence had wondered if it might be wise to pass on cross-examining Banks. His testimony was not good for Lieberman, but it was not damning. Cross-examining him risked letting him say something more damning about Lieberman, like how many other times he had slipped Banks money to keep quiet about a female guest. She decided she had to finish what Underhill had started.

"Mr. Banks, I want to be clear about something. Did you see what was on the defendant's phone as he passed you by?"

"No, I did not."

"So, it could have been anything? An email, a photo, a text message, a Facebook post? Right?"

"I guess that's true."

"Thank you, Mr. Banks. No further questions."

Chapter 31

As Banks made his way from the stand, Underhill got to his feet. He said a few words of thanks to Banks before consulting the paperwork on his desk. He then looked up at Judge Gates and called Wade Hampton to the stand.

Cadence braced herself for what was bound to be a key battle. If she failed to land a blow here, Underhill could well have enough to win the jury over.

"Mr. Hampton," said Underhill. "Why did you hire Tessa?"

"It was pretty simple, really," said Hampton. "For some time, I'd wanted to try and attract a younger audience to *DC Watch*. Not at the expense of our established readership, mind you. It is vital to our growth, but I also thought there was no good reason the twenty-somethings of this world wouldn't be interested in politics. You just had to find the right way to deliver it to them."

"Is that what you saw in Tessa Reeves—a voice of the younger generation?"

"That's about it. She had done some great work as a freelancer and had built up impressive numbers on her social media accounts."

"Didn't other media outlets have their eye on her?"

"Yes and no. They most certainly knew about her but she was not very conventional. A bit too abrasive for the mainstream, I'd say."

"In what way?"

"She was afraid of no one. She confronted people in the streets and put the hard questions to them. She did not take a backward step, physically or verbally. On more than one occasion, there were scuffles. Now although her content was strong and incisive, this rebellious streak of hers was not exactly MSNBC material, if you know what I mean."

"I see," said Underhill. "Was she considered too unconventional?"

"That's putting it mildly. But I reached out to her and she came on board. I think she was looking for something a bit more mainstream, but no one came to her with an offer like I did."

"How was she as an employee?"

"She was a hard worker, no doubt about that. Independent. She liked to tackle her stories as though she was a one-man band. That's okay to some extent. In our game you have to be self-motivated and self-reliant. You have to go out and find stories. That's not as easy as some people think."

"But she was good at her job?"

"Yes, but she was very green in some respects. I'm proud to say I was her mentor and I encouraged her to focus more on her work than her style. I wanted her to focus on her writing. I didn't want her to just produce video stories all the time. It was a different balance than what she was used to."

"Now, I'd like to ask you when you became aware that Ms. Reeves was preparing a story on Tate Lieberman?"

"It was a month or so before she died. She told me she had a great story about how PR companies were becoming some of the most powerful players in DC. She told me she wanted to produce a story that showed how PR companies subverted our democracy."

"And Mr. Lieberman was to be part of that story?"

Hampton shook his head. "Lieberman and his company, which is called Berrins, *were* the story. Tessa had found out that Berrins had mounted various campaigns around the country on behalf of their clients, which were large corporations. Berrins produced TV commercials and websites that promoted those corporations' interests."

"Was there something wrong with that?"

"Not in an outright legal sense. But Tessa was convinced that some of their activities were undemocratic, possibly illegal."

"Is that what she was seeking to bring to light—these illegalities?"

"Yes."

"Mr. Hampton, when did you learn that the defendant was aware of what Tessa was up to?"

"She had called him a few times and he ignored her. Then she called and left a message itemizing some of the claims that had been made against him and citing some of her evidence. She said she wanted to give him an opportunity to respond."

"Did he call her back?"

"No. He called me. And we, er, talked."

"Could you please recount that conversation?"

"It wasn't much of a conversation. It was mostly Lieberman just yelling at me, demanding to know what that 'little bitch' was up to. He said that if I ran the story he was going to sue for defamation. He said he was going to eradicate Tessa, take me down, and destroy my publication."

"Eradicate Tessa. Were those his exact words?"

"Yes."

"Was that the only time he threatened you or Tessa?"

"No. He sent us both a threatening email and he sent Tessa an abusive text. He may have also left an abusive voicemail message, I'm not sure."

"What was your response to these threats?"

"I made it clear to him that he did not get to decide which stories we ran."

"But you didn't run Tessa's story, did you?"

Hampton shook his head. "No, I did not."

"Why not?"

"Well, as it turned out, Tessa was thinking bigger than any of us had given her credit for. She wanted to produce a three-part series."

"What was your response?"

"She had not fleshed out the series thoroughly at that stage. All she told me was that she knew of other ways that private companies were buying the loyalties of elected officials. The theme of her series was how democracy was being eroded by the actions of various companies."

"Is that the type of article you wanted from her?"

"Of course it was," Hampton said. "But you have to be very careful with these kinds of stories. Get it wrong, and you pay a high price."

"What did you do?"

"I put Tessa's story on ice until she gave me more details about the next two stories. If we were going to make a song and dance about this series—you know, promote it heavily—then I had to feel confident she had the goods."

"What was her reaction to you holding the story?"

"She didn't like it. But I think she knew I was right."

"Mr. Hampton, at this stage were you aware Mr. Lieberman had sent a threatening message to Tessa?"

"I was not aware of the messages he sent directly to her, no. As I said, he sent us both an email with the threat to sue but it was only in the text message that he sent Tessa, which I have now seen, that he threatened to kill her."

"So she didn't tell you?"

"No," said Hampton before smiling ruefully. "She probably didn't want me to worry. I wish she'd told me."

"What would you have done?"

"I'd have gotten the police involved," said Hampton.

Underhill lifted his hands. "I have no more questions for the witness, Your Honor."

Judge Gates turned to Cadence. "Do you wish to cross-examine the witness, counselor?"

"Yes, Your Honor," said Cadence. She got to her feet and took up a pile of documents and crossed behind Underhill on her way to the lectern. She placed the documents on the top of the lectern and gripped its edges with both hands.

"Good afternoon, Mr. Hampton," she said. "So let me get this straight, you had no idea what Tessa had planned for the series, is that right?"

Hampton was looking very comfortable on the stand. If he had any qualms about being cross-examined, it did not show. Cadence was pleased to see him so at ease. The last thing she wanted was for him to clam up.

"Tessa was very protective about her work," he smiled reminiscently. "She didn't let anyone see what she didn't want them to see. Me included. Journalists can be like that. It's like the rest of us at the office were the enemy. Especially Luke Everson, our gossip writer."

"Is that right?"

"She didn't mind so much that her story was on hold when I told her Luke's would never run before hers."

"Was there a crossover between the two stories?"

"Some, but her story was far more important."

"So you never knew what she had planned for the other two stories, is that right?"

"No. I asked her to prepare a thorough brief—"

"But you did read her early draft of her story, didn't you?"

"Yes, but it was only a high-level summary of—"

Cadence picked up a piece of paper and held it up. Hampton stopped talking.

Cadence's eyes were on the document. "She showed you the early draft of her story, though. Right?"

"Her draft? Yes, I had a look, but it did not cover everything."

Cadence frowned. "It covered enough for you to know specifically what she wanted to write. Isn't that so? I mean, don't the first few paragraphs say that the first story in the series would focus on Tate Lieberman's firm Berrins, and that the next two would focus on Senator Ron Nagle and Zellus Pharmaceuticals?"

Hampton did not know what to say. Cadence waited, knowing that his acknowledgement of the story would mean she would not have to file the draft as evidence or give Underhill the chance to stall, and counter.

Hampton looked at Cadence. "I'm not sure—"

"Not sure. Isn't it clear cut. It's in the draft that you read."

"I can't go into the details of what Tessa intended to write," said Hampton. "She never got to finish any of those stories. But yes, you are right, at a high level those were the topics she wanted to explore."

"The topics she wanted to explore? Don't you mean the subjects she wanted to investigate?"

"Of course, I do. And she had my full support. But as I told her, we would need ironclad proof of any wrongdoing that we reported."

"Did you put Tessa's story on ice before you read her draft?"

"Let me see. Yes, I'm pretty sure I did."

"Did you know whether Tessa had already been in contact with Senator Nagle about her story?"

"No, I did not."

"Did Senator Nagle ever express to you any concern about Tessa contacting him?"

Hampton's eyes tightened, as though it might help him read Cadence's mind. "No, he did not."

"Didn't he barge into your office the very morning you put Tessa's story on ice?"

"No, that's not true."

"What is not true? That he stormed into your office or that he shouted at you?"

"We had a brief argument."

"What about?"

"Objection," said Underhill. "The witness is not on trial here."

"Sustained," said Judge Gates. "Stick to the case at hand, counselor.

"Yes, Your Honor. Mr. Hampton, Tate Lieberman was not the only person to complain to you about Tessa's inquiries, was he?"

Hampton hesitated. Then his confidence seemed to have been restored, as though he had struck upon the right course of action. "To be honest, Senator Nagle was not happy."

Hampton followed with a mild laugh. He obviously felt he had made a reasonable concession to Cadence's questioning.

"Nobody likes bad press, right?"

"No, that's right."

"Especially when you've got the midterms coming up, right?"

"Ah. Yes, I see what you're getting at. Yes, Senator Nagle was up for reelection, but it was of minor concern."

"Of minor concern to you, maybe. Did he tell you to kill Tessa's story?"

Hampton scoffed. "Don't be ridiculous. No."

"So it was just a coincidence that he was in your office yelling at you about something he was not happy with?"

"You're making too much of this."

"Really? Was it possible that other people had as much, if not more, to fear from Tessa Reeves' work than Tate Lieberman?"

"No, I wouldn't necessarily—"

"I asked if it was possible."

"Of course, it's possible. No one likes to have their secrets exposed."

"I bet they don't," said Cadence. "Nothing further."

The first day of the trial was done. As Cadence took her seat and began sorting her papers, Tate Lieberman reached over and tapped her forearm. "Whichever way this goes, I'm okay with you being my lawyer. I want you to know that."

Lieberman's words took Cadence by surprise. For just a second, Cadence considered that Lieberman was letting his kinder, gentler self show. Then she saw his face go sour.

"I think you and I both know we're not going to win," he said grimly. "Not a chance in hell."

Lieberman's words remained stuck in Cadence's mind as she made her way back to the office. Not even her client believed in her. She expected to reach her office to find Alan Henshaw waiting for her there, ready to tell her how disillusioned their client was and how Cadence might be throwing Hardwick and Henshaw's reputation down the drain.

When she heard her cellphone ring as she neared the office, she expected it to be Alan, fresh off a grim update from Lieberman, eager to give her a dressing down at the earliest opportunity.

When she looked at the screen she saw with some relief it was Bob.

"Please tell me you've got some good news," she said as she stopped to talk.

"I'm afraid I can't," said Bob. "I thought about waiting for a better time to tell you, but you need to know now."

Cadence's heart sank. She expected Bob was about to tell her he was resigning as of now and she was mortified at the thought of losing his support and help.

"You're not leaving, are you? Can't you just wait until the end of the trial?"

"No, don't be silly," he said. "I'm not going anywhere. But Monica Cordoba is dead."

"What?" Although the Cordobas had never been far from her mind, the news came as a shock. "How?"

"She overdosed on pills," said Bob. "Her driver found her unconscious in her hotel room. Looks like either suicide or a careless mishap. Most likely the former."

Cadence's mind began to race. Although she was deep into trial mode, she still scanned the news headlines. She had seen nothing.

"When did this happen?"

"Just now. I've been looking into Simon Cordoba while you've been in court, and one of my police contacts gave me a heads up. There will be online stories soon, I'm sure. Just thought you should know."

For a moment, Cadence was locked in a daze of painful reflection, pangs of guilt and shame kicking at her insides. She wondered what role she played in Monica's death. Maybe none but then again maybe she was the catalyst. And now young Ben was about to bury the only mother he had ever known.

Cadence had felt self-loathing before but now her thoughts about herself appeared to have sunk to their lowest possible point.

"Cadence? You there?"

"Yes, Bob," she said weakly before rousing her strength. "Thanks for letting me know. I'm about to hit the office. We'll talk later, okay?"

She hung up and marched into the foyer. She was doing what she always did when she wanted the world to swallow her whole.

She got back to work.

CHAPTER 32

When Phoebe Baker was called to the stand by Underhill, Cadence could not help but think of the woman sitting behind her. This was sure to be the most challenging day in court for Kelly Lieberman, and Cadence would not have blamed her if she had refused to attend. Yet there Kelly Lieberman was, immaculately dressed, beautifully presented and stoically calm. Only moments before she had turned up to court on the arm of her husband. What a downright fool he was, Cadence thought.

Although the courtroom floor was carpeted, the click clacking sound of Phoebe Baker's high heels filled the air as she crossed the well to the witness stand. If Underhill had suggested to Baker that she should tone down the sexiness, Baker was deaf to such advice. Her skirt suit looked painted on, and her low-buttoned blouse barely contained her cleavage. Evidently, she figured that if she was to play the role of mistress in this ordeal, she was going to play it to the hilt.

To Cadence, Phoebe Baker was not someone to dismiss. She had told Lieberman to cut her off completely. Although this might raise her ire, Cadence told him, it would at least prevent him from giving her fresh ammo. If he kept his distance, Phoebe Baker would be pretty much a known quantity in court.

Cadence bowed her head to sneak a glance at Lieberman. She was alarmed to find him shooting daggers at Baker.

"Tate," she whispered urgently. He snapped out of it and turned to his lawyer. "If looks could kill... my God. Get a hold of yourself. You can't let the jury see you looking at her like that."

Lieberman seemed to think her words over for a moment. Then he nodded and gave her a wry smile. "Sorry," he said. "But the truth is I would like to see her—"

"Don't you dare," Cadence cut in. "Force yourself to think about something else."

"Okay, okay," he said, his head lowered now while he rid himself of the look of disdain. "I'll be good."

Gerard Underhill looked as though he could hardly wait to draw his witness into the juiciest parts of her testimony, but he was smart to draw it out. He had Baker recount the origins of her relationship with Lieberman. She said she was an event organizer and her company had been booked by Berrins several times. She said things between her and Lieberman went from business to pleasure quickly. She said at first he told her that he was divorced. Then he admitted that he was married and had only taken his ring off to put her mind at ease. More like to get into her panties quicker, she added.

Several times during Baker's testimony, Lieberman muttered furiously that she was lying. Each time, Cadence had to remind him that he had to keep his emotions in check and stay calm. He did so, but she heard him breathing deeply with almost every sentence Baker uttered.

"So in the end, you knew he was married," said Underhill. "Why did you continue on with the affair?"

"I was in love with him and I thought he loved me back. He always said that secrecy was of the utmost importance. He made me swear not to tell a soul about our relationship."

"Did he tell you why that was necessary?"

"In one sense it was normal," said Baker. "I mean, he was a married man and he didn't want his wife to know. But he made me swear on my mother's grave not to tell a soul, not even my best friend, Caroline. He told me his wife would ruin him if she found out."

"I see," said Underhill. "And you agreed?"

"Yes. No one knew about our relationship until now, really."

"Now, Ms. Baker. Let's go back to the night in question. Where were you?"

"I was with Tate at the Fairbanks Hotel. He booked the room under a false name and I got there before him."

"What time was that?"

"I got there just after eight o'clock."

"And then what happened?"

"I waited. Tate called to say he was held up, but he got to the room by half past eight or so. Then we opened a bottle of champagne, drank a little and made love. We didn't even make it to the bed. That's how we were with each other."

Baker lowered her eyes at the last revelation. The courtroom was dead silent. Everyone wanted more details, no doubt. Underhill had other ideas.

"Ms. Baker, the defendant initially told the police that he did not leave the hotel room until almost midnight."

"Objection, Your Honor," said Cadence. "Mr. Underhill is testifying. The defendant has revised his statement to the effect that he left the hotel room."

"Thank you, Ms. Elliott," said Judge Gates. "You need not have added your own testimony to your objection. Objection sustained. Mr. Underhill, I do expect a man of your experience to know full well not to testify."

"It was an unfortunate slip, Your Honor," Underhill said. "Ms. Baker, did the defendant leave the hotel room?"

"Yes, he did. At about quarter to ten he said he had to go out. He was on his phone before then and was getting worked up about something."

"Do you know what he was getting worked up about?"

"No. But he swore."

"He swore?"

"What did he say?"

"He said, 'I've got to do something about that little bitch.'"

Cadence heard Lieberman hiss. "She's lying," he whispered through gritted teeth.

"Do you know to whom he was referring?" asked Underhill.

"No. But I asked him, and he told me to keep my nose out of it. He then said he had to go out. That he had to meet someone. It was important and it had to be now."

"Did he say who he was meeting? Where?"

Baker shook her head. "No. He told me nothing about it. He just said that he'd be back soon."

"And what time did he return?"

"It was after midnight. He was a little out of breath, as though he had been running. He was distracted and he grabbed a bottle of scotch from the mini bar and poured it into a glass. Then he threw it down in one gulp."

"Did he say anything to you by way of explanation?"

"No. Nothing. He seemed more excited than distressed, if you know what I mean. Anyway, the scotch seemed to calm him down. He just looked at me, looked at the television and said, 'What are we watching?' Then he poured us champagne and sat down on the couch and asked me to sit next to him."

"I see," said Underhill, stroking his chin. "Now, Ms. Baker, did the defendant ask you to do anything for him?"

"He wanted me to, you know, go down on him while he watched TV. Is that what you mean?"

"No, I should have been more specific. After that night, when did you become aware the defendant was a person of interest in the case of Tessa Reeves' murder?"

"He called me after the police went to see him," Baker said. "He told me that he said he was at the hotel with a friend. He wanted me to lie and say I was not there. That was what he said at first. But then he told me he wanted me to lie for him. He said that he had told the police he was with me in the hotel room from nine-thirty until morning."

"What did you say?"

"I said I can't lie. Then he got really angry. He told me I had to. He asked me if I loved him and I said yes. Then he asked me again. So I agreed."

"Did you lie to the police to cover for the defendant?"

"Yes, I did. I wish I hadn't but that's what happened. After that I was not in contact with Tate for a few weeks. He said we shouldn't see each other."

"When did you hear from him again?"

"When he learned I was going to be a witness for the prosecution."

"What happened?"

"He called me. He was furious. And then he swore at me and threatened to kill me."

The courtroom's energy shot up, the muffled chatter between excited onlookers sounding like an electric hum. Cadence tried not to shoot a glare at Lieberman. She did not have to ask if Baker was telling the truth. One look at Lieberman and she could see he had not listened to her and was now paying the price.

"Ms. Baker, unfortunately, I'm going to need you to be more specific. What did he say to you? What were his exact words?"

Baker bowed her head. "He said, 'If you testify against me, I'll kill you, you mother-effing b-word.'"

The muttering of the gallery threatened to break into outright banter when the crack of Judge Gates' gavel snapped everyone back into quiet obedience. No one in the gallery would have given up their seats for a thousand dollars.

"He said that to you?"

"He didn't just say it, he wrote it," Baker said. "I was reading word for word what he wrote in a text message to me."

As Underhill took a moment to let Baker's words sink into the jury's collective mind, Cadence turned to Lieberman coolly.

"Is that true?" she whispered through a fake smile.

Lieberman lowered his chin to his chest. "Yes."

What a disaster. Thoroughly avoidable, if he had only followed his lawyer's clear advice. Cadence did consider objecting to the text message as being material not in evidence, which would have compelled Underhill to share it with her before trial. But she kept quiet. Underhill played it beautifully.

Cadence stared down at her pad in front of her. All the text she had written became a blur. This case was over. Suddenly she felt that she no longer had a fighting chance.

"Thank you, Ms. Baker," said Underhill, before looking over to Cadence with a broad smile. "That will be all from me, Your Honor."

"Ms. Elliott, do you wish to cross-examine the witness?"

Up until a few minutes ago, that was the plan. Cadence had intended to get up and discredit Phoebe Baker on the stand, showing the jury that she was speaking against Lieberman purely out of spite, that she still loved him and was little more than a jilted mistress who never had her story straight. But there was no point.

"No, Your Honor," said Cadence.

With that, Underhill announced that Phoebe Baker was his last witness. "The prosecution rests, Your Honor."

Judge Gates checked his watch. It was almost half past four. "We will begin calling witnesses for the defense tomorrow morning, nine o'clock sharp. I presume that suits you, Ms. Elliott?"

"Yes, Your Honor. Perfectly."

Cadence began gathering up her documents. She could hardly bear to look at Lieberman.

"I'm sorry," came Lieberman's voice. "I should have listened to you."

"Yes, you should have listened to me," she said. "What else is there that don't I know? Actually, you know what? Don't answer that. I'd much prefer to have Gerard Underhill throw me another surprise. Letting your ego cloud your judgment has worked out brilliantly so far, hasn't it?"

"Cadence, I—"

She held up her hand. "Enough, already. I'll see you tomorrow. It's our turn to call witnesses."

"I really think I should testify, Cadence," Lieberman said, putting on the mask of sheer confidence he must be used to falling back on at work. "I can clear a lot of this up."

"Tate, I've said it before and I'll say it again, letting you testify is your quickest route to prison. The fact that you still can't see that makes it all the more true. You think you can win this jury over? With what? Your pure charm? The jury knows that you're a serial cheater. They know you threatened to kill two women to save yourself. And that's nothing compared to the damage Underhill will do to you in his cross-examination. If we give him a shot at you, it's game over. So, in case this isn't getting through, you're not testifying."

"As far as I recall, it's my decision."

Cadence stopped packing her briefcase and looked Lieberman dead in the eye. "A few moments ago you said you'd listen to me."

Lieberman struggled to find the words. "You're probably right," he said. "No, I mean you're right, Cadence. Whatever you say."

Cadence turned to Lieberman. "Get some sleep. We've got a big day ahead of us."

As soon as she was clear of the crowd, Cadence took out her cell phone and called Bob.

"Hey," Bob answered. "How'd it go today?"

"Not great, Bob," Cadence said. "I'm calling witnesses tomorrow and I'm afraid I don't have enough firepower to win this thing."

"Anything I can do?"

"Where's Danielle? I need her to help present the evidence against Nagle. As it stands the jury only knows one possible suspect—Tate Lieberman. I have to get them thinking there's more to it. And that's not all she can help with. If anyone knows who Tessa's source was, it's Danielle."

"That's exactly what I was thinking," said Bob. "But I've had no luck getting hold of Danielle. I can't and that's because she doesn't want me to. She's no longer at her dad's place in Florida. I've been down there and I've checked. She could be anywhere."

Cadence turned to face away from the street traffic and saw a woman a few yards away standing dead still and looking at her.

"She's not anywhere, Bob," Cadence said. "She's right in front of me."

Chapter 33

"I didn't think we'd hear from you again," said Cadence as she shut her office door. Danielle was seated holding a cup of coffee Cadence had gotten for her. After such a rough day in court, Cadence might have been tempted to opt for something stronger. But Danielle's appearance put a spring back in her step. Bob arrived half a minute later.

"You dropped off the radar for weeks," Cadence said. "I haven't seen you in court and Bob said you never returned his calls. I thought you could trust us."

"Yeah, about that," said Danielle. "It's nothing personal. I do want to help you, Cadence, but I have never been sure of the best way. And, to be honest, I feel pretty nervous about being back in DC."

Cadence resisted the urge to immediately try and talk Danielle into testifying. She had to wait for the right moment. "I know you're scared, Danielle, and I appreciate you coming to me, but what I'd like to know is what you're scared of. As in, who?"

"Well, you tell me. After I saw you and Bob in Florida, someone broke into my apartment. It wasn't just anybody. They were looking for something. The place was turned upside down. How did they find me?"

Cadence looked puzzled. "We weren't followed. I'm sure of that. But maybe someone else followed the same path Bob took to find you."

"Well, whoever it was, I was glad I wasn't at home when they broke in."

"What did they take?" asked Bob.

"The only things missing were my camera and a couple of thumb drives."

"What was on them?"

"Nothing related to Tessa's stories. I keep all of that material on the cloud. They haven't stolen anything I can't replace or can't do without."

"What do you think they were looking for?" asked Cadence.

"Tessa's files. I think they wanted my phone and laptop. They could use them to access my cloud accounts."

"Who's they?"

"I think it's Wade. And Ron Nagle. Not them personally. They'd have paid someone to find me and try to get those files."

"So you think Wade told Nagle that he was next in line in Tessa's series?"

"Maybe but Tessa had already been asking questions about Nagle for weeks. Who knows who told him. But I don't think it was a coincidence that the day after Nagle came in and read him the riot act, Wade iced Tessa's story."

Cadence sat back and thought for a moment. "You know I've subpoenaed Nagle to testify."

"Yes," said Danielle. "I'm not surprised. I guess there was no chance he'd have done so willingly."

"That's not what he told the press," said Bob. "I don't know if you guys saw it, but he was quoted as saying that he had offered

Cadence his full assistance and that a subpoena was little more than Lieberman's lawyer showboating."

"Danielle," said Cadence, "I'd like to know what's so damning in those files."

"I only know about half the contents. There's a lot there."

"Why don't you and Bob go through them and see what you can find?" said Cadence. "All we need are the key parts that got Nagle so worried. Then I might be able to use that against him. We need something strong but at this point I'm reluctant to make Nagle the key point of my trial strategy."

"What do you mean?" asked Danielle.

"As it stands, I just can't allow the jury to only believe that this was a homicide. I need to keep other possibilities in play. The first witness I'm calling is a physics expert who is going to testify that we can't rule out suicide."

Cadence had tried to choose her words carefully, but she knew by the expression on Danielle's face that her words were not being received well.

"There's no way Tessa killed herself," said Danielle. "No way in the world. You can't say she did."

"Danielle, it's not about whether she did or not. It's about whether it's a possible and plausible explanation. But I'm not going to lie. I would have to frame it as a story. Wade told me Tessa had been deeply upset by her friend's death and that her piece on youth suicide only seemed to make things worse. She had taken leave for mental health reasons. So, one could argue that she was in a frame of mind that would make her a candidate for suicide. Again, I'm not saying—"

"No," said Danielle. "You can't do that, Cadence. It's not true. I understand what you mean about your defense strategy but if you push the suicide angle the media will run with it and I can't let that happen."

"I get it, Danielle," said Cadence. "I know it's upsetting for you but that's why I'm telling you this now. There's another life at stake—Tate Lieberman's—and I'm bound by my oath to defend him with everything I possibly can. Now, that's what I have to prepare for tomorrow."

Danielle stared hard at Cadence, her eyes wet with tears and her jaw hardened.

"Maybe you can help take the suicide argument off the table, Danielle."

"How?"

"You're a journalist. You've got those files and you've got one of the best journalists who ever worked in DC beside you. Find me something in those files to make Ron Nagle tremble and I'll ditch my suicide strategy."

"Like what?"

"I don't know. You need to find it and tell me. I don't care if we're here all night but there's got to be something that triggered Nagle into storming Hampton's office to get the story killed. What was it?"

"We'll find it," said Danielle.

"Good," said Cadence.

"We're going to need more coffee," said Bob. "Let's go."

It was half past one in the morning when Danielle and Bob appeared at Cadence's door. Danielle was holding up a piece of paper.

"Good news. You can call off your expert," said Bob. "We found it."

Chapter 34

Despite having less than four hours' sleep, Cadence was buzzing. The river of coffee she drank had helped but it was the tightrope she found herself walking on that had really got her blood pumping. She was placing an all-or-nothing bet and it filled her with equal parts adrenalin and dread.

The late change in strategy was a bold move. She wondered if she could still keep her plan B, the suicide argument, up her sleeve.

She informed Judge Gates and Gerard Underhill that her order of witnesses had to change because she was moving the expert down the list. To them, it would seem like she had just put him on hold. But she knew she could not use him.

Her two strategies were impossible to stitch together. She could not argue that Tessa Reeves spent her last night ambitiously chasing her story and then argue that she was emotionally frayed enough to kill herself. The suicide angle was no longer an option. But no one else needed to know that just yet.

It was pleasing to hear Underhill grumble and gripe about her witness reshuffle. Naturally, he overplayed the disruption it caused him. Really, it did not matter to him. He was not the one who had to build a new story now. He just had to shoot Cadence's down. The only change he had to make was to rearrange his ammunition.

When Judge Gates told Cadence to summon her first witness, she cleared her throat and called Danielle Farrell.

The jury watched Danielle with some curiosity. Although she was twenty, her youth was a striking change from the witnesses they had seen so far. Sometimes a trial may seem to be somehow unsuitable for the young, but Danielle was poised and her expression fearless. She took the oath like it was routine and she surveyed the whole courtroom without showing a hint of nervousness. Cadence knew Danielle well enough to know she hid her nerves well. And it took a few questions for Danielle to find her voice. Within a few minutes, Cadence felt she had made the right choice.

Such confidence could be undone in a second, though. She imagined Gerard Underhill was licking his lips in anticipation of testing just how tough this Danielle Farrell girl was.

"Danielle," Cadence said, "how long were you working at *DC Watch*?"

"I was there eighteen months."

"What was your position?"

"I was the junior reporter."

"And what was your relationship to Tessa Reeves?"

"I didn't know Tessa before I got there but we hit it off instantly. She was a few years older than me, but we got along so well. We really understood each other. I worked alongside her—our desks were next to each other—and eventually I worked under her direction."

"So you looked up to her?"

"Very much so. She was a great reporter. She was sharp and fearless and driven. But she had a softer side. She could be super funny. I mean, she knew what she wanted and she was going to do everything she could to get it."

"What did she want?"

"To be a great investigative reporter with a string of Pulitzers to show for it."

"You said you worked with her. Were you working with her when she died?"

Danielle nodded but had to swallow before she could speak. The memory of her time with Tessa was becoming more potent, as were the pangs of grief. "I was helping her out on her project. She had come up with the idea months before and told me about it then. I was sworn to secrecy, but it was a great story."

"What was the story about?"

Cadence heard Underhill stir behind her to her left. He was no doubt searching for an objection but was unable to find one.

"It was about the way PR companies in DC are undermining our democracy."

"I see, and how did that concern the defendant?"

"Mr. Lieberman was essentially a case study to show how public relations firms are taking over from lobbyists as the greatest influencers on the actions of our elected representatives."

"What do you mean?"

"Objection," cried Underhill. "Relevance. The finer details of Tessa Reeves' story are not relevant to her death."

"Your Honor, I would argue the exact opposite," said Cadence.

"Overruled," said Judge Gates. "Please answer the question, Ms. Farrell."

"Up until a few years ago, the main way that people who weren't elected got the ears of congressman and senators was through lobbyists. These lobbyists walk the corridors of power here inside the Capitol, and also in the White House. They are essentially insiders for hire. But their paymasters are mainly companies and corporations with very deep pockets who want to make sure that government decisions don't harm their business interests. This could be at the federal, state and even local level."

Danielle paused and took a sip from a bottle of water Cadence had made sure was put there for her. The courtroom was in utter silence hearing Danielle speak. Few present were accustomed to hearing perceptive insights from a young woman who looked like she was just out of college.

"Please continue when you're ready," said Cadence.

"Now what has happened in recent times is an alternative to conventional, direct lobbying. Companies are now using PR firms to persuade the minds of the people who put those politicians in power. They are creating glossy public awareness campaigns to get voters on their side of an issue."

"And Tessa thought there was something wrong with that?"

"Yes. We both did. These campaigns use every slick marketing tool under the sun. They come at a price only big companies can afford. I'm talking websites, TV ads and news stories that are little more than press releases. And it involves pressuring or paying local elected officials to do their bidding. And in the process, the average American voter gets screwed."

If anyone had expected Danielle to apologize for her language, they would have been disappointed. She just sat and waited for Cadence's next question.

"The court has already heard that Tessa planned to write more than one story. Could you please unpack that a little?"

"Sure. Soon after Tessa started researching, she realized it was a bigger story than just one man and his PR company. She wanted to probe the companies and the politicians involved."

"So how did her plans change?"

"She wanted to produce a three-part series. The first story would be on Tate Lieberman and Berrins. The second would be on Senator Ron Nagle. And the third would be on the pharmaceuticals company Zellus."

There was a slight murmur as the gallery absorbed this news. They all quickly quieted themselves to refocus their attention on the witness.

"I know you can't get into the finest detail here but what was the nature of Tessa's findings?"

"She had material that would expose criminal wrongdoing by—how should I put this?—both individuals and companies."

Again the flutter of hushed words erupted and abated.

"Now, Danielle, you said you worked closely with Tessa. How close?"

"I was the only person she trusted."

"Do you mean in the world or in the office?"

"When it came to her work, both. She didn't trust any of her colleagues except for me."

"Did she trust her editor, Wade Hampton?"

"Objection," said Underhill. "Hearsay."

"Your Honor, the witness is not just an acquaintance of Tessa Reeves. She was her trusted coworker and confidant. Her views on the workplace and Tessa's frame of mind are vital to us understanding what happened in the last hours of her life."

"Overruled, but keep it tight, counselor. Answer the question, please."

"She trusted Wade up to a point. She only told him what she wanted him to know. He supported her original idea. But she told me he was wary about her expanding the series."

"Did she say why?"

"Yes. She said his jaw dropped when she told him she wanted to expose the connection between Zellus and Senator Nagle. She knew Wade and Senator Nagle were close."

"When did she tell him?"

"The day before she died."

"I see. But why would he express interest in publishing a story that might damage his friend Senator Nagle?"

"I don't think he intended to publish the story any time soon. I think he was stalling. But the truth was if he didn't publish it, Tessa would find an outlet that would."

"What happened after she told him?"

"She told him in the morning. She came back to her desk and told me that Wade had not responded well to her intentions for the rest of the series."

"Did anything unusual happen that day in the office?"

"Yes. Senator Nagle appeared that afternoon. He just marched straight into Wade's office and started shouting at him. Well, he was shouting at first but then he kept his voice down. None of us heard what he said to Wade but a few minutes later he stormed out."

"Senator Nagle stormed out?"

"Yes, and he gave Tessa a look that could kill. Sorry, I shouldn't use that expression."

Cadence was not unhappy she did. For the jury to think Senator Ron Nagle held a deep hostility towards Tessa Reeves, however remotely, was critical to her argument.

"Did he say anything to Tessa?"

"No. He just marched out."

"What happened next?"

"Nothing really. We all went back to work."

"Danielle, had you seen Senator Nagle in the office before?"

"Yes. Quite a few times. He seemed to treat it like his property in a way and Wade didn't seem to mind."

"Is that unusual?"

"Well, I guess this is DC and there were a few stories that Tessa and I were sure were fed to *DC Watch* by Senator Nagle. You know, he'd come in then the next day or so there'd be a story quoting an inside source at the Capital."

"Stories written by Wade?"

"No. By Luke. Luke Everson. He wrote the Cloakroom column that covered the inside gossip on DC's movers and shakers."

"I see. And did anything happen the day after Senator Nagle's visit? The last day of Tessa Reeves' life?"

"Wade called her into his office and said he wanted to put her project on hold."

"What was Tessa's reaction?"

"She was angry and she was devastated," said Danielle.

"Did he say he was killing the story, or putting it on hold?"

"On hold, but Tessa was convinced it was as good as spiked. She didn't think Wade had the guts to publish it."

"Did Wade give Tessa an excuse?"

"He said Tate Lieberman had complained, and that they had to be extra careful to avoid a defamation suit."

"So what did Tessa do?"

"She wanted to get more information to make her story stronger, more compelling. And if Wade didn't want it, she figured someone else would. So she got in touch with Mr. Lieberman and told him she had to see him. Then they made plans to meet at the club."

Cadence had to think on her feet about her next question. The court had already heard that Tate Lieberman had threatened Tessa. She knew Underhill would go for the throat on this, confirming Lieberman as the one and only primary threat in Tessa Reeves' life.

"Danielle, did you speak to Tessa before she went to see Lieberman?"

"Yes."

"Can you tell the court what happened? What kind of a mood was she in?"

"She was just so determined to get stronger material for her story. She called him and he responded."

"But hadn't the defendant received threatening messages from Mr. Lieberman?"

"Yes, that's true and it wasn't like she had no reservations about seeing him. She was nervous but she was determined to get a one-on-one interview, all on the record, no holds barred. She said Lieberman had agreed to that."

"Was she scared about going to see the defendant?"

"A bit, I think," said Danielle. "I don't know for sure. She's pretty brave. More than most people I've ever known. But one thing I know for sure was that nothing could have stopped her from going to meet him. I don't know the exact details of the correspondence between them, but she was in a go-for-it kind of mood."

"During the time that you worked with Tessa, did she ever go somewhere that scared her?"

Danielle thought for a moment. "The only thing I can think of is when she was doing a crime story. She had to visit some very shady characters, but she was very clear with Wade about where she was going, and she was very, very careful."

"Thank you, Danielle," said Cadence. "No further questions."

Gerard Underhill took a page of handwritten notes up to the lectern. He laid it on top and took a long look at Danielle. His body language projected skepticism about this witness's words. After a few moments, he shook his head and tapped his chin.

"Ms. Farrell," he began, not bothering with any introductory pleasantries. Again, the way he treated her was how he wanted the image of Danielle Farrell to be shaped in the minds of the jurors. "Who was it that made a direct and malicious threat to harm Tessa Reeves—Senator Ron Nagle or Tate Lieberman?"

"Tate Lieberman, but like I said Tessa wasn't—"

"Ms. Farrell, do you still work at *DC Watch*?"

"No, I left."

"You left the day after Tessa Reeves' funeral, isn't that right?"

"Yes."

"And you haven't been back to the office, have you?"

"No."

"And you have no intention of working there again, do you?"

"No."

"Is it true that you stole all the research and documents Tessa Reeves had gathered in preparation for her story on the defendant and others?"

The gallery buzzed as one, as though a switch had been flipped.

"No, I didn't steal any documents."

"Tessa Reeves didn't keep her essential research documents on her work computer, did she?"

"I don't know."

"Really? Ms. Reeves stored all her important files on the cloud, isn't that right?"

"I don't know about all of them."

"Didn't she keep them in a Dropbox account?"

Danielle was visibly nervous. Cadence had told her to expect Underhill to come on strong and try to discredit her. Preparation was one thing, being poked and prodded by a hostile prosecutor was another. Now she knew that she was a fly in the spider's web. She straightened herself and nodded formally. "She kept some documents in a Dropbox account. I don't know about all."

"But everything to do with this particular story was in there, wasn't it?"

"I can't say for sure."

"Really? Isn't it true that Ms. Reeves gave you access to that account?"

"Yes."

"And isn't it true that before you left you took it upon yourself to remove them?"

Danielle bowed her head slightly, her eyes were downcast as well. "Yes."

"So you stole them?"

"They were Tessa's files."

"No, Ms. Farrell. They were work files." Underhill picked up a sheet of paper from the lectern and held it aloft. "As per Ms.

Reeves' contract, and yours, any work done on company time, on company equipment, belongs to the company. It's very clear that that data did not belong to you. You stole it."

"That was a misunderstanding. I have not been asked by Wade for anything."

"How do you know what he wants from you? You took a leave of absence and never went back, isn't that right?"

"Yes."

"And Wade Hampton, your boss, tried many times to contact you, didn't he?"

"I don't know."

"Yes, you do. You refused to respond to any attempt he made to communicate with you, isn't that right?"

"Yes."

"You took what was not yours to take and you never intended to give it back, isn't that right, Ms. Farrell?"

"I'm not sure."

"But you stole from your boss, didn't you?"

"That's not the way I thought of it."

"Of course you don't think of it that way. But you lied to him, didn't you?"

"Yes."

"And you lied here today, didn't you?"

"When?"

"Do you want me to remind you of your lie? In court, lying is called perjury. And when you testified to the court that you… it was a lie, wasn't it?"

"Yes."

"Just a few more questions, Ms. Farrell, and I must remind you that you are sworn to tell the truth. Did Tessa Reeves speak to you after she received those threatening messages from the defendant?"

"Yes."

"Did she take those threats seriously?"

"Yes."

"Seriously enough to fear for her life?"

"She changed her—"

"I'd ask you to please answer the question. Yes or no. When Tessa Reeves was threatened by Tate Lieberman, did she fear he might do her harm?"

"Yes."

"Thank you, Ms. Farrell," said Underhill, as though she had just delivered his lunch. "Nothing further," he said, giving Danielle a look of grave disappointment. He then returned to his desk. As he did, he locked eyes with Cadence and couldn't help but give her a half smile.

The tightrope she had chosen to step out onto was swaying violently. Not that anyone but her knew it. The nausea in Cadence's stomach was so powerful she struggled to keep a straight face and a straight back. Somehow, she managed to present a calm face to the world—a world that was about to witness her first catastrophic failure as a lawyer.

She needed time to process what Underhill had just done. She needed time to think. That she got to her feet without losing her balance was a major accomplishment.

"Your Honor, I'd like to request a recess to confer with my client in private," she said.

"How long, counselor?" asked Judge Gates.

"Half an hour," Cadence said hopefully.

"That would take us right up to lunch," said Judge Gates. "Let's call it ninety minutes. Okay?"

"Thank you, Your Honor."

As everyone jostled to leave the court, Cadence sat herself down and turned towards Lieberman, or more to the point, with her back to Underhill. She did not want to see the prosecutor gloat. Nor did she want him to see how shellshocked she was.

Discrediting Danielle, while useful, was not Underhill's main objective. By getting her willful removal of Tessa's research documents on record, he had rendered those documents as being inadmissible. The plan that Cadence had hatched the night before, the damning information Bob and Danielle had unearthed in the dead of night were now of no use to her. Her strategy had been gutted before it had barely started. She could not have felt more foolish to have taken such a risk.

And now she had to break it to her client.

Chapter 35

To find Tate Lieberman regarding her with disdain was nothing new to Cadence. Over the months she had known him, they had not gotten closer at all. All along, he maintained his entitled grievance at having to defend himself against criminal charges. And now that Cadence had made it clear that Underhill had the upper hand, the reality of him being convicted was starting to sink in for real.

"This is supposed to be a court of justice," he yelled at Cadence, throwing his hands up and looking around the now empty courtroom. "Is this some kind of perverse joke? When I contacted Alan, I was assured that this matter would go no further. He told me that he'd take care of it. Wrong. Where is he now? Where is Jackie? They left it all to you and look at where it's gotten me."

Lieberman leaned forward and slammed both hands on the table. The sound made Cadence jump. He glared at her, his face almost glowing red. "I'm an innocent man, goddammit."

There followed a pause that Cadence did not quite know how to fill. She did not think the case was lost. She was not giving up. But she knew Lieberman would ignore any words of reassurance she could offer.

Kelly Lieberman, who was seated next to her husband, filled the silence. "Innocent man," she scoffed. "Don't make me laugh. You may not be guilty of murder but there are so many things you are guilty of."

The three of them had shared a cab from court and Kelly did not say a word the entire time.

A stunned Lieberman turned to his wife. "Sweetheart—"

"Don't sweetheart me," she said. "And don't you ever forget that I'm here for show. How dare you try and take it out on Cadence. It's always someone else that's to blame, isn't it? Someone else who's in your way. Me. Your string of whores. And now your attorney, who you have done so little to help. You have been in denial all this time. Your vanity has kept you from helping the most important person in your life right now. It's never occurred to you, but you owe her a groveling apology."

Under Kelly's cold glare, the bluster seeped out of Lieberman. He nodded and turned to Cadence. "She's right," he said. "I should have treated you better. I should have trusted you from the start and put my faith in you. I treated you like the enemy."

Kelly waved a finger at her husband. "No, you treated her how you treat everybody—as an underling whose only purpose is to kowtow to you."

Lieberman nodded slowly. "Yes. I'm sorry, Cadence. What can I do now? Tell me."

"Well, for a start—"

Cadence's words fell away as Kelly raised a hand. "I'm sorry, Cadence. But I can't be silent anymore. I need to tell you something that may be of use to you."

"What is it?" asked Cadence.

"Ron Nagle is on the stand next, isn't he?"

"Yes."

"Well, as it happens, I've got a confession to make."

Cadence nodded, but she was mentally keeping track of time. They only had ninety minutes to regroup. Up next were two key witnesses—Ron Nagle and Luke Everson. She needed to shine the spotlight on Nagle as the possible instigator of Tessa Reeves' murder. The jury needed to be convinced that no one had more to lose than Nagle did by Tessa's stories getting published. She wanted to make sure the current conversation stayed on topic.

"Is it something related to this case, Kelly?"

"Oh, very much so," she said before turning to her husband.

"Tate, the reason I have come to court every day to play the dutiful wife is not because Cadence asked me to. Under different circumstances, I would have stood back and watched you fall."

"And I do appreciate your support, Kelly," Lieberman said. "I really do."

"Tate, there's no roundabout way to say this. Ron and I had an affair that lasted three years."

"What?" blurted a stunned Lieberman.

Kelly ignored her husband and turned to Cadence to expand on her revelation.

"To me, it was only a dalliance," she said. "And a payback, of sorts. If I didn't have such an unfaithful husband, I would never have considered it but perhaps I can't lay the blame entirely at Tate's feet. It was fun, for a while. I was not aware of how serious Ron's feelings for me were. He was not going to divorce Rosemary—that would almost certainly ruin his hopes for reelection. But he was in love with me and so he became intensely jealous of Tate. He said he was going to destroy Tate."

"Really? How?"

"Public humiliation, I imagine," said Kelly. "He knew I had vowed to divorce Tate and more if he strayed again. And I think I know how he aimed to do it."

"How?"

"At one point he boasted to me that he had used *DC Watch* a few times to undermine his rivals."

Cadence was busy making notes. "How?" she asked without lifting her eyes off her yellow legal pad.

"I don't know exactly but I heard him on the phone once talking to someone that I assume was the editor. Wade Hampton. The tone of the conversation sounded like a deal—a quid pro quo. Ron was saying that the story needed to be out the next morning and he was clearly pressuring Wade."

"You said it was a deal? What was he offering Wade?"

"He said something about a couple of his staff members. That's right, it was his Chief of Staff Zach Levine. I asked him and he said Zach was going to help him through the midterm election but then he was moving on."

"So you're saying Nagle offered Hampton the chief of staff gig if he got reelected so long as Hampton ran a hatchet piece on Tate?"

"He never said so to me directly but, yes, that's what I believe was planned."

"Do you know if Ron was doing anything illegal?"

"Nothing specific. But he did tell me that a certain bill was sure to be defeated. I'd have to look it up. But he knew in advance."

"I need the details," said Cadence, looking at her watch. "But there's no way Judge Gates will extend the recess."

"It's okay, Cadence, you don't have to ask," said Kelly. "I'm willing to testify."

"There's not enough time," said Cadence. "I'm going to duck outside and call my investigator, Bob. I need to find the names of Ron's rivals. Then I'll come back in and I want you to tell me as much as you can."

"Okay, Cadence," said Kelly. "And don't worry, I'll be a lot more forthcoming than my stupid husband, I promise you that."

"Great," said Cadence.

"I still don't understand why you have been supporting me in public," said Lieberman.

"I came to realize that while you may be a fool, Ron Nagle is evil," Kelly said. "Being out in the public eye and seen supporting you was a message mainly for him, so it was clear that I would not let him ruin you like he did to others."

"Guys, I need to duck out," said Cadence. "I'll be back in five."

"No worries," said Kelly. "And just so you know, I'm not done yet. I have more to share. But I'm wondering, if I don't testify, how are you going to use what I've told you?"

"Leave that to me."

Cadence met Bob as he came out of the elevator.

"Listen," she said. "I've got to prepare for my Nagle examination. There's something I need you to do."

Chapter 36

Nagle sat in the witness chair looking over the courtroom as though it was his dominion. He had a pleasant smile on his face and an outward appearance of calm. He was clearly a man assured of his own importance. His tailored suit was navy blue and double breasted, his silk tie gold. His belly may have been soft but he was, in his early sixties, a man in his prime. Six packs and push-ups did not get you the kind of peak state Nagle had attained. The highest levels of power, prestige and admiration were his benchmark goals. And in many ways, he was just getting started. Heck, there were presidents and cabinet secretaries in their seventies and eighties.

"Thank you for your time, Senator Nagle," said Cadence.

"Happy to be of service," he said, returning Cadence's smile. Few people but Cadence knew he did not mean a word.

"Senator Nagle, would you say the editor of *DC Watch,* Wade Hampton, is a friend of yours?"

"I guess you could describe him as a friend," said Nagle. "But this is DC, Ms. Elliott. Most relationships are, one way or another, centered on mutual interests."

"How long have you known each other?"

"I don't know exactly. About five or six years, I'd say."

"So, it's primarily a business relationship, is that right?"

"Yes."

"Could you please elaborate on that relationship for the court?"

"He edits a political website, I'm a politician," said Nagle. "I thought it would be obvious. But in case it's not, Wade will sometimes ask for my opinion on one subject or another. From time to time, he'll be exploring a topic of which I know something about. He may come to me for a quote—a comment—or to get my angle on some matter like a bill that's about to be voted on."

"I see. So that's it, he just gives you a call or you meet up?"

"Yes," said Nagle, as though he thought Cadence was extremely perceptive. "Just like most people communicate. We have phones we can use for the job, if we can't meet face to face."

After speaking, Nagle sat there regarding Cadence with a patronizing smile that had the jury smirking along with him. His eyes shifted to the left and he practically beamed with the knowledge that he had them on his side.

"Senator Nagle, the day before Tessa Reeves died, did you make an unannounced visit to Wade Hampton's office?"

"You may say unannounced. I'd say I dropped in."

"Was there something urgent you needed to talk to Mr. Hampton about?"

"I wouldn't say it was urgent."

"If it wasn't urgent, why didn't you call?"

"Wade Hampton and I are friends."

"No, you are not friends first and foremost, as you have made clear. You said your relationship with Wade Hampton was primarily work related. I can have the transcript read if you like."

"I know what I said. I—"

"Did you make an appointment to see Mr. Hampton?"

"Don't be silly. Wade's always got time to see me."

"Really? Even if he's on a deadline, you can just stop by his office whenever you like?"

"Yes," said Nagle, running his tongue over his top lip.

"Did you ask Mr. Hampton's receptionist if he was free?"

"Objection, Your Honor," said Underhill, getting to his feet. "Relevance. How do these spurious details have anything to do with the murder of Tessa Reeves?"

"I'm getting to that, Your Honor," said Cadence, holding Nagle with her gaze.

"Get to it with no further delay, please, counselor," said Judge Gates. "Overruled."

Having successfully tested the patience of Nagle, Underhill and Judge Gates, Cadence decided the time was right to change tack.

"Your Honor, I'd like to ask your permission to treat the witness as hostile," she said. "He has been subpoenaed by me to appear here today and I believe I will get to the point faster and with more accuracy if I could treat the witness as hostile."

Nagle shot Judge Gates a look. There were many politicians in DC who had law degrees under their belts. Nagle was not one of them.

"If I allow Ms. Elliott to examine you as a hostile witness," said Judge Gates, "it means she can ask you leading questions. It's normally an allowance made for attorneys only when they are cross-examining a witness."

"I think I am being open with my answers, Your Honor," said Nagle. "I think Ms. Elliott is the only person in this room who thinks I'm being hostile."

"Senator, in the courtroom, hostile does not mean there's a conflict. It just allows the lawyer to get a witness to address specific points of evidence. I think it would be for the best in this instance."

"I see," said Nagle, nodding and turning back to Cadence. He looked at her now in the same way as when she confronted him at the Zellus conference.

"Thank you, Your Honor," said Cadence. "May I proceed as requested?"

"You may. Granted."

"Senator Nagle, is it true that you barged into Wade Hampton's office?"

"No."

"Did you make an appointment?"

"No."

"Did you ask Mr. Hampton's receptionist if he was free?"

"No."

"Were you angry about something?"

Nagle switched his relaxed demeanor back on.

"You know, Ms. Elliott," he said. "I don't recall."

"But you marched into his office without knocking, slammed the door and began shouting at Mr. Hampton, isn't that right?"

"That sounds quite dramatic."

"It's how witnesses have described the event. You were angry with Mr. Hampton about something, weren't you?"

"Maybe I was upset."

"What about?"

"You know what? I can't remember."

While Nagle's demeanor indicated he was being honest, to most people in the courtroom it seemed like a sly move, an all too convenient lapse in memory.

"You were aware, though, that Tessa Reeves was preparing to write an investigative story about you and your relationship with Zellus Pharmaceuticals, weren't you?"

"Yes, I was."

"That's what you were angry about, wasn't it?"

"Mr. Hampton and I don't always see eye to eye."

"Did you order Mr. Hampton to kill the story?"

"I have no such influence over what Mr. Hampton does or does not publish," said Nagle with conviction. "Maybe I was unhappy with what he was not publishing. There have been times when I've said that to him. There's a lot that goes on in DC that goes unreported. And for the good of the public, I have on occasion pointed out such lapses in Mr. Hampton's publication."

"Have you ever asked Mr. Hampton to publish a story attacking your rivals?"

"Don't be ridiculous."

"Is that a no, Senator Nagle?"

"Yes, it's a no."

"Senator Nagle, you know the defendant's wife Kelly Lieberman, don't you?"

Nagle's face flinched. The question completely blindsided him.

"I beg your pardon? Do I know Kelly Lieberman? What kind of a question is that?" For a second, Nagle seemed to forget there were realms of the world where his power and standing did not bend everything to his will.

"A very simple question. A yes or no would suffice."

"Yes, I do know Kelly Lieberman. Our paths have crossed at functions a few times."

"Your paths more than crossed, didn't they, Senator Nagle. Isn't it true that you had an affair with Kelly Lieberman for the better part of three years?"

The gallery practically erupted, in the most self-restrained manner possible. Some of those in attendance could not stop themselves from speaking out and Judge Gates' eyes flicked over his courtroom to identify the culprits. Again, the disturbance was brief and although Judge Gates raised his gavel, he did not have to use it.

"How dare you," shouted Nagle, the corners of his mouth white like he was foaming at the mouth. "This is outrageous."

"Objection, Your Honor," cried Underhill. "Relevance. This is nothing but an outrageous attempt to slander Senator Nagle to distract attention from the defendant."

"Ms. Elliott?" said Judge Gates, his eyes glaring at her. "I won't allow you to make a tabloid circus of my courtroom."

"Your Honor, my line of questioning will lead directly to the circumstances surrounding the death of Tessa Reeves. This will be evident shortly."

Judge Gates pondered Cadence's response for a few moments while Nagle looked at her with barely suppressed outrage. "I'll allow it," Judge Gates said finally. "Please answer the question, Senator."

Nagle's head swiveled from the judge to the attorney. A full-blooded protest sat on his tongue, but he thought better of letting it loose. His eyes fell upon Kelly Lieberman. She stared back at him impassively.

"Yes," he said reluctantly.

"And Kelly Lieberman ended the affair approximately one month before Tessa Reeves' death. Does that sound right to you, Senator Nagle?"

"Yes."

"Senator Nagle, did you tell Kelly Lieberman that you fed Wade Hampton stories to attack your rivals?"

"I don't recall," said Nagle, presenting Cadence with a look of smug defiance.

"Did you tell Kelly Lieberman that you were going to feed *DC Watch* a story about her husband's infidelity with Phoebe Baker?"

"I don't recall."

"How convenient. So you deny feeding such a story to Wade Hampton?"

Nagle's mind worked furiously to try and find a way to emerge from this exchange with his reputation and reelection hopes intact. Yet he drew a blank.

"Mr. Nagle, I must remind you that you are under oath and that you must answer the question," said Cadence.

"I did not feed Wade Hampton any stories," he said. "Like just about every person of influence in DC, I gave journalists information off the record. It's up to them how they use it, if they use it at all. Everyone does it. It's how the world works. Have you never heard of backgrounding?"

"Thank you, Senator. That's interesting, but what concerns this case is that you knew Tessa Reeves was investigating you, didn't you?"

"She had some baseless allegations. I told Wade I'd come down on him like a ton of bricks if he published."

"By that do you mean you threatened to sue him?"

"Exactly. I wasn't going to stand by and let myself be defamed."

"So Wade Hampton agreed to hold the story because you demanded him to, isn't that right?"

"Yes. That's how it works. It didn't mean that she would never write her story."

"No, that's exactly right. Someone made sure she never got to finish it, didn't they?"

"How dare you," shouted Nagle. "I had nothing to do with her death."

"I didn't say that but what you have confirmed is that Tessa's story was spiked because you told Wade to spike it not because of any threat made by the defendant, Tate Lieberman. Isn't that right?"

"You're asking the wrong person."

"No, I don't think so. I'm asking you. Wade Hampton did what you told him to do, didn't he?"

"I don't know," said Nagle. "I never asked him. But maybe he took what I said to heart. If you ask me, Wade did the right thing. But I did not feed him any story."

"Yes, you've already told us that. No further questions, Your Honor."

When she returned to the defense table, she saw Bob had arrived and was seated next to Kelly.

Underhill stepped up to cross-examine Nagle and somewhat managed to reinflate his standing in the eyes of the jury, but Cadence was confident she had done enough damage. She would not need to call Kelly as a witness.

After Underhill's cross, Judge Gates adjourned court for the day. Cadence suggested to Lieberman that the four of them should go back to her office for a debrief. Lieberman hesitated before saying he needed a drink.

"I'm going to pass, Cadence," said Kelly. "I've done my bit for today."

"You most certainly have," said Lieberman, looking as though he was still processing the shock of her confession. "So, I don't get it. Did you want to stop Nagle from burying me so you could have the pleasure of doing it yourself? Is that it?"

Kelly met his gaze with a flat expression. "No, my dear. I did it to help you. There was a time when I would have done everything within my power to ruin you for your infidelities but now, I don't care. That doesn't mean I'm not hurt. I just have no need for vengeance and outrage. But, I could not stand by and allow that man to make this ordeal worse for you."

"Do you think he framed me?" asked Lieberman. "Do you think he had Tessa killed?"

"I don't know," said Kelly. "Isn't that what you think, Cadence?"

Cadence nodded. "Yes. Well, it was up until today."

"What do you mean?" Kelly asked.

"You'll see," said Cadence. The Lieberman's exited the courtroom together—Kelly performing her last duty of the day. Bob joined Cadence at the defense table.

There was a look about Cadence that got Bob's attention.

"Cadence, what happened? You look like you've solved the Matrix."

Cadence squinted at him curiously, her mind spinning almost audibly. "Maybe I have, Bob," she said. "Tell me—how much of Nagle's testimony did you catch?"

"I came in when he was denying that he fed Wade Hampton dirt on his rivals."

"Yes, well that's the very thing I'm stuck on," said Cadence. "That was interesting, wasn't it?"

Bob shook his head. "No, not really. He lied. He committed perjury but you are never going to be able to prove it. It's not like Hampton is going to tell you."

Cadence shook her head. "No, Bob. That's just it. I don't think he was lying. I think he was telling the truth."

After a moment's thought, something clicked in Cadence's mind. She quickly bent down and snatched up her handbag and began rummaging through it urgently.

"What on earth are you doing?" asked Bob.

"Looking for Tessa's killer," she said without looking up.

"In your handbag?"

"Yes."

One by one, Cadence emptied the contents of her handbag onto the defense table. She then turned the bag inside out, shook it and inspected every inch of it.

Suddenly she froze. "Oh my God. I found it."

"What?"

Cadence held the bag close to Bob. "See?" she said. "Under here."

"An AirTag? What's that doing there? Did you—"

Bob already knew the answer to the question he was about to ask but Cadence shook her head firmly.

"No, it wasn't me who put it there," she said. "Someone hid it so they could follow me and try to kill me. Remember that car I told you about? The one that tried to take me out after my run. I thought Monica was behind it. She denied it when I challenged her and now, I know she was telling me the truth. And I think Senator Nagle was telling the truth."

"Dear God, Bob," Cadence said as she returned all the items to her handbag. "But now I'm going to get it right."

"What do you mean?"

"I know how to win this case," she said. "Oh, and I know who killed Tessa."

"Cadence, you need to focus on the case first and foremost."

"I know, Bob," Cadence said. "Let's head back to the office. We've got a big day tomorrow. But just wait for me a minute. I need to step outside and call someone."

"Who?"

"Wade Hampton."

Chapter 37

Like many people, Luke Everson dressed for court like it was for Sunday church. Most times Cadence had seen him he was the image of the disheveled journalist—weeks overdue for a haircut, five days late for a shave. Today, he had addressed everything from head to toe, so when he walked through the gate anyone would think he presented the nightly news as opposed to hammering out his gossip column from the shabby confines of *DC Watch*. Every reporter knows the importance of appearance, especially those who know they will never be in front of the camera.

Everson had given Cadence a quick nod and as he sat there waiting for her to begin, he appeared ready and eager. After taking in his surroundings, he straightened his back and looked at Cadence with an air of being ready to both oblige and impress.

As far as Cadence knew, this was Everson's first appearance at the Lieberman trial. She had expected him to come for both Danielle's and Hampton's testimony. But whenever she scanned the gallery there was no sign of Everson. She did not think he was disinterested or unsupportive, she simply presumed that someone had to keep the news site running.

"Mr. Everson, you were a colleague of Tessa Reeves, weren't you?"

Everson bent forward a little into the microphone. "That's right. I got there a few years before her."

"And what kind of reporter did she strike you as?"

"Well, there was no doubt that she was in a hurry to make a name for herself," he said. "She was not shy about promoting herself but some of her stories were a little rough around the edges. Before she came to *DC Watch*, that is. She needed a bit more polish.

"Did you have a role to play in her development?"

"Not formally but Wade wanted the way we did things to rub off on Tessa. Though that never really happened."

"What do you mean?"

"Tessa was kind of dismissive of older people. Practically anyone over thirty-five was a Boomer to her, and I guess that made her arrogant in an immature way. Impudent, that's what she was. Not all the time but—"

"To you?"

"Yes. Look, I don't want to talk her down at all. It's just that under pressure, sometimes our negative qualities come out. I mean, she could be nice. She just didn't seem to want to engage much with her colleagues."

"Except for Danielle Farrell?"

"Yes. Exactly, except for Danielle, who was more her age."

"Did Tessa talk to you about the stories she was working on?"

"Occasionally, but she usually did not share much."

"Was there a sense you were competing with each other even though you worked for the same publication?"

"Yes," said Everson. "That's not unusual in newsrooms. But we were on different levels, experience wise."

"That seems a shame. Did you and Tessa ever work on anything together?"

Everson thought for a moment but shook his head. "No. I got the picture pretty early on that she did not want my advice, which was fair enough."

"Was a hyper competitive culture something that your editor Wade Hampton bred at *DC Watch*?"

"Yes, to a degree. But, like I said, it was nothing unusual in the journalism game."

"Mr. Everson, were you in the office the day before Tessa Reeves died?"

"Yes, I was."

"Did you see Senator Nagle come in?"

"Yes. I did. He and Wade had an argument, but I have no idea what it was about. But after that both our stories were put on hold."

"Could you tell us what your story was about?"

Everson paused and thought it over. "Under normal conditions, I'd refuse to tell you under my rights as a journalist, but I know that the gist of my story has already come out in this court. My story was about the defendant Tate Lieberman. It was about the fact that he was having an affair with Phoebe Baker."

"That was your story?"

"Yes. Was being the operative word. Now it's old news."

The morning's papers were all over the Lieberman-Nagle love triangle. Nagle now had a shocked and disgusted wife on his hands and his midterm chances were shot.

"But back then, you wanted to run the story and Wade refused. Is that right?"

"Yes."

"Why?"

"He said there was a conflict with my story and Tessa's. He said he was giving Tessa some time to bolster hers."

"How did you feel about that?"

"I wasn't happy. But later I felt maybe it was a good thing."

"Why?"

"Well, look at what happened to Tessa. I believe if my story was published my life would have been in danger. I was nervous about exposing Tate Lieberman. I'd been warned that he might react violently."

Everson's words took Cadence by surprise. She had discussed what she wanted to cover over the phone several times and he had never mentioned that he feared what Lieberman might do.

The murmuring of the gallery lasted a few moments as Cadence paused to recalibrate. She had made it abundantly clear to Everson that his role as a witness for the defense was to highlight the culture at *DC Watch*. His last response seemed to indicate that he had forgotten that.

"The court has already heard that Wade Hampton decided to hold the stories only after Senator Nagle's visit," said Cadence.

"Well, I wasn't privy to the timing of everything," said Everson. "But I was aware that Tate Lieberman had threatened Tessa. Wade told me. And he was extremely concerned. And he had every right to be. But putting the story on ice wasn't enough to save Tessa."

Cadence looked puzzled. Her expression silently conveyed her disapproval. She did not expect to have her witness go out of bounds like this. They had agreed that Everson's testimony would focus on the work culture at *DC Watch*. She did not call him as a witness to make things worse for Lieberman. The hint of smugness on Everson's face indicated he knew very well what he was doing and that he had intentionally gone off-script, so to speak. For some reason, he seemed to be enjoying his defiance of the agreement with Cadence.

What Everson did not know was that Cadence was actually pleased with his performance. He had no idea what was coming.

"Mr. Everson, I just want to turn our attention back to Senator Nagle's visit."

"You mean away from Tate Lieberman's clear threats of violence?"

Everson's comment was provocative. It certainly made the jury members sit up straighter. Suddenly, they were wondering if they had missed something. Something about Cadence Elliott seemed to bother the witness.

"Mr. Everson, you seem to be implying that you were in as much danger as Tessa Reeves."

"Well, I think that is self-evident."

"Are you saying you feared for your life because you were preparing a hatchet job on the defendant?"

"Objection," called Underhill. "If that's not badgering the witness, I don't know what is."

"I'll be the one to draw such conclusions, counselor," snapped Judge Gates, stopping Underhill in his tracks. "The objection is sustained nonetheless."

"I'll rephrase, Your Honor," said Cadence. "Mr. Everson, are you saying you feared for your life because you were preparing an expose on the defendant?"

"Yes."

"Yet here you are. You're still with us."

"I count myself lucky," said Everson firmly.

"No doubt you do," said Cadence. "Mr. Everson, how did you get your job at *DC Watch*?"

"There was a vacancy, I think. I went for an interview and got the job. Pretty standard."

"Really? Weren't you recommended to Wade Hampton directly?"

Everson's face went blank as the air of certainty leaked from his bearing. "That doesn't mean that's why I got the job."

"Really? But who recommended you?"

The long pause that followed made it clear that Everson wanted to pass on the question. That was not an option.

"It was Senator Nagle."

"Oh, I see. You must know Senator Nagle well then?"

"Quite well. We go back a ways."

"You go back a ways? What exactly is your relationship with the Senator?"

"I'm his wife's nephew."

"Ah, so Uncle Ron got you the job. That's nice."

Everson shifted in his seat, and remained quiet, thinking better of retaliating. By now he knew Cadence was onto something. He just did not know what, nor what she knew.

"Where were you working before you got the job at *DC Watch*?"

"I was in Boston. I worked on a paper there."

"Okay. Did you write stories for Senator Nagle there too?"

"What?"

"Mr. Everson, did Senator Nagle ever ask you to write articles that were designed to damage his political rivals?"

"That's ridiculous."

"Is it? Last year, didn't you write two stories that did serious political damage to Senator Nagle's opponents?"

"I don't know what you're talking about."

"One story was on Senator Mike Carney," said Cadence. "The other was on Congressman Tim Scheller. Both were vocal opponents of Senator Ron Nagle. Both are no longer in politics in no small part due to what you wrote about them."

"Politics is a tough game."

Cadence was on the verge of asking Judge Gates to allow her to treat Everson as a hostile witness, but she held off. She wanted to bide her time a little more, though. She was not convinced it was necessary.

"Mr. Everson, do you recall who gave you the tip-off that prompted you to produce the story on Lieberman?"

"I just came up with it myself. Through my contacts."

"If you did publish that story on Mr. Lieberman, do you think it would have dealt him a savage blow personally as well as professionally?"

"I have no idea."

"Really? If you have no idea of such a story's impact, why on earth would you say it put you in danger, just like Tessa?"

"Because powerful people can hurt you if you hurt them."

"I see. But your story was not in the same league as Tessa's, was it? She was putting together an in-depth investigative piece, the kind that wins awards. You're the *DC Watch* gossip writer. Not quite the same thing, is it?"

"You're trying to get me riled up."

"Oh, I'm just getting started. Your Honor, I would like to treat Mr. Everson as a hostile witness."

"Go right ahead, counselor. Granted."

"Objection, Your Honor," said Underhill. "Relevance. Ms. Elliott is deviating well beyond the case at hand."

"Your Honor, I'm trying to give the jury a thorough understanding of Tessa Reeves' last moments. As a man who worked with her and competed against her, Mr. Everson here has a unique perspective that must be examined."

"Overruled. Please continue, counselor. I'd like to see where this is going."

Everson's eyes were glued on Judge Gates as he spoke. When he turned back to Cadence, his eyes were alert and fierce and his body was rigid. Clearly, he knew that he had unwittingly stumbled into Cadence's trap.

"Mr. Everson, you said that you and Tessa had a natural rivalry, and that it was normal for reporters to treat each other that way, isn't that right?"

"It happens everywhere."

"Like in your previous job at *The Boston Sun*, right?"

"Yes."

"About that job. Is it true you were fired for physically assaulting a female reporter?"

Everson's face turned red and his eyes glared at Cadence. "No. That was a misunderstanding."

"Really? Is that what Trevor Norris, your former editor, would say? According to the office memo, you had to be pulled away from her. It says you were unhappy that she seemed to be moving up the ladder faster than you. Is that right?"

"That was his take on it. You haven't heard my side of the story."

"I'm sure you do have a story, but I don't really need to hear it now. I wonder how you coped with working with such a young and promising reporter as Tessa Reeves? Here you are writing gossip, while she's producing groundbreaking reporting."

"She was doing no such thing. She was young and naive and stupid."

Everson had spoken before his better judgment could take hold of his verbal reins. He tried to smile, as if it could defuse the intensity of his outburst.

"I'm sorry, but I feel like I'm the one on trial here."

"No, not yet you aren't," said Cadence. "But can you tell the court whether Senator Ron Nagle asked you to do something to thwart Tessa Reeves in her pursuit of her Zellus story?"

"No."

"Did you take it upon yourself to do him a favor and it got out of hand?"

"Objection," cried Underhill. "Badgering the witness."

"Sustained," growled Judge Gates, glaring at Cadence. "Watch yourself, counselor."

"I have nothing further for the witness, Your Honor," said Cadence. "Oh, except this. I just wondered if Mr. Everson knew how this AirTag ended up in my handbag. It's curious, since that was how Tessa Reeves was followed. And even more curious since Mr. Everson's colleague Danielle Farrell had written a story about how criminals were using the devices to track their victims."

"Is that a question?"

"You were assigned the follow up to that story, weren't you, Mr. Everson?"

"What if I was?"

"Well, I wonder if you could tell me how you feel about the fact that I've given the AirTag I found in my handbag to Detective Hudson, who is seated here in court today. He's going to run a DNA test on it, so I imagine he'll be asking you to submit a sample."

Everson shrugged. "Fine."

"Good then. Oh, and please don't delete anything on your phone. I'm sure Detective Hudson will want to study all its data. You know, any calls between you and Senator Nagle. And any indication that you used your phone to track AirTags. Because that will all be there. I'm sure you'll be fine with that, won't you?"

Everson gave a weak smile and nodded but it was clear to everyone that his mind was working overtime. Suddenly, he reached for his phone.

"Bailiff!" cried Judge Gates.

In half a second, a tall and intimidating bailiff was at the witness stand. He wrapped his arms around Everson and pulled him out of the stand like a prized catch. Another bailiff was at the ready, and Hudson had burst through the gate.

"You bitch!" Everson cried. "You bitch! I'll get you. This is bullshit. I'm going to sue your ass."

Cadence, still at the lectern, looked on with passive curiosity as the bailiffs dragged Everson out of the courtroom.

Much of the gallery was now standing. They could not contain themselves and were talking excitedly about what they had just witnessed.

The crack of Judge Gates' gavel took the noise down a notch but not enough for his liking. "Silence," he cried as he struck it down again. "Silence. Everyone be seated immediately or you will be thrown out. This is a courtroom, not Dodger Stadium."

In less than ten seconds the entire crowd in the courtroom sat in quiet obedience.

"Your Honor," Cadence said.

"What is it, counselor?"

"The defense rests."

Chapter 38

It was amazing the difference a trial win made when she walked back into the office. A delirious swell had carried Cadence out of the courtroom, through the clamorous throng of media up the elevator to the refined, almost stately, confines of Hardwick and Henshaw. There was, however, no champion's welcome up front, no gauntlet of popping champagne corks and rowdy cheering. That was not the Hardwick and Henshaw way. She received admiring looks and a few congratulations from her colleagues as she made her way to the office, but as she approached Alan and Jackie were there, beaming at her and applauding.

"Fifteen minutes," said Alan, whose round face was lit with cherubic joy. He clapped his palms together under his chin before releasing them to take firm hold of Cadence's right hand. "Fifteen minutes. That's a record."

"We're almost sure it's a record," said Jackie, closing in to kiss and embrace her protege. "But I can't recall a verdict being returned faster than that in DC. Well done."

With that, Jackie and Alan parted to let Cadence into her office. The sight of a phenomenal bouquet of flowers on her desk stopped Cadence in her tracks. Off to the side was a stand with an ice bucket containing a three-hundred-dollar bottle of vintage Krug. The taste at Hardwick and Henshaw may well have been refined but it was not subtle. Cadence had expected that whatever grief she had gotten from Alan since taking the case would evaporate the moment the case was won. He would be, of course, expecting any friction to be swept away like water under a bridge. Five years ago, Cadence would have been grateful to have passed the test and eagerly awaited her next case. Now she was a little more circumspect. She would not soon forget her feelings about moving on from the firm, win or lose.

But such a decision was for another day.

She placed her bag on the floor and stepped over to smell the flowers. Jackie closed the door behind her while Alan reached for the champagne. "These are stunning," Cadence said. "Thank you."

"No, thank you," said Alan as he pressed his thumb into the cork. "I was amazed. We all were. None of us saw that coming."

The cork shot from the bottle with a satisfying pop and Alan proceeded to fill the three glasses on the desk.

He shook his head. "When did you suspect Luke Everson was the killer? You had Nagle in your sights from the get-go."

Cadence took the glass and raised it to her bosses. "Cheers. Here's to justice."

"Indeed," said Alan.

"To justice," said Jackie. After taking a sip, she said, "Well?"

"It's true," Cadence said. "I was convinced that Nagle was behind Tessa's murder. He had far more to lose than Lieberman. But something occurred to me after I cross-examined him. I did not think that he would risk perjury by telling an outright lie and I thought I had let him off the hook when I questioned him about feeding stories to *DC Watch*. I assumed that whenever he sought to exert influence on that publication, he leaned on its boss and editor Wade Hampton. I went over the transcripts and I realized that my wording allowed him to conceal that the person he fed stories to was Luke Everson, and that he did so directly. I assumed it went from Nagle to Hampton, who then commissioned Everson to write the story. But I realized Hampton was kept out of the loop. I called him after I left court that day and he confirmed it."

"So Hampton wasn't Nagle's patsy?" asked Jackie.

"I totally thought he was," said Cadence. "Bob had heard that Nagle was needing a chief of staff if he was reelected and Hampton was going to leave *DC Watch* to join Nagle. But it was Everson who was promised that gig, not Hampton. It was then I realized that if Tessa ruined Nagle's reelection chances by publishing a searing exposé, then Everson had nowhere to go. He was a bitter man whose career had stalled, and he would have hated and envied Tessa more than anyone could imagine."

Cadence continued to tell Alan and Jackie that while her suspicion had shifted to Everson, she did not think she would be able to get him to confess in court.

"In the end, I didn't have to," she said. "I realized he must have stuck an AirTag in my handbag with gum when I was at the bar buying him a drink. And from his reaction in court, I don't think he was smart enough to delete the tracking data he used to follow Tessa, and then me."

Jackie raised her glass to Cadence. "Here's to you, my brilliant girl."

They all clinked glasses again. After taking another sip, Cadence moved to her chair. "I don't want to drink too much. I'm expecting a call from Detective Hudson. He might have the results from the DNA test. And I'll have to give him a statement about the attempted hit and run and threats on my life. He wants to add attempted murder to the charge of the homicide of Tessa Reeves."

"How did he feel about you doing his job for him?" asked Alan.

"I wouldn't go so far as to say that," Cadence smiled. "But I did tell him, 'I told you so.'"

"Now, look," said Jackie. "We'll leave you to wrap up things here but if you've made plans for tonight, cancel them because we're taking you to dinner. Just the three of us. We'll be leaving at five-thirty sharp."

"Five-thirty?" said Cadence. "That's a bit early for dinner, isn't it?"

"This will be no ordinary dinner," said Jackie. "We're heading outside the Beltway. There's something important we'd like to discuss with you and we thought what better place to do that than The Inn at Little Washington."

"My goodness," said Cadence. "It must be important." She had of course heard about the Michelin 3-star restaurant. Located an hour's drive away in the small town of Washington, Virginia, it was reputed to offer one of the most extraordinary dining experiences in the US.

"We can finish the bottle in the limousine on the way," said Alan, returning the cork to the bottle. "It'll keep."

As Alan and Jackie left her office, Cadence took a deep breath and savored the moment. This was what success felt like. She had pulled something out of the hat to win the trial and she had the city at her feet.

She sat down and reflected on the past few months. And the person who came to mind was not Tate Lieberman. Make no mistake, she was thrilled to have saved him from the most horrible existence. She shuddered to think how an arrogant, pampered man like him would fare living shoulder to shoulder with hardened criminals. No, the person who sprang to mind was Kelly Lieberman.

After the three of them had stood outside the courtroom facing the press, they said their farewells. Lieberman had begun thanking Kelly and went to hug her, but she repelled him.

"My job is done, Tate," she told him. "I meant what I said. You're not staying at the house. You can book yourself a room at the Fairbanks until you find somewhere else to live. I'll be filing for divorce as soon as I possibly can."

Lieberman was speechless, not with shock but with something that looked more like regret. He seemed half-inclined to try and keep the matter open for discussion but he knew Kelly well enough to know that such a move was futile. A resignation came over him. Surrender, maybe. "If that's what you want," he said. "I understand but I'm so grateful that you stood by me. I mean it, Kelly. I don't know if I could have gotten through this without you."

That her husband was sincere only made their situation all the more lamentable. "Don't mention it, Tate. You need to start thinking ahead. As do I. We've both got to lawyer up, I'd say. But can we try and keep it civil?"

Lieberman nodded. "Of course."

With that, Kelly looked at Cadence with a wry grin. "Know any good divorce attorneys, Cadence?"

As Cadence shook her head, Kelly took her hand. "You are an extraordinary young woman, Cadence Elliott. I'd like to keep in touch. Maybe we could have lunch some time. On me."

Cadence nodded. "I'd like that."

Alan Henshaw was at his gregarious best at dinner. He engaged with Cadence and explained himself without ever apologizing for how he treated her. It was not as though Cadence felt Alan had overstepped the mark, she just felt he had let his own emotions and business interests take precedence over trust and faith in one of his most capable attorneys. Jackie chimed in to smooth things over, and the whole process was charged by the pleasure of dining at The Inn. Everything about the restaurant was extraordinary.

It was after they had ordered their deserts and a bottle of Sauternes, that Jackie held Cadence with the most affectionate gaze.

"Cadence, as Alan mentioned earlier, there was something that we would like to discuss with you."

Cadence laughed. "Well, you certainly have me intrigued. I think it must be something good, given this excursion away from the Swamp and this extraordinary meal. It would be cruel to lay some bad news on me."

Both Alan and Jackie joined her laughter before Jackie assured Cadence that it was good news.

"Cadence, you've been with us for nearly five years," Jackie said. "I know we've got every cent of our money's worth from you. I've been thrilled to watch you grow and you just keep going from strength to strength. I know it's been extremely difficult for you but even though Alan may have lost his composure once or twice, we never lost faith in you."

Cadence thought to herself that that was not how she remembered things. But what did she care?

Jackie continued. "We are so impressed and so pleased with how you handled this case that we would like to offer you a thirty-thousand-dollar bonus."

Cadence felt the blood rush to her head. A thirty-thousand-dollar bonus. That would sure go a long way to consigning the memory of a tetchy Alan Henshaw to the past, and it certainly took the urgency out of Cadence sounding out who else in DC might like to employ her.

"That's not all that we wanted to say," said Jackie. She looked at Alan before speaking. "Now as much as I'd like to draw this out and tease you, sweetheart, I can't. The truth is, we'd like to offer you a partnership."

Cadence almost gagged. Most lawyers would be happy to make partner at age forty. To make partner ten years earlier was very rare. Anyone who made partner by thirty was clearly an outstanding practitioner of law. The thought of such an honor made Cadence's head swirl a little.

"I don't know what to say," said Cadence with a gentle laugh of wonder and disbelief. "That's not what I was expecting. I mean, I was not expecting to get fired—but a partnership. My goodness."

Alan and Jackie sat wordless as they watched the idea sink into Cadence's mind. As Cadence pondered the offer and what it meant, the pause in the conversation grew to a length approaching awkward. They obviously did not think Cadence would have to think too long about whether or not to accept.

"You don't have to answer tonight," said Jackie, needing a little effort to keep her smile at full beam.

"No, Jackie. I'm not unsure," Cadence said. "Of course, I'll take it. Thank you. Thank you both. I'd love to become a partner. Nothing could make me happier."

Alan and Jackie's relief was palpable. The conversation then sprang into how it would work and how Cadence would get a new office and a handsome budget with which to renovate it. Cadence was overjoyed and felt as though she was truly being embraced as someone who would play a leading role in the firm's future.

Alan looked at his watch. "It's only ten o'clock. What's say we finish off with brandy. One for the road, eh?"

Cadence was never much of a brandy drinker, but she was not about to say no.

After the waiter had disappeared to get the drinks, Alan leaned into Cadence.

"There's something else I need to tell you," he said. He was more than tipsy—they all were—and Alan was in his most buoyant of moods. He looked the picture of the happy drunk. "You are a gift. A gift that keeps giving."

His words sounded harmless but they had Cadence confused. "What do you mean?" she asked.

"Your performance for the cameras today," he said, waving a hand. "Brilliant. I don't think you know what a striking force you are, my dear. The camera loves you. Everything you said was perfect. And you refused to try and humiliate Underhill. You were conciliatory and quietly triumphant. I know Jackie and I have asked you to bear in mind that you are always representing us and today, Cadence, you cast Hardwick and Henshaw in the brightest, most beautiful light. And I say, bravo."

"Bravo," echoed Jackie, as the waiter delivered the brandy.

"And yes, you are the gift that keeps on giving," said Alan. "I say that because your appearance on TV may just have landed us a major account."

Cadence raised her eyebrows. "Really? How did that happen?"

"Simple," said Alan, getting set to enjoy the telling. "I took a call from someone who saw you on TV, who told me how brilliant you were to win that case and how impressive you were on camera. So impressive that he picked up the phone and told me he wanted to discuss the prospect of Hardwick and Henshaw handling all their commercial law. It's a very large account, Cadence. It dwarfs anything Lieberman could have been for us. And to be honest, I think we dodged a bullet because Berrins will be damaged goods."

"You don't think it will survive?" asked Cadence.

"It will survive, I'm sure," said Alan. "But I think they'll struggle to keep their big clients. And without them, Berrins will be a much leaner outfit. So we can just let Berrins fade in our rear-view mirror. Okay? So we have you to thank for that, and then this massive account falls from the sky. And all because of you."

"Really?"

"Yes. He mentioned you by name. I mean, he will be a business client, but he told me that he had a potential criminal matter looming that could use the attention of one of the finest brains in DC."

"You mean me, you want me to take the case?" asked Cadence, adopting the appropriate humility. She had no idea where this was going but it sounded good so far. She thought the brandy may have been one drink too many, for all three of them.

"Of course. Of course," he said. "He says it's rather urgent. He wants you to go and see him tomorrow morning."

Cadence's thoughts immediately shifted to how she would be feeling the following morning. It was not going to be pretty. Given the champagne, cocktails, wine and brandy, she was guaranteed a stage-five hangover. She was a little annoyed that Alan had not told her earlier.

"What time tomorrow morning?"

"Ten o'clock. Is that okay?"

Cadence breathed a sigh of relief. "Of course. That's totally fine."

"Good," said Alan before his face turned serious. "Now I don't want you to think I'm underestimating you but as managing partner I need to say that there will be a lot riding on this meeting."

"Alan, I know the score. I'm fully aware of who I represent and that he is a client of great value to you."

Alan shook his head. "Not just to me. And not just to me and Jackie. But to you too, my dear. As a partner you will have a much bigger stake in the growth of the firm, and the responsibility that goes with it."

"I get it, Alan," said Cadence. "I won't make a misstep. Trust me."

"I do," said Alan, digging a hand into his inside jacket pocket. "I really do. Here. He sent me his business card and told me to give it to you. He'll have a car pick you up outside our office. Ten o'clock sharp."

"Alan, this is starting to sound way too sound familiar," Cadence said laughing. "Please don't tell me it's another Tate Lieberman. It would be far too soon."

"I can't tell you exactly what he's like," said Alan, "because we haven't met face to face. We had a long, very promising chat, though, and he sounds extremely charming and very smart. So I really do think you'll find him an entirely different prospect than our friend Mr. Lieberman. Do what you do best, my dear. Dazzle him."

Alan slid the card over the tablecloth towards Cadence. She picked it up immediately and read it.

In an instant, her blood ran ice cold, her heart rate escalated and she found herself fighting the urge to be sick.

The name on the card was Simon Cordoba.

Chapter 39

"Ms. Elliott?"

"Yes."

That was the entire conversation between Cadence and Simon Cordoba's driver. It took only a few minutes to get from Hardwick and Henshaw to Cordoba's Clarosol office in Rosslyn. But it was long enough for Cadence—still nauseous and downright scared—to replay over and over again the events of the previous night, trying to remember the exact words Alan had used. It seemed clear to her that Cordoba had presented himself purely as a prospective client and had said nothing bad about Cadence. She felt somewhat helpless, that Cordoba had found a way to get her to walk straight into his lair. What could he do, though? She had asked herself this question a thousand times. Was he saving himself the trouble of sending another hitman after her? Could he possibly just make her disappear? At first, Cadence thought it was unlikely but then what was to stop them saying, after she had been reported missing, that they had had a productive meeting and that she had left to deliver the good news back to Alan and Jackie.

Suddenly, she thought how stupid she was not to go with her first instinct and ask Bob to accompany her. And what? Put his life in danger? Have him disappear too, and launch his wife and daughter into inconsolable grief? No, the right thing to do was to go it alone. Standing on the pavement as the driver pulled away, Cadence felt profoundly alone. More alone than ever. She steeled herself and felt the strength of her spirit fortify her body. This was it. This was her chance to say everything she wanted to say. She was going to tell him exactly what kind of a man he was, tell him that she was not some stupid teenager who lived in a trailer park who bred children for a price like some pound mutt with a fresh litter. She never even got to hold her son, such was the cruelty of his deeds. Such thoughts prompted an upswell of emotion that could have reduced Cadence to tears on the spot. She shook her head and fixed her eyes on the revolving door that led into the building and marched forward.

The Clarosol office was on the eighth floor and the elevator door opened onto a large foyer dominated by a curved reception desk. Behind the two women answering calls via headsets was a large, curved screen that ran through a series of images that must have been Clarosol projects. They presented that kind of comforting sentiment that the future was safe in their intelligent, capable hands.

Cadence applied her mind to the task. There was no other choice than to play it straight. Simon Cordoba had said he needed her services, and that was that. She could not begin to imagine what he was thinking. The way Bob had described him had never left her memory. He said Cordoba was regarded as some Godfather figure—an outwardly cool and cultured man who was capable of utter ruthlessness. Then there was Alan, practically swooning over Cordoba's charm.

They offered Cadence a seat while she waited for Cordoba. Cadence remained standing. After a few words, the receptionist got to her feet and came around from behind the desk.

"Please," she said. "Follow me."

It was a gallows walk for Cadence. Her fear and anxiety were maxed out, yet beneath was a burning defiance ready for a fight. She was both child and warrior at once, occupying the peak state of both fight and flight. She did not mind. In fact, she considered being at once vulnerable and dangerous to be one of her core strengths. It's what took that trailer park kid all the way to partner of a highly respected law firm in record time. No one had to tell Cadence Elliott she was a force to be reckoned with. Not anymore, at least.

The receptionist opened the door and showed Cadence in. As Cadence entered, she closed the door behind the visitor.

Greeting Cadence was first and foremost a spectacular view of DC through a series of floor-to-ceiling windows that flooded the office of Simon Cordoba. She turned her head to see a large desk to her right behind which sat the man himself, his fingers forming a triangle under his chin, his eyes dark and unblinking and his face as blank as could be. She had seen photos of him before, social functions mostly where his smile dazzled the camera yet prompted nothing but dread in Cadence. To her, with his short hair slicked back, his olive skin clean shaved and gleaming teeth, he was a perfect villain. Now the menace she saw in him seemed to fill the room.

"Come and take a seat, Cadence," he said, his voice light and calm but firm, like that of a doctor who could never be surprised by whatever mysterious ailment might be afflicting you.

Cadence crossed the carpeted space, watching him constantly. He did the same. Eye contact all the way. He had the will to not let his eye stray downward to take in any aspect of her feminine appeal. Only when she was seated did he blink, slowly. He lowered his hands and looked upon her like she was a problem that he was compelled to fix in a manner that could not be avoided. Cadence instantly knew that what Bob told her about this man was true.

"I think it's okay for me to call you Cadence, don't you think?" he said. "Let's not pretend we are strangers. So please don't feel the need for anything formal like Mr. Cordoba. Agreed?"

"Yes," said Cadence.

"Fine. Now, I have a few things to say to you and I am certain it is the same for you. No?"

Cadence nodded. "Yes. I have plenty to say to you."

"Could I suggest that I go first, as I do believe that what I have to say will give you some food for thought."

The fear and ready-to-pounce adrenaline in Cadence subsided a little. "That's okay with me."

Cadence took a moment to look around the room.

"It's just you and me," said Cordoba.

"And an eighth-floor window that for all I know I might be thrown through," said Cadence.

"Is that what you think? That I brought you here to kill you?"

"Let's just say it's right about at the top of the list of possible reasons why you wanted to meet. It's not like you haven't tried before."

Cordoba's forehead knotted with confusion. "I'm going to come back to that, but if you don't mind, I'd like to continue."

"Go ahead."

Cordoba lifted a jug of water and poured out two glasses. He leaned over his desk and placed one in front of Cadence. He took a sip to show her there was nothing to fear.

"What I have to tell you is difficult," he said. "It's difficult because it is personal, it is private, and it is painful. But I need to tell you these things. To begin, I must tell you about my late wife Monica."

"I heard what happened to her," said Cadence. "I'm sorry."

"No, you're not," said Cordoba. "I'm going to be as honest as I can with you and I invite you to do the same."

Cadence nodded her approval.

"You see, I could not say that I knew my wife intimately, as in her mind and character," he said. "And that's because we married not for love but for practicality. I was rich and gave her the promise of a wealthy life. She was well connected and, as I am an immigrant from Argentina, she could offer me permanent residency in the country that I have come to love as my own. So you see, we had a deal. Rather American in some ways. And I am at heart a businessman. I do whatever I can to grow and grow and grow in strength. I never back down.

"In a sense, I was on the run from Argentina. Part of that was I was trying to escape my family name. My family has a past, you see, Cadence, and I wanted no part of it. I wanted to forge my own way in the world. I was young when I came to America and very soon I realized that my finances did not match my ambition. I needed to make a big play to get moving and there was only one source of such an income. And that was my inheritance."

Cordoba explained that his family was very traditional. His father and grandfather were practically royalty back in Argentina. They mixed with the Perons, and enjoyed a life of luxury most Argentinians could only ever dream of. And in America, when he needed seed money to launch his business, there was only one source. He was dating Monica at the time, and he knew that while her family was wealthy, they were tight with their money. He actually had a lifeline waiting for him—an inheritance worth tens of millions of dollars that would be passed on to him upon his father's death. The problem was his father was dying, with only a matter of months to live and there was a strict condition Cordoba had to meet to gain access to his inheritance. He had to have a son. That was how conservative his family was. If he did not produce a son and heir to ensure the survival of the family name, then he would not get one cent of his inheritance. So he found himself in a situation. His father would be dead in a year at most, and if he did not produce a son then his inheritance would go to his elder brother.

Cadence's demeanor was transformed by the unexpected candor with which Cordoba spoke. She believed he was being completely honest with her. Yet she could not let her guard down entirely. Who knew what kind of a ruse this could turn out to be.

"Now, the basis upon which our marriage was built was mutual benefit, not love. So Monica and I quickly found that we were not very well suited as a couple. Nevertheless we did what we could to produce a son. Twice Monica miscarried and we became fearful that my father would die before we could produce a child."

"You mean son," said Cadence flatly. While respecting Cordoba's honesty, she could not help but find his pact with his wife offensive.

"Yes, a son," Cordoba conceded. "And as luck would have it Monica got pregnant. And soon afterward it was confirmed that she would be having a boy. Well, once we had achieved that goal together, we proceeded to go about our lives separately, all the while living under the same roof, of course. We had separate rooms. And I took lovers, as I'm sure she did."

"I'm going to cut in here," said Cadence. "Are you saying you did not know your wife faked her pregnancy?"

A pulse of surprise ran over Cordoba's face. "How did you know?"

"It doesn't matter how I know. But do you really expect me to believe that you had no idea she was faking?"

"I do not expect you to believe what I'm telling you," said Cordoba. "I'm telling you I have no reason to lie. What you accept to be true is ultimately up to you. Can I continue?"

"Yes."

"I was shown all the results from Monica's checkups," said Cordoba. "As you can imagine, my father, even though he was dying, took a keen interest in his progeny. I sent him ultrasounds and scans. And eventually the doctor set a date for the birth. The baby would be delivered by C-section, so it was scheduled like any other appointment. I was able to tell my father what day his grandson Ben would be born."

Cordoba reached out and took a sip of water. "Cadence, you should know that Monica and I separated a few months before she died."

Cadence refrained from saying that she had figured that out already. "Why did you separate?"

"Our marriage was not sustainable, as you might understand," said Cordoba. "But I will get to that. Now where was I?"

"The date of Ben's birth."

"Yes, the date was set and as it happened, I was called away on business. But I returned to find a beautiful boy in Monica's arms."

Cadence was filled with revulsion. No matter how civil and honest Cordoba was, the ghastly truth he spoke of did not just concern the fate of a loveless couple, it told the fate of an innocent third party, a young teenage girl named Cadence Elliott living sixteen hundred miles away.

"But as you said, the boy was not my son," said Cordoba. "However, from that moment on I was his father and I felt more blessed than any man alive."

Cadence remained impassive to Cordoba's sentiment. Without thinking she had folded her arms. She was not about to invite him to speak but she wanted him to hurry up and finish. Not that she knew what she was going to say when it came to her turn.

"It was only after Monica died that I found out the truth," said Cordoba. "My wife had paid for a woman to be our son's surrogate mother, with my semen. She fooled me by wearing maternity clothing and doing everything she could to make it look like she was pregnant. I was convinced and never doubted her. I even found out that she had a prosthetic belly that she had custom made. And as much as I hate to admit it, she had me fooled. But as the birth date approached the surrogate mother had a change of heart. She disappeared."

"So there is a woman out there with your son," said Cadence. "I bet you fear she will come for your money."

Cordoba's eyebrows lifted. "No, that won't be happening. Among the things I came to learn was that this woman died in a car accident."

"You mean your wife had her killed," said Cadence.

Cordoba paused for a moment. "I don't know that, Cadence. But it may well be true."

"My God, what a vile woman."

"I'm not going to defend Monica right now, but I would like to say she was not without virtue. Still, after the surrogate abandoned her, Monica and her doctor—"

"Dr. David Osbourne," said Cadence.

"You found that out too?"

"Yes," said Cadence, barely able to hide her contempt from the man sitting across the desk.

"She and Dr. Osbourne had to find a replacement," said Cordoba. "They searched the country's adoption sites looking for the right child. He had to be newborn on or close to the set date. He had to be at least partly Hispanic. And, of course, it had to be a boy. And I'm afraid that's how they found you. They struck a deal with your mother, and as soon as your baby was delivered, they flew straight back to DC and pretended that Monica had had a homebirth. Soon after that, Dr. Osbourne had the birth certificate authenticated, which he had the power to do."

A wave of grief welled up inside Cadence. She did not want to humiliate herself by crying. She needed to set her vulnerability aside and go on the attack.

"You stole him," said Cadence, tears welling in her eyes. "I never got to even hold him. How could you be so cruel?"

Although Cadence took Cordoba at his word, she could not regard him as blameless. He was as guilty as anyone else involved in this callous, money-hungry ruse.

"I'm sorry, Cadence," said Cordoba. "I know it makes no difference that I was not part of the plan to take your baby. But I wanted to tell you that what you must believe in your heart is right. While the birth is now considered official by law, the process leading up to it was indeed criminal. Both my wife and Dr. Osbourne committed a federal offense in transporting your baby across state lines. The birth of your son should have been certified in Denver."

"What about the papers my mother signed?"

"There were none," Cordoba shook his head. "They paid her and told her if either she or you ever came anywhere near them, you'd be killed."

"Are you saying you only just found all this out?"

"Yes," said Cordoba. "After Monica died, I wanted to put together a photo album for Ben. We managed to access Monica's computer, and so in the process of looking for photos I discovered a chain of files and emails that set out the entire plan. Piece by piece, I put her deception together."

"Does Ben know about me?"

Cordoba nodded. "He knows you in the sense that you are a woman Monica despised. I'm sorry but I'm just being honest. He told me he had noticed a woman matching your description watching him from a car. He said one time Monica chased you away. But your name and that of your mother Tina were mentioned in the files that I found. So I knew who you were. I just didn't know where you were or what you looked like. So I hired an investigator, who found security footage of you at The Line Hotel where Monica was staying after we separated. And then when I saw you speaking on television after you won the trial, I knew I had finally put a face to the name."

Cordoba leaned forward and pressed a button on his phone. "Bring us some green tea, please," he said.

Leaning back in his chair, Cordoba looked out through the window. "Cadence, none of this is fair and I can understand that you hate me. But what we do next is of utmost importance. Because together we need to decide what the future will hold—for you, for me and for Ben. We are inextricably bonded now, although he doesn't know it."

"I want my son back," said Cadence, tears overflowing onto her cheeks. "He was stolen from me and I want him back."

Cordoba nodded. "I understand, and I get it, but I urge you to consider this. As terrible as it may sound to you, Ben is my son. That is all the two of us have ever known. I love my son. He loves me. He is the best thing that has ever happened to me."

"He was first and foremost the means by which you were granted a fortune," said Cadence.

The door opened and the receptionist brought in a Japanese porcelain pot and two small cups. After she left, Cordoba poured the tea.

"You are telling me something I have already admitted to you," said Cordoba. "I gave you something I knew you would be inclined to weaponize. But you are deeply hurt. I won't pretend to know anything about the depth of pain you have endured all these years. And I'm truly sorry but I must speak frankly about the reality of the here and now. Cadence, I must tell you that I would not give Ben up for anything, not even you. Not without a fight.

"So you have been right all along. Ben was taken from you illegally and this cannot be altered. You can of course fight for custody, but you'll have no documentation, no proof, and hence no grounds to pursue it. I would say you are almost certain to lose.

"Yet even if you secure some kind of evidence, I'm not underestimating you—you may well do that—then we will go to court, and I will fight you every inch of the way. And what impact will that have on Ben?

"And let's say you do win custody. That victory will be at least five years away, once we've gone through all channels, right up to the appellate court. By that stage Ben will be 15. If he is not happy that you have won, in a year's time he could legally leave you and come and live with me. Cadence, I put it to you that this is an outcome that serves none of us well."

As much as Cadence did not want to believe it, she knew Cordoba was speaking the truth. A court battle would be the most destructive and ugly way for her to win custody of Ben. This was assuming she could take Cordoba's word that he and Ben were close. As much as she hated to believe it, she had to accept it was possible.

"I suppose you have some kind of deal to offer me," said Cadence.

Cordoba nodded. "Yes, I do," he said. "My proposal is this. I introduce you to Ben. We could say you are advising me on matters of law. But we take it slowly. He will probably recognize you and start asking questions. I give you my word that I am open to him knowing every bit of the truth that he deserves to know, but we must proceed cautiously. Ben believes that Monica and I are his natural parents. But when he asks questions about you, he should be given honest answers. However, I suggest it would not be good for him to know the whole truth about his mother."

"You mean the truth about her being a—?" Cadence cut herself off. "I'm sorry, I need to think of her less as someone who tried to kill me. She was Ben's mother."

"Yes, the only mother he has known," said Cordoba. "I won't try to argue that she was a saint. She was not the most affectionate of mothers. She and Ben had a strained relationship but he loved her. And he has just lost his mother, so I'm begging you, if you agree to my proposal, that we proceed very, very slowly."

"What does he know about me? What has Monica told him?"

"I don't know but I'm sure it wasn't kind," said Cordoba. "But that is not what is important. What matters is that you have a new beginning. You and Ben. The both of you. The three of us, really. That is what I want to offer you. I promise not to stand in your way or impede the relationship you form with him. I want you to be together. You deserve that. I just hope you will not take the combative route. Either way, I'd like to hear what you propose."

Cadence wiped tears from her eyes and gulped hard. "I'd like to see Ben."

"Good," said Cordoba. He leaned forward and picked up Cadence's untouched cup. "Here. Have some tea."

Cadence took the tea and sipped. It tasted good and felt oddly comforting going down.

"How do you want me to introduce you?" Cordoba asked.

"I'll have to go back to work after this," said Cadence. "Was your offer to Alan just a ploy to get me here?"

"Not entirely," smiled Cordoba. "Your firm is highly regarded in business law, and I'm more than willing to take my business there. I understand that is not your field. But it's an option. I could say you're my new attorney."

Cadence shook her head. "No," she said.

"As a friend then?"

The tears came uncontrollably now. She had spent years upon years alone with her grief, her longing, her pain and her shame. The prospect that they could start to be soothed was profoundly sweet. But her tears were not just for her. There was a comfort in knowing—she was convinced of it now—that Ben had a loving father who had his best interests at heart.

"Yes," Cadence nodded. "A friend of the family."

"Okay, then," said Cordoba, "when you're ready I'll bring him in."

"He's here?" asked Cadence, feeling unprepared and suddenly inadequate. The moment she had waited for all her life was now upon her in the blink of an eye.

"Yes," said Cordoba. "I had hoped you would agree to my plan, and so I brought him to the office. We don't have to stay here. We could take the car down to the river. Take a walk and maybe get ice cream. How does that sound?"

"You didn't need to throw in ice cream to sell it to me," Cadence laughed. "But the answer is yes. I'd like that very much."

Cordoba smiled. "I think Ben would like that too."

THE END

AFTERWORD

I really hope you enjoyed *The Lawyer's Heart*. It gave me a great deal of pleasure to see Cadence in a better place. I know, it's only fiction, but I do get attached to my characters. Could I ask you to do a couple of things to help the book's prospects? First, please leave a review on Amazon. Second, please recommend the book to fellow readers. This kind of support means so much to me.

All the best,

J.J.

Printed in Great Britain
by Amazon